Treasons of the Heart

Treasons of
the Heart

Charlotte Lamb

COMPASS PRESS

★ OXFORD ★ MELBOURNE ★

Copyright © Charlotte Lamb 1999

First published in 1999 by Hodder & Stoughton

Compass Press Large Print Book Series; an imprint of
ISIS Publishing Ltd, Great Britain, and Bolinda Press, Australia
Published in Large Print 2000 by ISIS Publishing Ltd,
7 Centremead, Osney Mead, Oxford OX2 0ES,
and Bolinda Publishing Pty Ltd,
17 Mohr Street, Tullamarine, Victoria 3043
by arrangement with Hodder & Stoughton

**British Library Cataloguing
in Publication Data**
Lamb, Charlotte, 1937–
Treasons of the heart. –   Large
print ed.
1. Romantic suspense novels
2. Large type books
I. Title
823.9′14 [F]

**Australian Cataloguing in
Publication Data**
Lamb, Charlotte, 1937
Treasons of the heart/
Charlotte Lamb
1. Large print books.
2. Romantic suspense novels.
I. Title.
823.914

ISBN 0-7531-6362-4 (hb) 0-7531-6363-2 (pb)
(ISIS Publishing Ltd)
ISBN 1-74030-218-4 (hb) 1-74030-219-2 (pb)
(Bolinda Publishing Pty Ltd)

Printed and bound by Antony Rowe, Chippenham and Reading

PROLOGUE

PARIS
September 1937

PROLOGUE

The three men climbed into the back of the car together. "Hotel Meurice," one said in an accent the driver could not place. English? American? he thought, engaging gears. The other two he knew were German, both of them wearing sunglasses that hid their eyes. The company had told him he was booked to drive some important Germans around Paris: they would be on the next train from Berlin. He was to take them wherever they asked to go.

He had spat on the floor but he needed this job so he had arrived in good time to meet the train.

"Oui, M'sieur." In his mirror the driver kept glancing at the passenger who was not German. He had seen that face before — but where? A striking face, handsome, in a wild, reckless way, with reddish hair and brown eyes that held laughter as they met his.

The passenger grinned at him, winked, and at that instant he knew who was sitting in the back of his car.

Flynn. The famous Hollywood film star, Errol Flynn. What would his wife say when he told her? She probably wouldn't even believe him.

Traffic was heavy, but he knew the best short cuts and wove his way fast to the Rue de Rivoli, enjoying showing off his skill. Several times when he looked back he noticed a large, black saloon car right behind him.

Police, he thought irritably. Not that there was any sign, but he knew the look of their cars and the men in it had all the hallmarks of policemen. Big, unsmiling, watchful men.

He wouldn't be surprised if they switched on their siren soon to order him to stop and pull into the side of the road.

They didn't. But they were still there as he drove along beside the Tuileries railings, with the Seine sparkling beyond under a hot autumnal sun.

"Come back for us in two hours," he was told as the three of them climbed out when he parked outside the Meurice.

He watched them walk across the pavement into the hotel. Before vanishing, Flynn turned his head to glance at the Tuileries gardens where pretty young nursemaids in dark blue uniforms, with neat-turned ankles and fluttering white veils, pushed prams. Flynn gave a visible sigh, shrugging his wide shoulders.

He'd rather be in the park, chasing the girls, the driver thought, smiling to himself, even though the Meurice is one of the grandest hotels in Paris! Well, what red-blooded man wouldn't?

He looked into his mirror before moving off and saw the black car stationary behind him. One of the men in dark raincoats and trilby hats got out and walked into the hotel.

They had not been following him at all, the driver realised. They had been following his passengers. But

4

which? The two Germans or Flynn? Maybe he should warn them they were being watched?

But why should he bother? They hadn't even tipped him and, anyway, he wasn't putting himself out for a couple of Germans.

Inside the hotel foyer the detective went over to the *conciegerie* and conferred softly with the man on duty. A few banknotes slid into the porter's top pocket.

The detective listened impassively to what he was told, then went to sit down in a chair which gave him a good view of both the lift and the main exit back into the Rue de Rivoli. Settling down, he prepared for a long wait, opening a newspaper as cover behind which he could watch who came and went.

Upstairs, the doors of a suite opened. The three men from Berlin were greeted with warmth and friendliness by its occupants.

"My dear Herr Hess, it is good to see you. I hope you had a comfortable journey from Berlin?"

"Thank you, Your Royal Highness, indeed, we did. What excellent German you speak, I congratulate you."

"Thank you. I am proud of my German blood; speaking German is natural to me. You know my wife, of course."

"Your Royal Highness," Hess bowed to kiss her hand. She was wearing an elegant black dress which showed off her slender, graceful figure. A white carnation was pinned into the plunging neckline, just above the rise of those small, white breasts. She had real style, he thought. Hitler would admire her. Except that she was not a blonde. Unfortunately her colouring was Jewish.

But all their researches had not revealed any trace of Jewish blood.

"Your Highnesses, may I present the *Führer*'s secretary, Martin Bormann?"

They smiled politely. Bormann shook their hands. Hess saw a repressed shiver of distaste run through the Duke and sympathised.

Bormann was a real peasant: thick-necked, heavy of body, with small, greedy, cunning eyes. Barely literate, he had worked on a farm for a while until he was sent to prison for being accomplice to a murder.

Hess didn't trust or like him, but, as Hitler said, you have to work with the material you can get, and Borrnann was useful. Especially when there was dirty work to do.

The Duchess did not even try to disguise her interest in Errol Flynn. When she gave him her hand Flynn bent forward to kiss it, purring like some big golden cat on heat, his eyes on her low neckline. He was wearing a beautifully cut English suit. Of all of them he looked most at his ease in this luxury hotel.

But Hess was irritated. They must not offend the Duke, who was notoriously jealous and possessive about his wife. Maybe they shouldn't have brought Flynn? It had been Bormann's idea.

"If we take him along he'll occupy the wife while we talk to the husband alone. Flynn makes them all hot for him. Women can't resist him. And from what I've read about this little tramp, he's just the sort to start her juices flowing."

Hess had frowned but said nothing. Bormann's coarse

tongue amused Hitler, but did not amuse him.

The Duchess laughed. "I can see you live up to your reputation, Mr Flynn!"

"Errol, please, your Royal Highness," he said, smiling into her eyes.

Her husband smiled approval of the title, which, Hess was aware, the new King of England had refused to allow her to use. Baffling, all this English protocol, but in some ways Hess was supportive of anything that affirmed order and discipline in society. Too many admirable rules had been discarded in this century. It was time they were reinstated.

A servant appeared, pouring excellent white wine and offering them tiny, triangular sandwiches containing thinly sliced ham or cheese.

"This French stuff can't hold a candle to a good German wine, can it, your Highness?" Bormann growled. He took a fistful of the sandwiches and stuffed them rapidly into his mouth.

The waiter's face stiffened, although he kept his eyes averted from Bormann's face.

"The weather is very warm for the time of year," Hess quickly said, taking one of the minute sandwiches. "And Paris is looking beautiful."

The Duke dismissed the waiter. "We'll call for you if we need you."

The young man bowed, gave Bormann a stare of dislike and left the suite.

Flynn and the Duchess had drifted over to the window and were looking out over the Paris skyline. Although he was polite to Hess the Duke kept glancing over towards his wife.

"Your Highness, can we begin our discussions as soon as possible? We have to get back to Berlin today."

The Duchess heard his words, turned and said in her cool American voice, "Mr Flynn would be interested to see our suite, darling — shall I take him on a tour while you have a private chat with Herr Hess? That, after all, is the object of this visit, isn't it? And there isn't much time."

Hess saw the flicker of reluctance in the Duke's blue eyes, set deep in a sea of lines — from smiling, from hours in the sun, no doubt. He had been a very beautiful young man; he was fading into a frail, world-weary elegance.

But with well-trained courtesy he said, "Of course, darling, do that."

She tucked her hand into the film star's arm. "Wait until you see the bathroom!"

"I'm more interested in bedrooms," Flynn said, charm oozing out of him.

The Duke's gaze followed her as she and Flynn left the room. The door closed on them and the Duke sighed.

"Please, sit down, Herr Hess. I understand that you have known the *Führer* for many years. Tell me, how did you meet?"

"We served in the same regiment during the Great War. You, yourself, fought in the war, I know. You will realise what a bond can be forged between comrades in arms facing death together."

"Indeed. I made very good friends in my regiment. But I had the notion you were in the German

Air Force.''

''I joined the air force later.''

Hess left out the fact that he had taken part in the attempted putsch in Munich, had been jailed with Hitler, and shared a cell in the Landsberg prison with him. Nor did he tell the Duke that Hitler had dictated a large part of *Mein Kampf* to him while they were in prison.

Those had been the glory days, the time when he and Hitler were closer than brothers. Everything had changed since then. Lately, Hitler seemed to confide less in him and more in Bormann, his secretary. Hess increasingly felt excluded. He needed to pull off some tremendous coup to get back into Hitler's favour.

''I understand Your Highness is interested in visiting Germany to meet the *Führer?* I assure you, you would be most welcome.''

Half an hour later the Duchess and Flynn returned. The two Germans had finished their private chat with the Duke of Windsor and were again exchanging small talk while the footman poured more wine.

The Duke's head spun at the sound of the door opening. Hess saw his eyes narrow and glitter as the Duke registered that the white flower his wife had been wearing at her throat, above her breasts, was now in Errol Flynn's buttonhole, and that Flynn was smiling, the curling, mocking smile of a cat that has stolen someone else's cream.

PARIS

1999

CHAPTER
ONE

The moment she opened her front door Claudia Guyon knew a stranger had got into her apartment. She stiffened, turning icy cold.

It was midnight. There hadn't been a soul in sight outside on the quay. The only sounds had been the familiar slap slap of the Seine between its banks, the rocking of moored boats, the whisper of spring leaves on the dappled plane trees, the muffled roar of traffic on the city boulevards.

Down by the river at this hour you could almost forget you were in the heart of Paris, except that the thick smell of petrol fumes drifted down from the roads and hung in the branches of the horse chestnut trees among the five-petalled leaves, their creamy, blotched flowers just coming out. Candles, French children called them. *Les bougies,* shining most brilliantly at night among the dark green leaves.

There had been a spate of burglaries in this *arrondissement* recently, but she hadn't worried too much because she always took precautions. It was well-engrained habit to close the shutters and switch on the alarm before she left the apartment. In the three years she had lived alone here there had never been a burglary in her building; the security system was so good. But there was always a first time.

Maybe she should shut the door and ring the police? But would they come on such thin evidence? She was the sole occupant of this floor. If she screamed, nobody would hear her. In any case, if she was imagining things she would look ridiculous. Leaving the door open in case she had to get out again fast, she stepped out of her low-heel shoes and tiptoed, barefoot, into the corridor.

She leaned down to take a silver-headed walking stick from the umbrella stand by the front door. Her stomach screwed in tension, she gripped the heavy stick tightly and went to the open door of the sitting room.

She didn't put on the electric light. Trying to breathe quietly she looked hurriedly around the room.

All the shutters were closed, but even so the light from the street lamps on the quay outside slid through the airholes in the aluminium, making it possible for her as her eyes adjusted to the darkness to see that there was nobody in the room.

That morning, as always, she had spent an hour on housework. This room had been spotless when she had finished; it still looked that way.

But her conviction that somebody was here — or had been not long ago — was stronger than ever.

She crept on to her bedroom. That was empty too, and just as immaculate.

It was easy to see at a glance that nothing had been taken or moved because she had furnished this room in a stark Japanese style — white curtains, white cotton rug on the varnished floorboards beside her low Japanese bed. There were no ornaments. Just an electronic radio/ alarm clock on her bedside table, and a black Japanese lamp.

The built-in black wardrobe was still locked from outside; nobody could be in there.

The second bedroom was Hugh's; his furniture was heavy, dark, nineteenth-century mahogany. He had a French boat bed, draped with a deep blue duvet, curtains of maroon velvet. The steel shutters over the windows were kept closed except when Claudia opened the windows for an hour each day to air the room.

Hugh hadn't used it for months. He rarely came to Paris. No sign of intrusion there either.

The bathroom door was shut. Hadn't she left it open? A nerve jumping in her throat, grasping the walking stick in her right hand, she turned the handle with her left, her fingers slippery with sweat. The handle slid from her grasp and the door swung open suddenly. She gasped, ready to run, but the mirror on the wall opposite reflected only what she would expect the bathroom furnishings of the late seventies — aubergine bath, bidet, lavatory.

She looked at the kitchen last of all. It was tiny, no room for anyone to hide — not even a dwarf could have squeezed into the small refrigerator.

There was nobody in the flat at all. With a sigh of relief she closed the front door and bolted it, slid Hugh's walking stick back into the brass umbrella stand, picked up her shoes and went back into the sitting room. After switching on the light she stared round it again: painted pine furniture, which she had stencilled with a few, carefully placed, purple birds among curling green tendrils, purple cotton. Taking a deep breath, she grimaced with distaste.

There might be nobody here now, but there was no doubt about it. Somebody had smoked in this room since she had left the flat that afternoon.

Claudia never smoked. She didn't allow anyone else to smoke in her apartment, even at parties. She loathed the smell of cigarettes. Her mother, a chain-smoker, had died slowly of lung cancer.

The doctor had tried to persuade Madame Guyon to go into a hospice, but Claudia had begged her mother to stay at home for as long as possible, and had helped nurse her, although Hugh had hired a qualified nurse to oversee the medical side.

Her mother had been the only relative she had in the world. That long, slow death had been terrible for both of them. It had taken six, agonising months, and Claudia, then fifteen, could not forget watching her mother shrink until she was lighter than a child, all her ribs showing through the frail wall of her chest, fighting for breath as she tried to smile.

The smell of cigarette smoke had almost made Claudia throw up ever since, bringing back nightmare memories.

Because she had never smoked, she had an excellent sense of smell, which was essential in her job. That was why she was certain someone had smoked in here. Yet there was no sign of ash or cigarette ends.

''What had someone been doing in here, if they had not come to steal? It didn't make sense. Had he been disturbed? Had he only just broken in when she got

16

back? Had he left in a hurry, empty handed?

How had he got in, anyway? There was no sign of a break-in; the door hadn't been forced, the security alarms had been set, the shutters were all locked and barred as usual.

Hugh had a set of keys, of course. But Hugh did not smoke now, either, although he had, once. He had given up during those last months of Mama's life.

Hugh had been her father's best friend; they had once worked together on an American newspaper. After Papa had been killed in an African civil war he was covering, Hugh had given Mama and Claudia, his goddaughter, a home when the lease of their Paris apartment ran out soon afterwards.

Hugh was still a foreign correspondent for an English newspaper then; he had travelled a great deal and it had made sense for him to give Mama a job running his villa on the Cap d'Antibes. It meant he need not worry about the place when he was away for weeks. Even when he came back to France, he spent a lot of time in Paris.

He had given up his job on the newspaper when his first book was made into a film, but he still spent a lot of time in Paris, where he had many friends.

After her mother's death, however, he had stayed at the villa all year round until Claudia had finished her training at the best cooking school in the south of France. It was Hugh who found her a job in Paris at one of the exclusive hotels close to the Place de la Concorde. Hugh had tried to persuade her to get a job in Cannes or Nice, but she wanted to be independent. He had done so much for her. She felt she should stand on her own two feet now, although her pride didn't stop her accepting Hugh's offer of this apartment at a very low rent.

Having no wife or children of his own, he treated her as his daughter, and she thought of him almost as a father, a very glamorous and exciting father. As a child she had worshipped him, kept a scrapbook of his newspaper articles as he flew around the world, risking his life in war-torn areas, dodging bullets and avoiding landmines in far-flung corners of the globe.

Since her mother's death her love for Hugh had deepened; he was all the family she had. Neither of her parents had any relatives as far as she knew. Her grandparents were dead, her parents had been only children.

She knew Hugh better than anyone else in the world, and was certain that if he had been coming to town he would have let her know. He valued privacy for himself, he wouldn't invade her space without warning.

The apartment block had been built in the seventeenth century. A seven-storeyed, narrow, terraced house on a Seine quayside. The developer had made major structural alterations to the interior, but had left the exterior alone. He had sold the resulting apartments for a huge profit. Hugh had bought the whole second floor, high up enough to have a marvellous view of the river without an exhausting climb. She loved living here, could spend an age staring out of the windows up and down river, especially at dawn when the filigree outlines of the famous Paris buildings in view seemed dreamlike. The Ile de la Cité, floating like a stone-walled boat on the grey water, leafy with trees in summer; the miraculuous buttresses of the medieval cathedral Notre Dame beyond that, with an echoing vista of other landmarks, bridges, towers, spires in the distance.

As the adrenaline of tension drained out of her, Claudia yawned, very tired now. It had been a hectic day. She had cooked a wedding reception lunch for fifty people, and then a buffet for three times that many during the evening dance which followed. It had really taxed her inventiveness. Coming up with two very different meals for so many people meant careful planning and hours of hard work in advance.

She turned off the lights and went to bed. She had another big job on tomorrow, she needed a good sleep. As she stripped, washed and put on a thin white cotton nightshirt to climb into bed, her eye fell on the metal gratings low down on the outer wall.

Perhaps someone in another flat had had a party tonight? The smell of smoke could have filtered down somehow through the grating, which were meant to help the ancient walls breathe.

Of course. That must be it. She fell asleep a few moments later.

It was hard to wake up again when her alarm went off at seven the next morning. Bleary-eyed she forced herself out of bed and staggered off to the kitchen. Before showering she put on the coffee, and drank a cup, black, strong, unsugared, in between dressing, but didn't eat because she planned to grab a newly baked croissant at the market.

It was always cold in the food hall. The refrigeration kept the air chilly, especially first thing in the morning, even in spring. She put on jeans, a sunny, yellow lambswool sweater and comfortable flat shoes because she would be doing a lot of walking.

Her bronze hair was very short, naturally curly. In cooking you could not risk wearing your hair long. It got in the way in a kitchen, fell over your eyes, found its way into food. Very unhygienic.

Claudia preferred to wear her hair short anyway; it saved time, you just ran a comb through it now and then, no hassle.

At a quarter to eight she grabbed her wicker shopping basket. You couldn't be late for the market or you might miss a bargain — rare, wild mushrooms from the woods at Versailles perhaps, home-made, crispy farm bread dotted with olives or sundried tomatoes, freshly caught baby squid, langoustines, Merguez sausage, or a mountain cheese flavoured with thyme, sage or oregano. She wandered the market like a child at Christmas, never knowing what she would find, wide-eyed and hopeful.

Her van was in a lock-up garage five minutes away. Dashing along the quay with her eyes on the soft-misted river she ran right into a photographer who stepped back into her path from setting up a tripod.

''*Merde!*'' he grunted.

''Look where you're going!''

''*Désolé*, didn't hear you coming,'' he muttered.

She picked up a trace of an English accent which she recognised from listening to Hugh most of her life.

Hugh had never quite lost his accent despite his almost perfect grasp of French. This man, too, spoke French fluently, and he certainly looked far more French than Hugh, but that accent was unmistakable.

The eyes watching her were black and had a smoulder like a banked-up fire. Temper! she thought. A typical Frenchman in a temper? How had he got that slight English accent?

"Hallo!" he said on a long breath.

"Hallo to you," she replied, amused by the way he was staring at her.

Maybe he had lived in England for a long time? His hair was as black as his eyes, thick and wavy, long enough to reach almost to his shoulder. He had French skin, too, olive, but tanned gold. His high, winged cheekbones and wide mouth promised passion as well as temper.

When he smiled she distinctly felt her heartbeat quicken.

"Could you help me out? I work for a London magazine."

So she had been right! He did live in England.

"I'm doing a photo session for an article and I want to get some shots of the river. But the Seine is old and grey and you're young and beautiful. Will you stand here for a few seconds to give me a human focus?"

"Do you always flatter people like that?" she asked, laughing.

"Only women." His sidelong glance had a teasing glint.

"I think I guessed that! Look, sorry, love to, but I

haven't got time, I'm in a terrible hurry to get to the market.''

She wished she could hang around. When was the last time she had met a man this attractive?

''Please,'' he coaxed softly. ''It won't take long, I promise.'' Then he smiled, and that smile changed his face as a shaft of sunlight alters a landscape.

He was the sexiest man she had ever seen; not merely good-looking and charming, but intensely male. She felt like Eve discovering Adam in the Garden of Eden.

She caught herself up. But what if it wasn't Adam, just Lucifer. Didn't they say that Lucifer was the most beautiful of the angels, the sons of the morning? An archangel, full of arrogance and ambition, challenging God Himself, and flung out of Heaven by Michael. She had been listening to Hugh most of her life; he had never quite lost his accent despite his almost perfect grasp of French. This man, too, spoke French. The faithful archangel: she had a strong feeling all that fitted this man.

But she couldn't resist him. ''Okay, but be quick. I really am in a hurry.''

''Trust me,'' he said, stepping back to his camera.

Trust you? she thought. Every guy she had been out with had taught her not to trust. Twice she had thought she was in love, and twice she had been hurt. Wise women did not trust easily.

As he contemplated her through the lens, little needles of awareness pricked along her spine. This man made her feel intensely, dangerously conscious of being a woman.

"Could you put one foot forward, as if you're running?"

She obeyed, very self-conscious.

"Relax. Enjoy it. Look, swing the arm holding the basket — oh, yes, that's perfect. Look happy — no, don't smile, just look radiant."

"How do I do that?" She was amused, though, her face lighting up.

"Wonderful. Hold that expression, don't so much as breathe."

He focused on her, clicked rapidly. "Could you half turn to look at the river? Great." He took some more pictures. "Now look up at the sky. Oh, yes."

The sun broke through the mist and dazzled her eyes. It might be a fine day today, after all.

The photographer straightened. "That's it. Thanks, you really made those pictures. What's your name and address? I'll send you some prints."

"Never mind," she said, grinning, and ran. As he was English he would be going back to London, so where was the point in hoping to see him again?

He shouted after her, but she didn't stop or look round. She had to get to the market before the good stuff went. Early birds caught worms. Later ones just got squashed cabbage leaves.

When she got back to her flat an hour and a half later, he had gone as she expected. The quayside was full of men fishing.

One of them turned to look at her, then bent to take a mobile phone out of the hessian bag beside him. He was a thin, cold-eyed man with a mole just beneath his left eye which gave him a sinister look.

Now that it was too late she wished she had given the photographer her name and address. But what was the point? He probably wouldn't have got in touch, he would forget about her. She would never see him again.

The post was always here by this time; she unlocked her mailbox down in the hall. Some invoices from suppliers, a few paid bills from clients, some enquiries — the usual mixture.

One of the letters was for Hugh; the envelope bore the logo of the Hôtel Crillon, she noticed.

No stamp on it — it must have been delivered by hand. She must remember to put a stamp on it and forward it to Hugh.

She walked up the stairs. Just before she turned the corner to take the last steps to her landing she heard a click which was oddly familiar, then the faint echo of feet hurrying. There was nobody else on the stairs though, so it must have been somebody from an upper floor.

As she shut her front door behind her it suddenly dawned on her that the click she had heard had been the sound of her own front door closing.

She stiffened. Somebody had been in here again. She could smell cigarette smoke. What the hell was going on? Was she going out of her mind, was all this just a hallucination?

She hurried into the kitchen, dumped her bags, then went through the rooms. As before, nothing seemed to have been touched.

She glanced in at Hugh's bedroom and turned away,

then stopped and swung back, a cold shiver running through her. There was a sprinkling of grey ash on the floor.

She leaned on the wall, staring at it. So she hadn't been imagining things. Someone had been in the apartment.

The click she had heard must have been somebody hurriedly leaving. He hadn't passed her, so he must have gone upstairs. Was it someone who lived here?

She thought of the other tenants, but couldn't believe any of them were burglars. They were all too wealthy. To live here you had to have money. The only reason she could afford the apartment was because Hugh made it possible. She had nothing worth stealing, anyway.

Looking around Hugh's room she saw that a drawer in the Edwardian bureau was slightly out of line with the others. Claudia pulled it open. The contents, mostly letters, had been disturbed. Whoever had been in here had looked through them, then thrust them back in a hurry.

Her return must have surprised him at his work. But how had he known she was coming back before she even got up to this floor?

Obviously somebody must have been watching outside; must have given a warning. But who?

There had been those men fishing on the quayside. One of them had turned to look at her, then bent to get a mobile phone out of his bag.

She ran to the window to look down at the quay. There were still fishermen down there, but the thin man with the mole beside his eye had gone.

Had he given a warning to the man in her apartment

that she was coming back? But how would he have known she lived here? She had never seen him before.

A shiver ran down her back. Had he been watching her? She had heard of apartments being targeted by gangs who find out when a tenant is likely to be out for a long time, come with a removal van, and take everything worth taking, at their leisure. She had nothing worth taking, but other apartments here were full of antiques and jewellery.

What if these men were planning to rob others in this building?

She rushed to the phone and rang the police, was put through to the emergency number.

Her voice breathless, she told the woman operator what had happened.

"Was anything taken?"

"No, but I know somebody has been here because there was ash on the floor."

A pause, then the operator politely asked her, "Ash on the floor? What sort of ash?"

"Cigarette ash. And I don't smoke, don't you see? I don't allow anyone else to smoke in my apartment, either."

"Do you live there alone, M'mselle?"

"Yes."

"Do you have a boyfriend?"

Claudia crisply said, "No."

"But you do have friends who smoke?"

"Not in my apartment."

"Had the front door been forced?"

"No."

"The windows?"

"Locked and shuttered. There's no sign of damage anywhere. I have no idea how they got in, but I know somebody has been here. I thought maybe a gang were planning to rob all the apartments. Some of the other tenants are very rich."

"Have any of them noticed ash on the floor?"

Claudia went red. The woman was laughing at her.

"Are you going to send someone?" she asked angrily.

"I'll log this call, M'mselle. You will get a visit from the police, but we are rather busy today. Now, will you please ring off? This line is for serious emergency calls only."

Claudia hung up with a crash.

Her mind seething, she went to the kitchen, put on coffee, unpacked her bags with shaky hands. Stupid woman. She'd be sorry if other apartments here were burgled because she had refused to listen to a warning.

When she had calmed down later, she reluctantly admitted that she could see why the police operator hadn't taken her seriously. Nothing had been stolen. There were no signs of a forced entry, indeed they had gone to great lengths to leave no evidence of their presence here.

These were no ordinary burglars.

Hugh! she suddenly thought. Why hadn't that occurred to her before? He was rich, famous — he was still the owner of this apartment. What if the burglars thought he lived here? He had always been secretive, a taciturn man, never talkative, never answering questions, never volunteering anything about his past.

The press were always curious about that. Why did an Englishman live in France and never go home to England, even on a fleeting visit? Why did he refuse to talk about his family? He had never told her anything about them, she had no idea if he even had living relatives.

If the burglars had been in this apartment for some reason connected with Hugh, what had they been looking for? And would they be back if they hadn't found it?

She went back to the phone to ring Hugh, but nobody answered. Normally if he was going out, he left the answering machine on, but not today. She would have to try again later. She had a lot to do, she had to start work.

She was cooking dinner tonight for Rex Valery, one of France's favourite actors, and a dozen guests, in his ultra chic apartment in a futuristic block in the shadow of the Tour Montparnasse, which could be seen from almost any part of Paris, like a giant brown cigar looming over the city.

She enjoyed cooking for Rex. He was mad about food, yet he was very thin because he ate a mere morsel of each course. Most of his guests were the same, dieting eternally, but Rex mischievously encouraged her to offer rich food at his parties; a form of self-inflicted masochism for him and torment for his friends. Rex had a corkscrew personality; both kind and spiteful, sympathetic yet childishly cruel at times.

Siegfried arrived at six to help carry the food out to the van which, as usual, she had brought round ten minutes earlier and parked illegally outside on the cobbles to make it easier to pack.

Siegfried was a gifted jazz pianist, but Paris was a hard city for musicians; there were far too many of them, and far too few jobs; they had a tough time making a living. He needed to work at other jobs part-time to keep body and soul together, and waiters were always required in this city of restaurants.

Blond, very tanned, with rather cold blue eyes, he would get a lot of attention from Rex Valery's gay friends, but they would get none from him. Siegfried was totally straight, not to say a little puritanical.

His father was a Lutheran pastor in a quiet Rhineland village and Siegfried had taken on many of his father's moral attitudes. His French was fluent now, although he still spoke with a clipped German accent. You couldn't mistake his nationality.

Sniffing the air, he said, "What smells so good?" Siegfried had a very sweet tooth. "Chocolate? Is that the pudding I love?"

"My chocolate bombe, yes."

"In the big brass mould like a cathedral?"

"Of course — and it is still in there, so no peeking, keep it locked."

She handed him the large wicker basket which held the bombe in its turn-of-the-century mould, and a bowl of pears poached very slowly in a good claret with cinnamon, into which, when it had chilled in the fridge, she had stirred redcurrant jelly to deepen the colour to a jewelled red. There was a plastic lid clipped firmly around the top of the bowl.

Into his other hand she put a cool-bag containing a big

lidded basin of melon and lime sorbet.

"Carry them very, very carefully!"

Siegfried obeyed to the letter, his face frowning in concentration.

It only took them ten minutes to load the van. *En route* to picking up her kitchen assistant, Patti, from her flea-ridden room in a crumbling, dirty old house owned by an Algerian, in the backstreets below Sacré-Coeur, Claudia stopped by a yellow mailbox to post the letter to Hugh.

"Love letter?" Siegfried asked.

"No, it's for Hugh."

"Oh, your adopted father! I'd love to meet him, I admire his books so much. My English tutor, back home, gave me one, and I bought the rest myself."

"Next time he's in Paris I'll introduce you."

"Thank you, I would be so pleased. I will bring his books for him to sign, if he permits."

"I'm sure he would." Hugh was always friendly to his fans when he met them, although his publisher dealt with his fan mail because there was far too much of it, and Hugh couldn't reply to them all. He kept most people at arm's-length, apart from her, and Louise, his housekeeper, and his friends in Paris and Antibes.

Claudia drove on to Montmartre and picked up Patti. An American art student, Patti was nearly six foot tall, with the noble features of some African statue, smooth, flawless skin like black silk, hair shaved almost to her scalp and springing up in tight, tiny curls. Her eyes were huge, jet, with thin gold flecks around the iris.

She was living on a grant, and, like Siegfried, needed

to earn extra money to make her life here bearable. As well as helping Claudia, she modelled, dressed in exotic clothes, or in the nude, but earned more from Claudia than any of the artists she sat for because they were mostly poor and did not pay well.

In a wave of strong garlic she squeezed into the van next to Siegfried who fanned the air in front of his face, grimacing.

"What have you been eating?"

"Louisiana gumbo," she said defiantly. "I was feeling homesick, so I made a big pot."

"Any left?" he asked predictably. Siegfried was always hungry. He skimped on food to make sure he had trendy gear to wear, and worked so hard that he was permanently one meal under par.

"Sorry. My flatmates plan to eat the rest tonight." She dropped into her native tongue, her voice languorous and dreamy, swallowing half her words, "It was just like Mamma makes — ve' hot, ve' spicy."

Hugh had taught Claudia English when she was in her early teens, and she had studied it at school. She loved to hear Patti talking either in her native American, or her own version of French, a Creole patois spoken in Louisiana for hundreds of years. The dreamy tones were seductive, lilting like blues music. Claudia loved jazz.

A pity the English don't speak their language like that, Claudia thought, their voices are too stilted, too clipped, too self-conscious.

"I must get you to make gumbo for that party we're doing for the Besserault kid's fifteenth birthday, I'm sure she'd love it, she's into jazz and went to New

Orleans last year with her parents.''

''Sure, love to.'' Patti was always amiable; she did not have the energy to be difficult. Yet when she did lose her temper it was a hurricane, blowing away everybody in earshot.

The traffic was as appalling as ever. Paris was becoming a nightmare; cars bumper to bumper in every street, drivers screaming swearwords at each other as they swerved to overtake in a space barely big enough for a bicycle. For a French driver *force majeure* was the only way to drive. Storm your way through, regardless, with the reckless daring of the French cavalry in the Napoleonic wars. Take no prisoners. Never stop on a zebra crossing unless there's a policeman on it.

''I don't know why I don't move my business somewhere else!'' groaned Claudia. ''Some nice quiet country town.''

''Paris is such fun,'' Patti giggled. ''You'd miss it.''

''Miss this? Are you crazy?'' Claudia slowed at traffic lights and the car behind her, driven by a man obviously in his forties, leaped forward to drive through just as they turned red.

''Madman!'' she called after him. He gave her an obscene hand signal and vanished in a puff of exhaust.

''You could go back to the Côte d'Azur,'' said Siegfried.

''The traffic there isn't much better. Sometimes I almost think it's worse, especially in high summer.''

When they reached Rex's apartment the front door was opened by his live-in lover, a Chinese man, in his early twenties, very slender, no more than five foot, with fine, delicate features. He looked very chic in a black silk pyjama suit, with a totally shaved head and skin like oiled gold silk; his black almond-shaped eyes surveyed them scornfully.

"You're cutting it a bit fine. He expected you an hour ago. The guests will start arriving soon and he'll go crazy if everything isn't perfect, and on time."

"Everything is ready, don't worry."

Yuan looked sideways at Siegfried walking past, loaded down with baskets and boxes.

"That boy is too lovely. I hate him. If I catch him smiling at Rex I'll cut his throat with one of your kitchen knives, so warn him to keep his eyes to himself."

"He's straight, Yuan, he isn't interested in Rex, don't be silly."

"Every guy who sees Rex is interested in him. Women never understand men the way another man can." Yuan gave her a cold glance and with great dignity glided away with snake-like undulations, vanishing into the bedroom he shared with Rex.

"Keep him away from me!" Siegfried growled.

"Cute, but creepy," said Patti, unpacking the dismembered, marinated duck. "Say, how old is Rex Valery today?"

"Keep your voice down! That's the last thing he'll want talked about. He's terrified of getting old. Let's just say he won't see forty again! Ladle out the borscht next — use these salt-glazed white bowls. The dark red of the soup looks great in them."

Patti's eyes glowed. "Sure will, can I taste a

spoonful?''

''If you must. Put the sorbet into the green glass dishes then pop them back into the freezer. Where's the pâté de foie gras?''

Patti unwrapped it from its foil envelope, put out a finger to take a piece, stopping as Claudia said sharply, ''No! Don't steal any! It cost the earth. I only bought enough to serve the duck on.''

''Smells like heaven,'' Patti sighed, ladling borscht. ''You know I'd love to paint Rex Valery and his boyfriend. Dare I ask?''

''Why not? They're both as vain as peacocks, they'll be flattered.''

Patti's regal features took on the closest thing to excitement she ever revealed. ''D'you think they might say yes?''

Claudia laughed, shrugging.

''Probably not, but there's no harm in asking. Tell them how magnificent the portrait would be, say you'll put it in for the next school exhibition. The press would see it and it would be great publicity for Rex. I bet nobody has ever painted them together, Yuan would love the idea, he might talk Rex into it.''

''Rex won't mind publicity about him and Yuan?''

''Good heavens, no, Rex has never been in the closet, he didn't need to come out. He has always been very open about his sexuality.''

Patti put the bowls of borscht into the fridge and began dealing with the sorbet.

''So, will all the men here tonight be gay?''

''Most of them, I expect — but some of the actresses

who are coming are married or living with someone, so there may be a few straight guys.''

''All spoken for, though,'' Patti said mournfully.

''You're here to work, not pick up men!''

''All work and no play makes life tedious!''

Siegfried had been laying the dining table; he came back, red-faced. ''I wish those guys would keep their hands to themselves.''

Patti hooted and he glared at her.

''It isn't funny!''

''Now you know how women feel!''

''No, I don't. Women expect to get felt up, I don't!''

The kitchen door swished open and Rex Valery sauntered in; exquisite in white from head to foot: white linen suit, white shirt with a transparent ruff instead of a collar, high-heeled white shoes. His silvery-blond hair shone like a halo.

He gave Siegfried a beatific smile. ''Poor boy, did they scare you? *Ne vous vous désolez pas comme ça.* I told them to keep their hands off in future. They won't bother you again.

Siegfried gave him a haughty, unsmiling stare.

Pouting, Rex said to Claudia, ''Oh, dear, isn't he cross? But so gorgeous. You can't blame a guy for trying. How's the dinner coming?'' He looked around the kitchen, hysteria coming into his eyes. Rex panicked easily. ''Where is it? Haven't you started work yet? Most of the guests are here, and getting drunk already. I told you dinner at eight thirty.''

''Don't get stressed!'' she soothed. ''It's all ready. Most of it's in the fridge — you wanted chilled borscht, remember? I'll be cooking the duck while you're eating the salmon.''

Rex sighed dramatically. *"Merci à Dieu.* My heart nearly stopped! When will you serve the first course?''

"Half an hour OK?''

"D'accord. That will be fine. Oh, did I tell you a photographer is here? A glossy English magazine is doing an article on me. He sighed with pleasure and she smiled at his vanity. Rex loved publicity, especially if large photos of himself accompanied it, and they usually did, Rex saw to that.

"Wicked!'' Claudia said indulgently.

"Very flattering, to be well known across *La Manche,* my films do well over there, and you know how the English are about us — they love to pretend we don't exist, but they make an exception for me,'' he said happily.

"I know, they adore you over there!''

He gave her an approving smile. "They do, oh, yes. Their magazines are always writing about me. They've sent this gorgeous guy to take some pictures. He's utterly delectable, but straight, alas — why are all the men one really fancies straight?''

He stole another look at Siegfried, who went red. Rex sighed dramatically. "Oh, well, it's the tragedy of my life. Darling, you don't mind if he comes in here to take some snaps of you working, do you? They want to focus on my private life, not the cinema — my apartment, my friends, the lovely parties I give, which are so famous all over the world.''

"So long as he doesn't get in our way, that's fine.''

"Can I borrow lovely Siegfried to help this guy with his equipment?"

"If it's OK with Siegfried."

Rex gave him a coaxing, seductive look through his eyelashes. "Pretty please?"

Siegfried looked outraged, but with a sullen expression followed him out of the kitchen.

Claudia thought of the Englishman on the quayside early that morning — hadn't he said he worked for an English magazine?

But she didn't believe in coincidences that huge. It couldn't be the same guy.

The kitchen door swished open again. She looked round. First Siegfried, carrying a tripod. Behind him, swathed in cameras, the Englishman.

He stopped dead, staring at her. "I don't believe it!"

Neither did she. Her heart was beating with excitement, just behind her ribs, vibrating there like a wild bird trapped in a cage.

He was wearing evening dress this time; not new, or trendy, but very elegant, what Hugh called a penguin suit, black jacket and trousers, stiff white shirt, black bow tie.

Bon chic, the French called it, because they loved the high style of the English upper class — traditional, unchanging, perfected through the ages.

If you knew the right boutiques in Paris you could buy English cashmere sweaters in taupe or pastel shades, to be worn over white shirts striped blue or red if you were a man, and if you were a woman with a blouse with open lapels with which you wore one single string of lucent, glowing pearls. To complete the look you wore heathery tweed jackets and skirts. If you were a slightly built, svelte Frenchwoman the combination was brilliant; large English women looked like carthorses in tweeds, in Claudia's opinion, but they went on wearing them, apparently oblivious, year after year.

Paris fashion came and went in tides, in, out, always the latest thing, the newest designers — but classy English chic was always the same, always fashionable in France, as well as England; in town or country, especially with the old rich, the decaying nobility who no longer had power or money, but had that essential class you could not fake or copy.

"This is a piece of luck," he said. "I hung about on the quay for an hour, hoping to see you come back, but there was no sign of you. I was afraid I'd lost my chance of seeing you again."

Claudia was aware of Siegfried and Patti staring, all ears.

"I didn't even know your name," he said.

"Claudia," Patti supplied before she could speak. "Claudia Guyon. And I'm Patti."

He turned slowly to look at Patti. "And I'm Ben." His black eyes opened wide. "Good God," he said. "You're amazing too! I must have some shots of you, Patti — no, keep working, it will take me a while to set up and I want you natural, not posed."

Claudia tried to concentrate on her work, but was very aware of his every move. He began taking shots of Patti, the flashes making Claudia's nerves jump. It was like having a thunderstorm in the room.

She was terrified of storms. The day her mother died there had been the worst storm she could remember.

"Are you asleep on your feet?"

The Englishman's voice made her jump. Blinking, she pulled herself together.

"Sorry, I was thinking. We have to start serving dinner in a minute. Could you stop taking pictures? You'll get in our way, distract us."

"Carry on, just ignore me."

How could she do that when every nerve in her body was so conscious of him? Turning away, she huskily told Patti to hurry up.

Moving to the serving table the Englishman focused on the bowls of soup.

"Wonderful colours," he murmured. "Is that deliberate? Is the way food looks, the dishes you serve in, important to you?"

"You see food before you eat it, so how it is presented is obviously vital."

"You're an artist, as well as a cook, then?"

"I'm just a cook, but all the senses are involved in preparing and eating food — sight, smell, taste."

"Touch?" he asked, running a long forefinger down her back, from her bare nape to her waist.

An erotic shiver followed that light touch. She turned away hastily and made herself concentrate on her work.

When Ben had finished taking pictures of the borscht, Siegfried picked up the tray of soup and went out. Swinging her way, Ben began taking pictures of Claudia as she put the bowl of marinated duck next to the hob on which she had a pan of foaming, caramelising butter.

She slid the duck in and fried it on both sides quickly, then turned down the heat and left it to cook for ten minutes.

Another flash from Ben's camera made her start. ''Could you stop?'' she snapped. ''You're giving me a headache.''

''Sorry about that. But you get used to the flash after a while. Trust me. Rex tells me you're one of the most fashionable chefs in Paris. Everyone wants to have you cook for them. What made you choose the job?''

''I was taught to cook as a child, by someone brilliant, a great cook, who wasn't a professional.''

''Your mother?''

''At first'' She wished he would stop talking. How could she work with him demanding her attention?

''Your parents must be very proud of you.''

''They're both dead.''

His face changed, grew serious. ''I'm sorry. Did they die recently?''

''No, my father died when I was very small, and my mother when I was fifteen.''

''That was tough. Who brought you up after that?''

''My godfather.''

He looked surprised. ''That's unusual. But I suppose in France that's a closer relationship than it is in England? Was he kind to you?''

''Very.''

''Do you cook for dinner parties every night?''

''Several nights a week. Usually weekends. I prefer to limit my engagements. Then the clients think you're special and they're happy to pay high prices. It works

40

out better, financially.''

"How about lunch?''

"Yes, I cook lunch for people too, although not as often as dinner.''

"I meant, how about having lunch with me? Tomorrow?''

She was very tempted, yet she still hesitated. What did she know about him, anyway? How did she know it hadn't been he who had broken into her apartment? He had been outside on the quayside that morning, hanging about for ages.

"Well, I'm not sure I ...''

"You must know the trendy places to eat. Where would you like to go?''

Siegfried returned. "M'sieur Valery wants you in there now, taking pictures of him with his guests.''

Ben grimaced. "Talk to you again later, Claudia. Siegfried, could you help carry the equipment back to the salon?''

Sighing, Siegfried obeyed. "I'm at everybody's beck and call, day and night!'' he moaned, trudging after the Englishman.

Claudia didn't see Ben again for several hours. Once dinner had been served and eaten she and her staff had to wash and clear up. It was midnight before they finished. Rex Valery came into the kitchen briefly to congratulate and thank them before giving her a cheque, then Siegfried and Patti took the various baskets and boxes down to the van.

Ben walked into the kitchen a moment later and

found her alone.

"Have you decided?"

She faced it — she couldn't resist seeing him again, getting to know him better.

"I know a little bistro near La Madeleine — the Paris Cameo. The patron is an old friend, her food is mouthwatering, but it is expensive, if you were hoping to get this lunch on expenses!"

"Let me worry about that. Shall I call for you — what's your address?"

"No, I have to go shopping in the morning. I'll see you there, at half-past twelve."

"Okay, the Paris Cameo, near La Madeleine — at twelve thirty?"

"As they're friends of mine, I'll book it, shall I?" She picked up her jacket.

He held it while she slid her arms into it; she was intensely aware of that long, athletic body right behind her, his breathing warm on her nape, his hands brushing her shoulders. She could not remember the last time she had met a man who had such a powerful physical effect on her.

The party was still going on; music, laughter, raised voices. It would probably go on until the early hours, then Rex would sleep through the morning, waking sometime in the afternoon.

"You look tired," Ben said as he walked with her to the lift.

"I am! Cooking a dinner like that can be a strain. Anything can go wrong, your nerves are stretched until it's all over. My professional reputation is on the line with every meal I cook.''

"I know how you must feel. Every picture I submit has to be as good as it gets, or I may lose not just that job, but any chance of getting others.''

She hadn't realised until then that he, too, had been working all evening.

"See you tomorrow,'' he said, taking her hand and lifting it to his mouth, brushing a brief, warm kiss over her skin. Claudia felt the same intense response to the contact. The kiss was nothing much — and yet it produced a sort of earthquake inside her.

She dropped Patti and Siegfried, then drove home thinking about Ben. Hugh would say she was being superstitious again, and laugh at her, but it seemed so strange that they had met twice today. Coincidence, Hugh would tell her, but was there such a thing as coincidence? Or was it fate working?

Had she and Ben always been meant to meet? Would they have met, sooner or later, anyway? If not here, in Paris, then somewhere else? She might have gone to London for a weekend break, and run into Ben in some other way. If it was meant to happen it would, some time, somewhere.

After putting the van into the garage, she walked home very fast along the quayside. There was nobody about now. The Seine was faintly choppy tonight, the grey waves glittering under the streetlights.

Her mind was in a peculiar state, almost euphoric. She had totally forgotten about her unwelcome visitor. Half-asleep she opened her front door and stumbled into the dark apartment.

As she reached for the light switch she felt a movement, heard breathing, but before she had a chance to scream or run out again, somebody grabbed her.

CHAPTER
TWO

Something was pulled down over her head. She put up a hand to drag it away and touched warm, soft, almost furry material. What on earth was it? Primal terror rose up in her throat. She tried to scream but the sound was smothered.

"*Ta gueule!*" a man growled close to her. "Shut your mouth." He yanked her arms behind her, tying them very tightly at the wrists with what felt like masking tape.

Claudia panicked. She couldn't breathe. She tried to struggle but was grabbed and hussled backwards, hearing the man breathing thickly close to her. Even through the thing over her head she could smell garlic on him, and wine, coarse, rough, cheap wine of the type you could buy in bulk in hypermarkets. She wouldn't even cook with it.

In French he told her again to shut up. "If you don't want to wind up with a bullet hole in your head, bitch, shut your mouth."

His hands roamed over her body, fondling and squeezing her breasts, her hips, down between her legs. He was wearing gloves, thin, supple leather gloves that made her skin creep; it was like being touched by an animal on heat.

"*Pas mal, salope*," he muttered. "No, not bad at all, your tits. I'm a tit man, myself, not a leg man. I think before we go I'll give you one, darling. You'd like that, wouldn't you?"

Claudia retched with disgust and fear, fighting to get away.

Another voice nearby growled, "Tie her up, and come and help me. You aren't here to enjoy yourself."

"Okay, okay, I'm coming. I'll deal with you later, *chérie,* don't think I've finished with you."

He dropped her and she was helpless to stop her fall. But she didn't crash down on to the floor as she expected. Instead she fell on the couch, her head spinning with vertigo at the violence of the change in position. She bounced briefly, face down. Lay still, trembling. The thing over her head was some sort of cloth bag. Every time she breathed she sucked it into her mouth.

Blind and with her hands tied behind her, she was afraid to move. If she tried to run she would probably fall over, they would catch her before she got to the front door.

Only yesterday she had read of a burglary where the victims were trussed like sausages while the gang rifled their homes. They had not been found until the next day, and one elderly woman had died of suffocation. What the police called *saucissonnage,* sausage-making, happened every day in the wealthier districts of Paris.

She could hear the men ransacking the apartment, moving from room to room, opening drawers and cupboards. What were they looking for? This was the third time they had searched the apartment — if there was something here they wanted, why hadn't they found it already?

Oh, God, what would they do to her when they came back? She could not bear the thought of it.

When she heard them coming, icy sweat trickled down her body.

They stopped moving. One of them grabbed hold of her arms, jerked her up to her feet. She staggered, fell back against the man holding her and he pushed a knee between her legs, parting them violently, making her stumble and start to fall.

"I told you I'd be back, darling."

The smell of him filled her throat with sickness.

The other man angrily told him, "Stop clowning around! Playtime's over. Listen, lady, we want some answers, and we want them now. Is there a hidden safe? Where is it? Don't waste any more of our time. Tell us, or we'll beat it out of you."

Her voice muffled by the cloth bag, she whispered, "I don't know what you're talking about."

"Oh, I think you do. You'll tell us sooner or later. Save yourself some pain. The safe — where is it?"

The man holding her pulled her closer, his body pushing and writhing against her buttocks in a simulation of sex. Even through her clothes she felt the swollen flesh inside his trousers.

A scream rose in her throat but she swallowed it. She wouldn't let him see he had got to her even though she was shaking.

"There isn't a safe," she whispered.

"I can't hear you! Say that again!"

"There isn't a safe!" she said louder through the smothering folds of the cloth in her mouth which the other man was pulling tight as if trying to make her choke.

"I still can't make out what she's saying! Stop playing games with her, will you? We're here to do a job, not have fun with the bitch."

She felt fingers fumbling at the back of her head where the bag was tied. The folds of cloth slackened.

"Say again!"

She snatched breath, swallowed. "I swear to you, there is no safe. There's nothing valuable here. We don't have any antiques or jewellery."

He struck her round the head. Her ears rang with the blow, she was deaf for a second, tears rising in her eyes.

"We aren't kidding around!"

Were they going to torture her? Kill her? She had never been so terrified in her life. Fear made it hard to think; she was possessed with a dread of what might happen next.

"Now listen to me — we know he's got what we're looking for, and we want it back. Tell him that!"

"Just give me ten minutes with her, I'll get her to talk," the man holding her said. "She'll be begging to spill her guts when I've finished with her."

"You just want to fuck her, any excuse will do. Ever since you saw her outside this morning you've been drooling over her. I don't care what you do to women in your own time. But this is business, not pleasure. Get that through your head, you stupid bastard.''

"Look at that body! Don't you want her? Look, okay, you can go first. A nice little bonus for both of us. She'd sing like a bird afterwards.''

"We haven't got time! And anyway, I don't think she knows a thing. If she's only the tenant, why should he tell her anything? I never tell women secrets. They can't keep their mouths shut.''

"You just don't like women! You gay, or something?''

The other snarled like a dog. "You want a kick in the balls? Your trouble is, you can't keep your mind on your job. Let the bitch go. We have to get out of here.''

"*Merde.* Oh, OK, OK.''

He opened his hands and a second later she hit the floor with a cry of pain.

From above her the other said, "Tell Hepburn to give it back. Right? Or next time I'll let my friend loose on you. And you'll wish you were dead afterwards. He's no Prince Charming.''

The other man laughed throatily. "She'd have the time of her life and be begging for more. Every woman loves a bit of rough. I bet you do, eh, darling?''

A foot kicked her hard in the ribs and she jerked in agony, groaning aloud.

"OK, that's enough of that. Listen carefully, M'mselle. Tell Hepburn it has to be given back. Or you'll pay the price. As you see, my friend enjoys beating women up.

They began to move away. She lay on the floor, shaking, listening to their footsteps departing. The front door opened, was clicked softly shut.

Claudia was too scared to move in case they came back. When she was sure they had gone, she scrambled to her feet, let her head droop and shook it until the bag fell off. The lights were on everywhere. She blinked, swaying as her knees gave under her.

Leaning on a chair back for a moment, she waited for her breathing to slow down. Her teeth were chattering with shock. Her face felt hot, feverish, yet she shivered with cold at the same time. Her ribs hurt like hell whenever she took a breath.

And how was she to free her wrists? They had wound wide brown masking tape around both wrists.

Going through to the kitchen she managed to get a carving knife out of a drawer. Holding it behind her, she began to saw, slowly and gingerly, afraid of cutting her wrists. The tape gave way, layer by layer.

At last the final strand broke. She dropped the knife back into the open drawer. Her arms hurt as she brought them forward. She sat down and massaged her wrists for a minute to get the blood flowing again.

Then she hurried to the front door, put the chain on, a painful sigh of relief escaping once she was sure she was safe.

Now she could ring the police. They couldn't think she was imagining things this time. She had the evidence of her bruises.

She picked up the phone and dialled the emergency services. The call wasn't answered straight away. While she listened to the ringing it suddenly dawned on her that it might be dangerous to involve the police.

She had to talk to Hugh first.

She slammed the phone down again.

Was Hugh mixed up in something illegal? Something dangerous?

"Tell him to give it back!" they had told her.

Give what back? What did Hugh have that they wanted? Who were they, or who did they work for?

Before she called in the police she must talk to Hugh to make sure it was safe.

She dialled the number of the villa with shaky fingers, but there was no reply. The phone rang and rang.

Fear jumped in her throat.

It was so late. Where on earth could they be at this time of night?

Had the villa been burgled too? Had something happened to Hugh and Louise?

Should she ring the local police? Get them to go round to the villa to check they were OK?

She hesitated, biting her lip. The local Mafia were involved in so many businesses on the Riviera — both legitimate, jewellery, hotels, casinos, to the vice which ran in a dark seam beneath the surface of the glamorous life; drugs, illegal gambling, prostitution. If Hugh had somehow got mixed up in something shady he might not thank her for involving the police.

What if he had been researching for a book about the South of France Mafia? She remembered Graham Greene's book *J'Accuse* — he had fallen foul of a criminal element in Nice and had been threatened.

She put the phone down — she would try again later.

A hand on her aching ribcage, she went round the

apartment. Again, they had done their work without leaving any evidence of their presence, except what they had done to her. They were professionals; knew exactly what they were doing.

How could Hugh be mixed up with them? And in what?

She went into the bathroom to strip, see what damage they had done. A bruise across her diaphragm was beginning to turn blue. She felt it tentatively, wincing. It hurt to breathe.

There were a couple of other bruises on her hip at the side where she had fallen, and some deep, dark red fingermarks on her arms and shoulder, where the man had held her.

You could not see the damage to her mind.

She felt dirty. She had a shower, as hot as she could stand it, wishing her mind would stop flashing her images of the man running his hands over her, his body jerking and grinding into hers as he stood behind her, breathing thickly with excitement.

She towelled herself and put on a nightdress and robe to cover the body he had fondled.

Then she poured herself a glass of brandy and swallowed it in two gulps, gasping at the heat of the spirit in her throat.

The coldness inside her began to ebb. She was feeling a little better.

She dialled Hugh's number again. This time she got his answering machine. He and Louise must have come back and gone straight up to bed.

She didn't waste time, just burst out, ''Hugh, the flat

has been burgled. I don't know what they were looking for, but they said to tell you to give it back — whatever that means. There's no sign of a break-in, and they were wearing gloves, I'm sure there will be no fingerprints. Nothing has been taken, either. Shall I call the police? Ring me, Hugh, as soon as you can.''

She hung up, made herself a hot-water bottle, and before she went to bed she piled chairs up against the front door.

They wouldn't get in again without waking her and giving her time to call the police.

In bed she lay listening to Paris outside, the wail of a police car in the distance, traffic in the city, voices on the quayside, a woman's breathless laugh.

She would never get to sleep, she was too scared and worried; her body ached all over. If only she could stop trembling. She was so cold, too. Despite that hot shower. She closed her eyes and did breathing exercises to calm herself. Breathed in through her nose with her mouth closed, out with her mouth open. Wouldn't let herself think or remember what had happened. Just breathe.

Warmth percolated through her, her body slowly relaxed.

It only seemed five minutes later that she was woken by a loud ringing of the door bell.

She sat up, shaking. The noise didn't stop. Dazed and bewildered, she got up, fumbled for the lacy gown that matched the white satin nightdress she was wearing, and was amazed to see the sun had risen.

For a second she could not understand why there was a

pyramid of chairs leaning against the front door, then she remembered last night, her heart leaping with shock.

Had they come back?

But they wouldn't ring the front-door bell.

It couldn't be Hugh, could it?

Hands shaking, she began taking down the chairs. The bell rang again noisily, in an impatient, peremptory way, and she jumped, dropping the last chair with a loud crash.

She had to stop that noise. Her head was splitting with headache. She opened the door with a jerk, keeping it on the chain as she peered out.

''Ben?'' In her relief, she took the door off the chain.

He stared at her with the same blank incredulity she was feeling.

''What are you doing here?'' she asked him, and by then his face had changed. He looked her up and down, his mouth hard and contemptuous as he took in her sleep-flushed face, her nightdress, her tousled hair.

Why was he looking at her like that?

''How did you get my address? Did Rex give it to you?''

He pushed her aside and walked in without a word.

''Hey, what do you think you're doing?'' Bewildered and angry, she shut the front door and went after him.

He was striding through the apartment, looking into every room. She couldn't believe he was behaving so badly. At the door of her bedroom he stopped, stared at the tumbled bed, then at her, and that look on his face made ice crawl down her back.

''Where is he?''

She was beginning to feel she was living in a nightmare. Her world had been turned upside down and she never knew from one second to the next what was going to hit her next.

Was Ben part of whatever was going on?

"Who?" she asked warily.

"You know who I'm talking about! I know he lives here, so don't lie to me."

"Lives here? Who?"

"Hugh Hepburn!"

So it had not been a coincidence that they had met twice yesterday. He had been hanging around on the quay deliberately. Probably even knew she would be cooking dinner for Rex later. Coincidence hell. She had been set up.

The worst part of it was, she had liked him. A lot.

"Hugh owns the apartment," she wearily admitted. There was no point in lying, after all. "But he isn't here, he..."

"Then where is he?" His eyes flashed to the bed. "Obviously only one bed was used last night, so the two of you shared it. Where has he gone?"

"What the hell are you talking about? He doesn't live here. I rent the apartment from him."

Ben stared tensely at her, those black eyes glittering. "You rent this flat from him? He doesn't live here?"

"No, he does not! I live here. Alone!"

"Then where does he live?"

"Cap d'Antibes."

He had seemed such fun, been so charming. How easy it was to be fooled by a man.

"Give me his full address, and telephone number." He pulled out a notebook and pen.

She threw dislike at him, face angry. "The hell I will. Hugh doesn't like visitors, especially unannounced visitors. Tell me where you're staying and I'll tell him you want to talk to him, he can ring you if he wants to see you."

"I left a letter downstairs for him — did you find it? Have you sent it on to him?"

Her eyes widened. "Yes, I have." So the letter had been from him? That had not occurred to her. But then why would it? "He can get in touch with you, if he wants to, then."

"I can't wait. I must see him today. I have to talk to him urgently. Ring him and tell him that."

The way he spoke to her made her teeth meet. She looked at the clock on her bedside table. It was just gone eight. Hugh always got up early. He ate breakfast at seven, went for a walk by the sea, began working at his desk by eight.

"He'll be writing by now, he doesn't like being interrupted when he's working. He'll have left the answering machine on and won't get any messages until he breaks for lunch."

"Then leave a message for him. Tell him I'll take the next plane to Nice and be at the villa sometime this afternoon. Now, give me his address."

Her curiosity got the better of her. "Do you actually know him? Or should I say, does he know you?"

"We've never met, no."

She gave him a scornful smile. "But you want to

56

photograph him, I suppose? He won't agree, he never does interviews with the press and hates being photographed.''

''He was a journalist himself!''

''That's why. He knows exactly how they twist what you say.''

''Well, I'm not after an interview, nor do I want to take photos of him. This is personal business, and I'm not discussing it with you. I have to speak to him.''

''If you don't know him, and you don't want to photograph him, why should he see you?''

''Just tell him it's Benedict.''

''Benedict? Not Ben?''

''Ben's the short version. He'll know who I am. Now, will you give me that address?''

''You can wait until he gets your letter. It should only take a couple of days.''

His eyes took on an angry smoulder, hot black jet. ''I haven't got time. This is urgent. I thought he would get that letter yesterday and ring me during the day, but of course he didn't. That was why I came here before breakfast this morning. I wanted to be sure of catching him in, I have to talk to him as soon as possible.''

She was fiercely curious now. What was he after? Was he involved with the burglars? Maybe he had sent them! Or was he also after whatever they were looking for? Had they sent him in here because they had failed?

It couldn't be a coincidence that he had turned up here this morning. All this had to be connected. What on earth did Hugh have that these men wanted? It must be something important, something explosive.

She felt so ill. Worse than she had before Ben had showed up. She couldn't stand here arguing much longer. Hugh would have to deal with Ben. The villa was well protected. The electronic security had been installed during the rebuilding, after the storm had hit the chimneys, the day her mother died. Hugh had paid for the best in modern security, and he had updated it last year.

Expensive villas on the Cap d'Antibes were always under threat from thieves breaking in to steal jewellery, electrical equipment, even furniture. A house nearby had lost its entire contents last summer; the owners had come back after a weekend in Paris to find everything gone. Neighbours, seeing the furniture being put into a removal van, had assumed the owners were moving to a new home.

But Hugh's precautions went further. Usually either he or Louise was at home, or, if they were both out, as they had been yesterday, the gardener/handyman, Jules, was always there, at work around the villa, or in his flat over the garage. It wouldn't be easy to get into the grounds. The gate was fifteen feet high, the walls topped with electrified wire that set off an alarm if anyone touched it. Now and then birds alighting on it set the alarm off and sometimes a local brown squirrel was killed by the electricity.

If Ben did manage to climb the wall or the gate, negotiating the electric wiring, or Jules, would deal with him.

Jules was not tall, but he was very, very strong, a squat, muscled man in his fifties with a face like an amiable gorilla, brown, hairy, wrinkled with sun and wind.

He had worked for Hugh for years; the two men liked each other and often played boules together. It had been Jules who had introduced Hugh to the real local people; the French who worked there, instead of those who came down for a few months for the sun from colder areas of France. They were the friends Hugh wanted, not the expats and luxury-seekers in their villas.

"Come on!" Ben insisted. "Give me the address."

"Bastide de la Mer, Chemin de Croe, Cap d'Antibes."

Ben scribbled down the address as she dictated it, then looked up. "I'm afraid lunch is off, I shall have to rush."

She gave him an incredulous, bitter stare. "You don't really think I would go out with you now?"

He grimaced, put out a hand to touch her arm in a placatory gesture. "Look, I'm sorry I turned nasty. I got the wrong end of the stick when you opened the door looking like that! I had no idea Hugh had moved out. Or that he had let the apartment. I wasn't expecting to see you. I thought..." His gaze ran over her again, sensual appraisal heating it.

"Oh, you made it obvious what you thought!" she interrupted furiously recoiling from that look. She had had enough of men.

"Claudia, I'm really sorry. I liked you on sight — really liked you. That was why I was so angry when you opened the door just now. I thought you must be Hugh's woman, and that you'd made a fool of me."

"Snap!" she said fiercely. "You certainly made a

fool of me!''

"It was dumb of me to jump to conclusions like that. I have a hot temper, and at the moment I've got a lot on my mind, personal stuff, I can't explain yet. Say I come back to Paris in a couple of weeks. Couldn't we meet, talk, get to know each other better?''

"You must be kidding! I never want to see you again. Now, get out of my apartment!'' She walked to the front door, her chest still painful when she breathed too deeply. Had that kick broken one of her ribs?

Ben stopped, staring at the litter of chairs. "What on earth have you been doing?''

"Mind your own business. Just clear off.'' She pushed him through the open door, shut it with a slam and put the catch back on.

It took her several minutes to put the chairs back into their customary places; each bend of her body made her flinch.

Why hadn't she heard from Hugh? Surely he must have listened to the answerphone tape by now? Maybe he hadn't bothered? That wouldn't surprise her. When he was writing he ignored the outside world.

His routine was unalterable; at his desk every day until lunchtime, when he ate a salad on the terrace above the pine-scented garden looking down at the blue swimming pool.

She tried again to ring Hugh, but only got the answering machine, so she made herself some black coffee, ate a fruit breakfast, and looked through her order book to check her next engagement. All she had for the next week was the teenage party, for which she planned to get Patti to cook something excitingly different.

Maybe she should go down to Cap d'Antibes to talk to Hugh face to face?

Could Patti and Siegfried cope without her?

After another long, hot shower she felt a little less stiff and painful. She dressed in white jeans and a navy-blue sweater, then cleaned the flat obsessively, feeling as if the men had left their fingermarks on everything, even though they had worn gloves.

Every hour or so she tried ringing the villa, and finally, at noon, Louise answered the phone, her clipped French lifting at the sound of Claudia's voice.

Small, brisk, busy, Louise had cooked for Hugh for years, and had taken over as housekeeper when Claudia's mother had become too ill to cope with the work. She had helped nurse Marie Guyon, had comforted Claudia through those terrible months. Claudia owed her a debt she could never repay.

"*Comment ça va, ma petite?* You haven't rung for weeks! We were beginning to think you had forgotten all about us."

"I left a message on the answering machine — didn't Hugh hear it?"

"I don't think so — I switched the answerphone off myself just now, but of course I didn't listen to the tape. He didn't eat breakfast. Made himself coffee before I was up, took an orange and an apple, and went into his study. Was the message urgent? Nothing's wrong, is it?"

"Well..." She hesitated, not wanting to tell Louise anything until she had talked to Hugh.

61

"Aren't you getting enough work?" guessed Louise.

"Oh, yes. Last night I cooked for Rex Valery."

"No?" gasped Louise, who never went to the theatre, but loved watching films on the television she had in the staff apartment at the back of the house, where Claudia and her mother had lived for all those years.

The bedroom and sitting room were furnished with solid nineteenth-century stuff like the furniture in Hugh's bedroom here. Claudia had often wondered where it came from; some of it was English in style, some French. It was mostly old and valuable. Louise kept it all lovingly polished and immaculate.

Claudia closed her eyes and saw it as she had throughout the years she had lived there, feeling homesick for the house, for the gardens, for the miraculous view through the pines.

"What did you cook for him?" Louise asked eagerly. Claudia had learned to cook in the villa kitchen, standing beside Louise while she beat eggs, whipped cream, sliced and shredded and cooked.

Claudia told her, and Louise sighed with gratification. "My duck? And that chocolate bombe I taught you to make? Ah, very good, I wish I had been there. And is he as charming as he always seems?"

"Exactly as he seems, he's a lovely man."

"Is it true he's . . . you know?!"

"Gay?" smiled Claudia. "Yes, he has a boyfriend who lives with him, *un type Chinois,* very chic, with skin liked oiled gold."

Louise clicked her tongue. "Ah, well, live and let live."

Normally Claudia would linger to chat with her, but today was different. "Sorry, Louise, but I really need to talk to Hugh, urgently, could you get him?"

"Of course, he's sitting out on the terrace, with a glass. Hold on, I'll get him."

His voice on the line a moment later sounded strangely English, perhaps because she had been talking to Ben that morning.

Normally it never entered her head that Hugh was English. He had lived in France for so long; his accent was so familiar.

"Claudia — how are you?"

"Okay, but..."

He picked up on her tone. "Is something wrong?"

"Yes, something scary happened. We were burgled."

"Burgled? What was taken?"

"Nothing, but ... I'd better begin at the beginning. It started the night before, actually. I came home and the whole apartment smelt of cigarette smoke. Well, you know, I don't smoke, and I hadn't had any visitors that day; even if I had I wouldn't have let them smoke, you know I hate the smell since..."

Gently he said, "Yes, I know. Me too. So someone had broken into the apartment?"

"That was just it — there was no sign of a break-in and nothing missing. I decided I must have imagined it. But when I got home from marketing next day I smelt smoke again, and this time there was ash on the floor."

"Ash?"

"You said that just the way the police did! Honestly, there was ash on the floor of your room."

His voice sharpened. "You called the police?"

"I called them, but they never came. They thought I was crazy, complaining about being burgled when nothing had been taken, just some ash left on the floor. They obviously thought I knew who had left the ash. I was so angry I never got around to telling them that one of the drawers in your bureau was open — I could tell that somebody had been reading the letters in there."

"Why the hell didn't you ring me at once?"

"I tried! The phone just rang and rang. The answerphone wasn't switched on, so I couldn't leave a message."

"Ah ... of course, Louise and I were at the local wine co-operative, all day, helping get the hall ready for the June dinner-dance. We had lunch with Georges and Michel, at the bar; came home mid-afternoon, then changed and went back for dinner. I remembered to set the answerphone when we got back."

"I know, I left a message on it — obviously you didn't listen to the tape before you went off to work?"

"No, sorry, I just went to my desk first thing."

"Well, that wasn't the end of it. I was working last night, and when I got back, after midnight, I walked in on them. Two men. They jumped me before I saw them, put a cloth bag over my head and tied my hands."

Hugh swore violently. "Did they hurt you?"

She felt her ribs, grimacing. "Not really — I got a bit of a shock, and a kick in the ribs, that's all."

He swore again. "The bastards. You must go to the doctor, check that they didn't break anything."

"What can a doctor do? You know you just have to

wait for a broken rib to heal. A few bruises, that's probably all that's wrong.''

"Did they say what they were looking for?''

"No, but they were searching your room again, Hugh. Before they left they asked me where your safe was, and I told them you didn't have one. I asked what they were looking for, but they didn't tell me, just said to tell you they wanted it back, whatever it is. And they left the apartment like a new pin. Hugh, there's absolutely nothing to give away the fact that they were ever here. They wore gloves; no fingerprints. If I called the police they wouldn't find anything.''

"Did they ask where I was living?''

She frowned. "No, which is odd, I suppose that means they already know?''

"Yes,'' he said flatly.

"But that wasn't the end of it, Hugh. At around eight o'clock this morning I was woken up by someone ringing the door bell. An Englishman forced his way in and searched the apartment.''

"An Englishman? You mean, the other two were French?''

"Yes.''

"Was this Englishman working with the first two?''

"How do I know? Maybe. But he was nothing like them — they were nasty pieces of work. One of them wanted to rape me.''

"Christ! You didn't tell me that!''

"It didn't happen, it was all just talk.'' She thought of the fondling hands, the excited breathing, and swallowed sickness, but made herself go on. "But the

Englishman was different. I knew him, Hugh..."

"Knew him?"

"I'd met him at Rex Valery's party — he's a photographer, he was taking pictures for an English magazine."

A silence fell, then, "Do you know his name?"

"Ben. I didn't get a surname."

"Ben?" Hugh sounded breathless, as if he had been punched in the stomach.

"He told me to tell you he was Benedict — does that ring bells?"

Hugh asked curtly, "What did he look like?"

"Well, he has your colouring and..." It suddenly struck her, and she said slowly, "Actually, he does look rather like photos of you when you were young. Could he be a relative of yours?"

"How old would you say he is?"

"A few years older than me. Not thirty yet, in his late twenties."

Hugh was silent again, then said abruptly, "Look, *chérie,* I'd like you to come down here, where I can make sure you're safe. It might be dangerous for you to be in the apartment alone for a few days."

"Hugh, what is this all about? You know, don't you?"

"I'll explain when you get here. Pack and come at once. Get a plane to Nice, take a taxi from the airport And, Claudia — keep your eyes open until you get here, don't talk to strangers, be very careful."

CAP D'ANTIBES

3 September 1939

CHAPTER
THREE

The sun was hot on his naked back as he walked to the side of the pool, watching the blue water flicker in the light. The weather was holding up amazingly well considering they were into September now. On the Riviera there was often a sudden drop into autumn in late August, although the weather usually improved later; winters could be very mild, while in England mists and rain turned to icy roads and snow.

A shiver ran down his spine at the thought of English rain. How he would love to be riding through English rain, mild, soft, gentle English rain, along the sandy bridle paths at Windsor between the oaks and ancient elm trees.

But he would not let himself think that way. He had made his choice. He couldn't have any regrets. In any case, he had always loved the sun. That was why they were here, on Cap d'Antibes, where summer lingered longest.

The sunrises were breathtaking. He had been out here, this morning, taking the dog for a walk. Across the tip of the Cap he had seen the orange ball of the sun swim up out of the sea on the misty horizon, and had paused with an intake of pleasure. The air had been fresh and cool; it had felt good on his feverish skin. He hadn't slept well last night. Some nights he barely slept at all. All his life he had been an insomniac, but since he had left England, it had grown so much worse that he barely noticed his lack of sleep any more. Only noticed when he occasionally got a good night.

This morning he had set off at a brisk pace, noting the elaborate webs of spiders stretched between some of the rose trees, a sign autumn was beginning.

Beyond the gardens lay a belt of close-set pines and date palms. He had walked through them, watching the black bars of shadow between the trunks. One detached itself and became a man.

"Guten Morgen, Hoheit."

He had felt a leap of alarm, had snapped. "For God's sake, Stevie, no German!" But he grinned with affection a second later. They had known each other since 1918 when Stevie's older brother, his fellow officer in the regiment, had got married. Stevie had been a very reluctant pageboy in a kilt; and he, himself, had been best man, also wearing the kilt. Whenever he thought of Stevie he saw that beautiful, sulky blond boy glowering as he walked up the aisle behind the bride, followed by a gaggle of bridesmaids in pale pink. First impressions never quite wear out.

"Thanks for coming, Stevie. Did anyone see you?"

"No, sir?"

"Sure?"

"Absolutely."

He had been an Adonis as a boy. He was an impressive man, now, with an upright, military bearing. Wide-shouldered, slim, clearly very fit, although his sleek blond hair had the merest trace of silver at the temples. But maybe the Riviera sun had bleached it. Stevie spent every spare free day here in his villa soaking up sunshine.

"Not a soul about at this hour, sir. Not on the Cap. Only the staff are up, and they're too busy cleaning the villas or gardening to notice anything happening beyond the walls."

Apart from the Hôtel du Cap, set in its own spacious grounds, and a couple of other, smaller, hotels, this was an area of detached villas. The people who stayed here were up half the night, often partying with each other, and slept until late in the morning behind high walls while their staff worked hard, cleaning, washing up, gardening.

"Good man. Look, Stevie, I want you to take care of something. Mustn't fall into the wrong hands. You can be sure they'll search my luggage."

"Of course, sir. I've already been recalled to the regiment, I leave for England tomorrow afternoon. But I have a safe place in the villa. Even if it is searched nobody will ever find it. Any messages for me to pass on before I leave?"

"I'll have a letter for you to code and send by radio. Come tonight, once the lights go out in la Croe. I'll let you in myself. Don't knock, just come up the seaward side, on to the terrace and wait by the library windows, I'll be watching out for you. Be very careful, Stevie. Make absolutely certain you aren't seen or followed. I'm being watched, but they leave once the lights are out.''

Stevie laughed, showing very white teeth. ''I know, I've seen them — the French or our people?''

''Oh, ours. They park in the lane and watch us through binoculars. Even the postman has noticed them and commented to our staff. They stick out like sore thumbs. Totally useless! Time they were properly trained.''

''Clumsy asses. I won't be using the road, I'll come over the wall as usual, through the pines, they won't spot me.''

Nothing moved or stirred among the pines or on the paths. All he heard was the crooning wood pigeons and the eternal cicadas chirruping among the pines, but he had felt the hair stand up on his neck in primitive uneasiness.

''Just remember, there are eyes and ears everywhere, you can't be too careful. See you tonight.''

He had barely taken a step away before Stephen had melted back among the pines; quicksilver, silent. Unlike the men watching the villa, he was trained to a hair and made no stupid slip-ups.

When he got back to la Croe he took his bath in the gilded stone tub with a swan's head at each end. His valet had put out for him a black short-sleeved shirt and white shorts, as he had ordered; a secret joke of his for Wallis, who smiled as she saw him walk into her soft pink and apricot bedroom; ultra feminine colours which glowed like the morning sky.

''Coffee, David?''

He kissed her cheek. ''Thank you, darling.''

Their images were fractured, broken up, twisted, and

reflected all around the room in the endless mirrors. Wallis had had the furniture painted in *trompe-l'oeil,* which he felt was so clever, such an original idea and so typical of her.

Even the hairbrushes on her dressing table were painted, not real, although, of course, she had real hairbrushes, silver or ivory-backed.

On a matching chest were painted mementoes of their courtship — his first invitation card to her, a piece of a love letter, a pair of long white evening gloves, a pair of his golfing socks. Some people looked askance — but only old-fashioned, dull-witted people — never their real friends.

Wallis's maid brought clothes out to be approved. Wallis took her time, frowning at the little black dress from Chanel.

"I don't want to look as if I'm sorry the war has begun!"

He silently shook his head at her behind the maid's back. They had to be very careful with remarks like that. Anybody could betray them.

Wallis hated the English now, especially those of the establishment who had rejected her and driven them out of England. Bertie and that wife of his; even Mama.

She made a face over a silver-thread Schiaparelli, settled on a cream Molyneux dress; beautifully cut linen designed on simple, elegant lines.

"I love you in that dress, darling," he said, getting up to leave so that she could be dressed.

"I thought you loved me whatever I wore, David!"

Her eyes mocked him as he kissed her hand. He still

did not feel certain of her; she eluded him like a will-o'-the-wisp.

In the corridor he passed her secretary, carrying a sheaf of letters to be answered.

"Good morning, your Royal Highness," she said with the little bob Wallis liked her to give them.

"Good morning, Gertrude. Her Royal Highness is getting dressed, she won't be ready for half an hour at least! Lovely morning, isn't it?"

His cheerfulness brought a startled look into her eyes. Stupid to forget. He must remember to look grave today. That is what people would be expecting; grim solemnity.

He took the small lift up to the penthouse, to his own quarters, which he called the Belvedere to remind him of the much-loved home he had had to leave behind and still missed. His secretary, Diana Hood, was waiting to deal with the usual huge pile of letters.

His time was strictly organised. That was how he liked it. Every morning the first thing he did was consult the schedule Wallis had drawn up the previous evening. The functions they would attend, plans for playing tennis or swimming, the names of visitors they expected, where they would lunch and dine and with whom. He was accustomed to living by a schedule. Blank spaces in his day sent him almost into panic. He had to know what to expect.

Everyone in England would be on tenterhooks waiting to find out what this day brought, but he had known for months, ever since he had visited Germany and met Hitler at Berchtesgaden. Oh, he had not been sure it would be war, had seen that it was inevitable. He had tried his best to avert this outcome. Nobody had listened or taken him seriously. They had smiled and shrugged away all his warnings.

So here they were again, on the edge of an abyss they could have avoided but for those grey old men who refused to understand what confronted them.

"Morning, Diana! I can see we have a lot to do this morning, so we'll get down to it at once. I want to fit in a swim later."

"Yes, sir."

He walked to and fro restlessly, checking other correspondence in files, glancing through books to make sure of facts, holding letters in his hand and dropping them on the floor once he had dealt with them. Diana took shorthand, standing up. He couldn't allow her to sit in his presence. As Wallis said, it would have been the thin end of the wedge. He must not lose sight of who he was, nor must his staff. Usually the floor was covered with letters by the time he had finished. Diana would pick them all up, take them away and file them.

While she typed up his letters he looked through the telescope, watching the incongruously calm, sunlit sea, the dazzling white of villas among the trees.

The decor around him was all blue and white too — curtains and chairs blue, and white covers on the sofa. These marine colours dominated the whole villa downstairs as well, but he had chosen to surround himself up here with memories of Fort Belvedere, his home near Windsor. Everywhere his eye alighted he liked to see the familiar objects he had had there. A ship's chronometer that had belonged to his father, a brass ship's bell, trophies he had won at golf and hunting, silver-framed photographs of his parents, of family and friends. He needed to feel at home. It eased the ache of exile.

He had not known how much he loved his own country until he was shut out of it.

A little breeze off the sea blew towards him the pungent odour of the *maquis*. This scent could be found everywhere around the Mediterranean.

Strongest early in the morning or after rain, the fragrance of pine and olive trees, juniper, myrtle, heath, mingled with the smell of herbs, spiky rosemary, thyme, basil, lemon-scented balm, mint, sage. As your foot crushed them when you walked, the aroma became overpowering.

Whenever he was anywhere else in the world he could close his eyes and almost believe he was back here simply by remembering that complex, marvellous perfume.

He glanced surreptitiously at his watch again. Seven minutes to eleven. Why did they always choose eleven in the morning? The last war had ended at eleven o'clock. He remembered that grey, November day, church bells suddenly ringing again, bare trees, wet roofs, skeletal leaves in the gutters, the mist, the sound of wild cheering outside in the streets, the tears that had sprung into everyone's eyes.

And then the parties had broken out. Champagne, dry and cold, bursting on his tongue, kisses, laughter, hope, the dancing, all night.

He had been twenty-four and had felt very old. On his last birthday he had been forty-five.

Forty-five. God. Downhill all the way from here.

He made for the lift again — time to change for a swim. Must appear calm, casual.

They were walking down towards the pool when one of the footmen in the red and gold royal livery ran out breathlessly gasping, "Your Royal Highness ... an urgent phone call, the British Ambassador calling from Paris."

"This is it," she murmured, too softly for anyone but him to hear. Graceful as a cat in her black swimsuit, which she had no intention of getting wet, her eyes hidden by dark glasses, she looked as calm as a saucer of milk, but he knew she wasn't. Her ulcers had been playing up in the night; she had been in agony, poor darling.

He walked back into the villa. In London, were they hoping it would never happen? Hoping the Germans would give in, back off, that there would be no war? The people would not want this war.

How many of them would die this time? He thought of the faces he had seen in Wales so few years ago. Coal-dirt bitten like ink into the etches of their faces, around the eyes, the mouth; gaunt, hungry, angry men who had yet sung as they lined the streets to greet him. The lifting up of their voices had brought tears to his eyes. He had felt so impotent. Nobody in London would lift a finger to help.

All the politicians had listened, nodded, sighed, smiled politely, but he had known they were secretly unmoved, indifferent. He had pleaded, protested, shouted, tried to insist that something ... surely ... something could be done for Wales?

Nothing ever had been done, nothing ever was. Now those men would be sent off to fight and die in agony for the country that had never done anything for them. All that talk about the war to end wars, and here they were again!

Well, at least he had nothing to reproach himself with — he had not got them into this stupid, pointless war with a nation which was closer to them in blood than any other; *Verwandtschaft*, kinfolk, *Brüder*.

He would never have gone down this road. He would have made peace with Germany. His roots went back into German soil, he never forgot that. He never would.

They had known that, those old men in London. That was why they had made up their minds to get rid of him. His teeth clamped tight. Oh, they would pay for that. For all the insults, the affronts, the coldness. It would soon be their turn to pack and go.

He lifted the telephone. "Hallo?"

The British ambassador to Paris sounded tired. Up all night no doubt, as he and Wallis had been. But his formality and distance was unchanged. "Your Royal Highness, there has been no response to the ultimatum. Britain is now at war with Germany."

"What do they want us to do? Go home?"

Home, home, his blood sang.

"I have no instructions as yet, sir," the ambassador said coldly.

But they would have to let him go back to England

now; they dared not leave him here.

"Well, thank you for letting me know so promptly."

Bertie should have rung him, not ordered someone else to do it. He had been trying to talk to Bertie for days, but was never put through. They had been so close once. This coldness hurt.

He blamed her, that sonsie housewife Bertie had married. Scottish as Haggis; provincial and narrow-minded. Wallis hated her, with good reason.

After the cool of the house his eyes flinched from the sun as he walked out again.

Wallis watched him alertly.

"We're going home," he said, fighting to sound calm, and dived into the pool.

The ripples spread, worldwide.

CAP D'ANTIBES

EARLY SUMMER 1999

CHAPTER
FOUR

So that was how they meant to play it, Hugh thought, standing at the window of his office.

He had been expecting a response sooner or later. His publishers knew about the book. He had talked to the head of the firm on the phone a week ago. Jarvis had been amazed, incredulous, had asked a hundred questions. This book was so different from anything he had ever written for them.

The grapevine would have started up within hours. He had been waiting for the news to spread, and for somebody to get in touch in an attempt to reason with him, plead for him to change his mind. Not that he would have listened or backed off, but he had wanted them to beg. That would have felt good, having them on their knees, admitting that he, of all people, had power over them.

But there had been no direct approach after all. Just this crude attack, the threat of what might come next.

That was not what he had been expecting.

He turned away irritably and paced the room, his eyes sliding over the photographs and maps lining the walls. A vast map of France, with red, white and blue pins stuck into it at intervals, a map of Spain with a few pins around Barcelona and the coastal area, another of Portugal with pins stuck into Lisbon and the border with Spain. Around each map were pinned pictures of people, some cuttings from ancient, yellowing newspapers.

He paused to stare at a photo of the Duke of Windsor standing beside Hitler at Berchtesgaden, Hitler's country retreat near Munich. The two men were smiling at each other while a crowd of people cheered and waved.

Oh, he should have guessed what reaction he would get when the news reached them. He knew them too well not to know how their minds worked.

Around the map of France were pinned postcards of towns; Paris, the forests beyond it, the royal palace of Versailles, white and gold like a wedding cake, the brooding, bloodstained old fortress of Vincennes, the boulevards at the heart of the city, the Champs-Elysées, the rue de Rivoli, the Place de la Concorde, and the Arc de Triomphe.

La gloire. That was printed on every Frenchman's heart. The glory of war, the glory of France. Even now. As a nation they had not changed much in centuries.

His gaze drifted on over the map and hovered over the hot south, the familiar valleys and woods he loved. Here he had pinned to the map photos he had taken himself of Antibes in summer, of Cannes in winter, the hotels like canyons of snow behind the palms, of the winding streets of Cap d'Antibes.

Further along the map he had pinned to the wandering line of coast, a late nineteenth-century postcard, hand-painted, faded and oddly insubstantial, of the tree-lined avenue of medieval tombs in Les Alyscamps at Arles. Many artists had painted it; he could have used a clear, hard, reproduction of a Van Gogh or a Gauguin, but he had preferred the sense of another time, of lyrical strangeness, which the old postcard gave him.

He had been working on this book for years, gathering together his materials from various sources in England and France. He hadn't written a word, however, until he had read something in a gossip column in *The Times*.

That was what he had been waiting for; reading it had galvanised him. The time had come. He must begin writing.

He had known for years what he must do. When had they discovered the danger they were facing? He had thought about that many times, wondering when they would get in touch and what they would say to him.

He would not listen, of course. They deserved what he meant to do to them. They had destroyed his life. He had waited years to get his revenge.

He ought to have guessed they wouldn't approach him at all. That was not their style. They wouldn't admit anything; they were too serpentine, devious, a race of vipers. But he hadn't expected that they might try to get at him through Claudia.

They must be very frightened.

Claudia rang the airport as soon as she got off the phone to Hugh. She was lucky; there was a seat on the next plane to Nice, but she had a breakneck race to get to the airport through a cloudburst of driving rain which made the usual horror of Paris traffic even worse. In rain people's tempers frayed, they took stupid risks, were in a hurry, in no mood to compromise or be patient with other drivers. Frenchmen hated the very idea of compromise. Their instinct was to triumph, not hang back and let the other guy win. Her taxi driver seemed to be on a seek and destroy mission, cutting up other vehicles, yelling, swearing, driving like a maniac.

She was relieved to get to the airport safely, and at least the plane took off on time. They flew through dark storm clouds until they were over the Alps, where the clouds finally dispersed and the sun came out into a blue, blue sky.

Claudia walked out of Nice airport into blinding sunlight and southern heat. Dazzled and already sweating, she joined the long queue for taxis. It was ten minutes before she got to the front. As she climbed into her taxi she caught a brief glimpse of a familiar face among the crowds thronging outside the palm-fringed white terminus building at the far end of the Promenade des Anglais.

Doing a double-take, Claudia couldn't be sure she wasn't imagining it. After the last couple of days her nerves were jumpy. Was that the man she had seen fishing on the quayside in Paris?

If it wasn't, it was his double — there couldn't be many men who looked like that. His thin, ferrety face had a furtive air as he looked around at everyone else, a cheap beige raincoat over his cheap grey suit.

"*Oui, M'mselle?*" grunted the taxi driver.

She pulled herself together. "What? Oh, sorry. Cap d'Antibes, please — the Chemin de Croe."

The taxi pulled out from the kerb. Claudia twisted round to get another look at Ferret Face. It was him. Definitely. The other man who had broken into her apartment had said something about him seeing her walk past along the quay yesterday morning, and she was certain he had hurriedly got out a mobile phone and made the call to his partner, inside her flat, giving the man time to get out before she reached her front door.

And here he was again. It couldn't be a coincidence that he should be in Nice, too. He must have been on the same plane. She hadn't noticed him, but then there had been hundreds of passengers fighting to get through the terminal building.

Perhaps he hadn't noticed her, either. Unless he had followed her here.

She was about to turn away when she saw Ferret Face step forward to join another man walking out of the airport. Shock made her turn cold and tremble.

Ben?

It couldn't be.

But it was. Ben, his tanned skin golden in the brilliant sunlight, lithe and very sexy, in well-worn blue jeans and a thin black T-shirt showing every muscle in his powerful chest, an overnight bag slung casually over his shoulder.

She saw him speak to Ferret Face, smiling. Her stomach turned over. Sickness filled the back of her throat.

They knew each other.

How did Ben know that man unless he was part of whatever was going on?

What was Ben doing here, in Nice, with one of the men who had broken into her apartment, tied her up, threatened her with rape?

It could not be a coincidence. He was searching for Hugh. So were the two burglars.

Her taxi turned out into the traffic heading out of Nice. She could no longer see Ben, but her head pounded with angry questions she would ask him when he turned up at the villa.

The taxi, in a haze of petrol fumes, took the busy coast road towards Antibes. Traffic along the Côte d'Azur was as bad as it was in Paris. They could only inch along most of the time.

They crossed the bridge over the Var, the brilliant blue of the sea glittering on the left, then they began passing favourite landmarks, the white pyramid apartments on the shoreline at Cagnes, like a flock of seagulls turned to stone, which always made her heart lift; then Vaubin's Fort Carre, massive and ugly, once the boundary of France and now forsaken by time. On the right the scrubby hills rose away from the sea, cluttered with terracotta-roofed, white-walled villas set among gardens where dark green, flame-shaped cypresses grew. Whenever she came back here she felt a welling of painful pleasure; nostalgia, home-sickness, delight. She had been born in Paris and chose to live there now, but this was home and always would be, all her life; this crowded, noisy, crazy cluster of little villages and towns beside the sea. Too many people, too many cars, beaches so crowded you couldn't fit a foot between the sunbathers, many of them almost bare.

It might now be regarded as dangerous to lie out in the sun, but these women did not seem to care, they lay with their naked breasts offered up to the sun's caress, their heavily tanned skin glistening with dark oil. Men as scantily dressed wandered past without bothering to look at the flesh so openly on display, yet stared at young girls wearing demure one-piece swimsuits, clearly wondering what they were hiding.

Tourists pushed along the narrow pavements. Cars hooted and drove straight at anyone daring to try to use the zebra crossings. Her driver swore gutturally as a red Fiat pulled out of a parking space, holding up their progress along the sea road.

"Merde! Espèce de salaud!"

The other driver, insulted at being called a rotten bastard, yelled back and made a one-finger gesture.

The taxi driver put his hand on the horn and kept up a blaring commentary as they drove on, making it impossible to think.

Frenchmen loved noise, the louder the better.

She couldn't see them yet, but, shimmering like a mirage in the bay of Cannes lay the Iles de Lerins, two islands some twenty minutes away by boat, with a strange, mysterious history. The Man in the Iron Mask had been imprisoned on the Sainte-Marguerite; she had seen the tiny cell where he had lived for ten years, and been horrified by the thought of being shut up there alone. It must have been a nightmare existence. She and her friends had talked about it for ages after a school visit. Who had he been? Why had he been forced to wear a mask, why was anyone who saw his face locked up too? It was one of those haunting stories you can't forget.

It had always been one of the highlights of the summer when she and Hugh took a picnic and went over on the hourly ferry among crowds of tourists, most of whom went back on the next boat.

But she and Hugh would wander away from the landing stage down to a rocky cove to swim, blinded by the dazzling whiteness of the rocks and cliffs. There was no shade to shelter you on the coast so after their swim they would walk inland into the deep shadows of the woods. They would find a cool glade among the pines and eat their picnic under a tree before taking a siesta, stretched out on their backs looking up at the blue sky through the branches. Later, they would trail sleepily back to the ferry landing stage and sail home hot, tired and happy.

"Gets worse every year," the taxi driver said over his shoulder. "Hell on earth. God knows why they come. Me, I take my holidays in the winter, in Norway. I love the snow. The white mountains, the calm people, the quiet roads. I ski and eat good food by a real fire, and let my head rest away from this madhouse."

Changing gear, he turned up into the small, wooded peninsula that was Cap d'Antibes, criss-crossed with wide roads and narrow lanes. Locally they were called *les chemins,* tiny, winding paths that ran up to the crest of the hill, the pine-shaded square around the ancient lighthouse, the Pharos, whose light for centuries had shone out across the sea.

"Chemin de Croe? How do I find that?"

She leaned forward to give him directions and he took the next broad boulevard heading towards the Garoupe, the beach on which so many famous people had sunbathed and swam in the Twenties; Cole Porter, Scott Fitzgerald, Rudolph Valentino, and many others.

The rich and famous no longer flocked to it in huge numbers. Other resorts had syphoned them off, the whole coastline had been opened up now, from the Italian border to Provence. Many new beaches had been created with lorryloads of sand, fully grown palm trees wrapped in wet sacking to keep them healthy until they were put into place, new blocks of apartments, palatial on the ground floor, marble-floored and high-ceilinged, but with mean, skimpy little rooms in the actual apartments. Nowhere to swing a cat, most of them.

Many of the old villas that had stood here on the Cap had been bulldozed away so that developers could make a fortune running up half a dozen new villas where one had stood, with none of the elegance, space or style of the old. There were very small gardens around them, too.

"That's modern living for you," Hugh had once said. "Cheap and trashy. Everything beautiful has to be destroyed so that ugliness can take its place. Rows and rows of ugly apartment blocks and villas."

"Money's at the root of it," she had replied. "That's all that matters to the developers, making money, and these days nobody can afford to hire staff, except a maid for a couple of hours, and a gardener who'll clean the pool and do the garden once a week. So they don't want big gardens or too many rooms. At least the people who

91

work here are doing well, the maids, especially, coin money. Visitors have to queue up to pay them hundreds of francs a week for the privilege of having the floor mopped and the sheets changed.''

''Don't tell Louise! She might ask for a rise!''

''I'm sure she knows, but she's been with you for years. This is her home, she doesn't have a family, or a house to pay for. Most maids are married women with brothers and sisters who need jobs. If anything urgently needs doing — a broken window repaired, a door painted — the maid always has a relative who can come at once. Of course they have to charge a special rate. Oh, everyone down here is doing just fine.''

''How do you know all this?''

''My friends have told me. The old days are long gone — when the rich kept lots of staff and had huge villas and enormous gardens. The only people who regret them are the rich themselves, who are no longer so rich and can't afford that lifestyle any more.

He had given her one of his angry, frowning stares. Hugh had a face that fell easily into a frown. His black brows had a sardonic arch to them, his eyes smouldered.

Was that why she had thought Ben's face familiar? His features lent themselves to anger easily, too.

''You're happy with what has happened to this coast?'' Hugh demanded sarcastically.''

''No, of course not! I hate the crowds of tourists, the cars and the overbuilding, but I can't stop it, so I prefer to ignore it. You either do that, or you go into politics and try to change things.''

''And get nowhere! All politicians are corrupt and

self-serving. They talk a lot about what they're going to do if you vote for them, but once you have, they put on their bibs and gather round the trough with all the others.''

Hugh was a disillusioned man who had no belief or trust in anything except the writers and painters whose work he was so passionate about. He had been that way ever since she could remember. She often wondered what had happened to him in England. What had darkened his mind and left him bitter and isolated? He might have quarrelled with the family he never mentioned, or perhaps he didn't have a family at all. He might be alone in the world, might have been orphaned long ago. Maybe he had been betrayed or rejected by a woman.

It could be a mixture of all those things. Or perhaps she was being too romantic. Perhaps Hugh had always been moody and disillusioned, even as a child? It might be his nature.

The taxi turned into the Chemin de Croe, which was just wide enough for one car at a time and had no outlet at the other end, so that you had to turn round to come back out again. On either side rose high walls behind which clustered trees hiding whatever lay within the grounds.

The Château de la Croe, in which the Duke of Windsor had lived for years, had been on the right. The Bastide was on the left, a white-walled villa built on several levels with terracotta tiles on the irregular roof. The driver pulled up outside the gate. Claudia paid him, got out, taking her overnight bag with her. The walls on either side, the trees bending over the lane, made it shadowy and chilly. Evening would soon be drawing in; when it was dark this lane had a sinister feel to it.

Shivering, she rang the bell, watching the taxi do a three-point turn and drive back in the direction from which they had come.

"*Oui?* Who is it?" Louise's voice said almost in her ear.

She turned and spoke into the security phone.

"It's me, Claudia."

"*Chérie!* Wait a minute, I'll open the gate."

The two high, wooden gates began to swing apart a second later, and she walked through into the sunlit garden. Behind her, in the lane, she heard the hum of another car's engine and glanced back. The gates were already closing, but she caught a glimpse of a white Citroën pulling up outside.

Had Ben or the burglars caught up with her? Or was this someone else? It could be a local tradesman.

She ran up the stone steps to the kitchen door, avoiding the clutching fingers of an almond tree she had always loved best in March, when its drift of pink blossom gave it a heartstopping beauty. She was too late for that; she could see tiny green nuts on the branches.

Through the kitchen window she saw Louise talking on the gate security phone. As Claudia got to the top of the steps, Louise hung up and hurried to open the door and grab Claudia into a warm, loving hug.

"*Ça va?*"

"I'm fine — how are you?" Louise looked older than she remembered; her skin was withered like a winter apple, golden but lined and collapsing inward. Her brown eyes were bright, though, and she was as thin and agile as ever. Hard work kept her healthy. She smelt of garlic and herbs — what had she been cooking?

Shrugging, Louise said, "Oh, me! As usual. Let me look at you!"

She held Claudia by the shoulders and stood back to stare at the short, glossy, curly bronze hair framing the face that would never be beautiful because it was too irregular; the proportions of her features all wrong, her eyes wide and far apart, her nose small and pert, the mouth below it much too full. Nothing matched. Her face was a haphazard collection of odd features. She had always wished, as a girl, that she had a classic face; everything in perfect proportion, framed by smooth black hair hanging to her shoulders.

"You look good. But thin, much too thin — do you eat?"

"Like a horse," she lied, because when you cooked all day you could rarely be bothered to eat.

Knowing that, Louise didn't believe her, sniffing her disbelief. "I know you. Cooks never eat enough. Well, you'll eat while you're at home and I'm cooking. I'm making cassoulet for dinner."

"I smelt it from the road!" Claudia inhaled the wonderful scent of garlic and duck, herbs, salt pork, tomatoes, Toulouse sausage and haricot beans filling the whole room. "Mmm, marvellous." No other food in the world had that strong, unforgettable smell, the very scent of the South.

The gate phone buzzed again, kept on buzzing, as if

someone had a thumb on it.

"Who is it out there?"

Louise shrugged, blank-faced, giving nothing away. "Some Englishman. Spoke French like a duck quacking. Wants to see Hugh, but Hugh said to let no one in. So I won't, and Jules is in his cave, ready if he's needed, if someone tries to climb in."

She went to the phone and said sharply, "Stop ringing, M'sieur, you're wasting your time. Go away."

Claudia looked down from the window over the high fence. She could see one edge of the white Citroën still parked outside, and a man standing by the gate, the wind blowing rough black hair back from a high forehead. As if becoming aware of her watching him, he stepped backwards into the road to stare up at her out of those fierce black eyes. Ben.

She had guessed it would be either him or Ferret Face, but the sight of him still made her throat jump with response.

She barely knew the man, but this intense physical attraction had been immediate and still happened every time she set eyes on him.

Turning hurriedly away, as angry with herself as him, she asked, "Is Hugh in his office?"

Louise nodded.

"I'll go and talk to him. After that, I'll come back and help you with dinner."

Louise's face lit up with the pleasure of having her here again, to work with in this kitchen where she had taught Claudia to cook.

"You can make the starter — how about melon and

papaya in kirsch? A good contrast, yes? And Hugh doesn't like heavy meals.''

''Perfect.'' Claudia kissed her cheek, as warm and wrinkled as a windfall apple, loving the familiar smell of locally made lavender soap and cologne. Louise bought it in Grasse on her monthly shopping trip there, at the factory where it was made, for half the price you would pay in the shops. She used it copiously every day, leaving trails of the scent in every room. They grew lavender in the garden, too; dried it spread out in the sun on calm afternoons, filled little bags with it to pop in among the linen, or into the chests of drawers in the bedrooms, and hung some high up in the rafters of the kitchen to keep flies down and perfume the air. It was there now, rustling every time the outer door opened, the pale grey-mauve withered heads mere ghosts of what they had been last summer, yet still putting out their perfume.

She ran up the winding stairs to the bay-windowed room where Hugh worked. Having heard her footsteps, he opened the door before she could tap on it.

She threw her arms round his neck and kissed each cheek three times; the family salute they always gave each other. In some parts of France people kissed twice on each cheek. You had to know the local custom. The ritual was deeply embedded, full of significance, cementing the family bond, fingering strangers, as language does, making it obvious that you do not belong.

''*Ça va?*'' they asked each other, another ritual, in every part of France.

His long, thin body was dressed in ancient, well-worn pale grey flannel trousers and a dark blue shirt. English style. Unmistakable. He had worn them both for years; she had often fingered the barely readable labels when they were being washed or going off to the cleaners. Savile Row. That was in London, she knew that. Hugh had several suits he had bought there, too, all of them old, but still elegant, although they were not up-to-the-minute, the way French suits were cut. These were English city suits, dark wool, pinstriped, smooth and expertly tailored.

His skin had a deep brown tan, his hair was powdered with silver where it had once been completely jet black. Like Louise, he looked older than she remembered. In her memory they were both always the age they had been when she was in her teens. For years they had never seemed to change. Now time was making slow inroads on them and she hated to see it. She wanted them to stay the same, for ever.

"I saw your taxi arrive." His dark eyes, so like Ben's, searched her face. "Are you OK?"

She nodded. "I'm over the shock of the burglary now and the kick in the ribs only left a bruise or two." She felt the place; it was still tender when she touched it, but she didn't give that away. It would worry him too much.

His frown deepened. "I'm sorry you had to go through that. I wasn't expecting it or I would have warned you."

How could he warn her if he wasn't expecting it? Did he mean he should have expected it? Why should he have?

"What is going on, Hugh?"

He turned away, face shuttered. "Don't ask."

She closed her mouth on the questions she wanted answered, and sighed, looking out of the window. Hugh's office was on the second floor and gave a clearer view of the road beyond the wall. The Citroën was still there. So was Ben, pacing up and down, staring at the house.

"That's Ben outside now."

"I'm not blind. I guessed it was him."

"But you didn't recognise him?" She was trying to work it out with guesses. "You've never seen him before?"

Hugh gave her a dry glance. "No, Claudia, I have never set eyes on him before. Did he follow you here? Was he on your plane?"

"I think so — I caught sight of him at the airport. But I had given him this address, so it might be pure coincidence. And one of the burglars is here, with him, the one who tied me up, kicked me."

"Is he out there now? I'll teach him not to beat up women!"

Alarm flooded into her. "No, I don't want you getting hurt! And, anyway, Ben seems to be alone at the moment. There's nobody else in the Citroën. But I did see Ferret Face with him at the airport."

"Ferret Face?"

She made a laughing grimace. "That's what I call the guy who tied me up. He has a face just like a ferret, pinched and spiteful. As my taxi drove off, I saw him and Ben talking — so they know each other."

"Do they indeed?" Hugh said in that cool, dry English accent she had never quite managed to mimic, however hard she tried, but which she loved. Like his style of dress, it was perfect; utterly English, unchanging.

"Yes, so, you see it has to be Ben who sent them to search the apartment, doesn't it? I certainly don't see him working for them. It has to be the other way round. What is he looking for, Hugh?"

At that minute Ben turned away, walked back to the driver's door of the Citroën. A moment later the car did a U-turn in the road and drove off.

"He's given up, gone away!"

"He'll be back," Hugh said.

"What do you mean? Who is he, Hugh?"

"Never mind. Come and sit down." He went over to his desk and sat down behind it in his scarred and faded leather chair. As a girl she had often sat in it and set it spinning round and round.

Today she took the old, sagging sofa he called his thinking couch, her body stretched out on the ancient cushions. Louise must have washed and dried the covers in the sun recently; they had a fresh, open-air lavender smell.

A weariness she had not been aware of took her over now that the tension had stopped. Hugh watched her, his chin balanced on his hands.

"Claudia, remember the day your mother died? The storm? The lightning struck the chimney and brought it down, and half the roof with it?"

The day her mother died, the weather had been oppressive; hot, sultry, barely a breath of air. In the afternoon they had heard the first slow, distant rumble of thunder and Hugh had said with relief: "The weather's breaking at last.''

She remembered vividly looking through the pines and seeing the lucent, purplish, grape-bloom of the sky; swollen, unearthly, flickering with white flashes, as if the whole world were tearing open, like a woman being split apart to give birth.

''Going to be a bad one.'' Hugh had walked out on to the terrace. It was raining over the sea already; hanging down in the sky, translucent grey curtains veiling the horizon. But it hadn't begun to rain on the Cap yet.

''Coming closer. Maybe we should go in.''

''You go.'' Hugh loved storms, but knew she was afraid of them. Down here, in the South, they were always violent, and nature's violence excited him. He loved strong winds, high tides, the lashing of trees in autumn gales.

A very tall, slim man, he was fit for his age; his skin deeply tanned from living in the sun for many years, but his silvering dark hair betrayed his real age. He must be over fifty, although she had never noticed him getting older.

She loved him deeply, but he was not a demonstrative man. She had learned not to show her feelings. That was another symptom of his Englishness; his embarrassment if she hugged him or said anything affectionate. He would go stiff, his face freezing. Yet she knew he loved her, too, even if he was too shy to show it.

As she had turned to go back into the white villa, eerily lit by the storm, lightning had torn down the sky and hit the great stone chimney, which had exploded with a noise like the end of the world. Stone and brick had flown out in all directions, crashed down through the red-tiled roof, fallen in cascades across the terrace, narrowly missing Claudia.

She had stood there, dumbstruck, as the noise had died away at last, and the clouds of dust had settled, staring at the destruction of the house.

Only when Hugh had begun to run had it dawned on her that her mother was in there.

''Oh, God, no, Mama,'' she had sobbed, following him up the old, polished wood stairs.

The debris which had come through the roof had fallen down into the attic, then through the plaster, into her mother's room and onwards into the salon on the floor below.

Claudia had seen the clutter of masonry on the floor before she had realised that none of it had come down on the bed. Her mother was lying on her pillows, paper white, her whole body trembling. Claudia had rushed to her; sat down, taking those cold, shaking hands into both her own, holding them tightly.

''You're OK, Mama, it's over now, don't worry.''

Her mother had not even seemed to see her. She just went on staring at the destruction of her room.

''Shock,'' Hugh had said. ''I'll ring the doctor.''

The doctor had come, at once, given Mama an injection to put her to sleep. Claudia had stayed with her for a while. When she had gone back downstairs she had found Hugh standing in the salon on the ground floor.

The room had been the heart of the eighteenth-century house, which had, originally, been a farmhouse, called locally a *mas,* with massive dark oak doors and small windows with shutters over them.

The walls had been built to withstand the wind; they still stood, and the windows were unbroken, but the chimney, the great stone fireplace, with its ancient iron roasting equipment, had all been destroyed. The room was full of heaps of stone, iron and brick. The antique rugs on the marble floor were torn and dirty, the air thick with dust which made them cough.

"Can it be rebuilt?" she had asked Hugh, sliding a hand through his arm and leaning on him, grateful for his strength and support."

"Yes, but it will cost the earth. Old houses are always the same. They eat money."

The ruined hearth seemed ominous. Claudia had been disturbed all night, hardly sleeping, sitting up in bed many times to listen to the silence outside. The storm had gone, moonlight lay in silvery sheets across the gardens, yet she still had a very uneasy feeling.

Several times, she had crept into her mother's room to check on her and had found her fast asleep.

When she had taken her mother tea and toast the next morning, Mama was dead, her fragile hands curled as if she had died fighting, as she had, in a way — fighting death for months.

"Of course I remember — how could I ever forget it?" Tears pricked her eyes. The lightning strike which had brought down the chimney had been no mere accident or coincidence. Her mother had died that night. The destruction of the family hearth had been a sign of what was to come.

"I'm sorry, that was clumsy of me, reminding you out

of the blue.''

Hugh did not believe in fate. He was rational, logical; but Claudia believed some things went deeper than logic, they came from the darkness of life, which reason could not reach.

She ran the back of her hand across her eyes and sniffed childishly. ''No, it's OK. I'm just so hyper after all the odd things that have happened over the last couple of days. Go on, what were you going to say?''

''Are you sure?''

She nodded. ''Tell me.''

''Well, the day after the funeral, I was restless, I needed to do something, to keep busy. Jules and I started to clear all that rubble from the salon. I shovelled it into a wheelbarrow and Jules took it off into the garden — he made a rockery of most of the stone, remember? While he was taking a barrowful out, I saw something metallic under a pile of red bricks from the upper chimney.''

She sat up against the cushions, eyes wide. ''What was it?''

''An iron box, about this big.'' He sketched the shape and size with his hands. ''It must have been hidden up the chimney and come down with it.''

''You never told me!''

''Once I'd seen what was inside, I felt it would be wiser not to mention it to anyone.''

''What was inside? Jewellery? Money?''

''Something beyond price. I'm not going to tell you more than that, Claudia.''

Slowly, she said, ''It must have belonged to whoever

sold you the villa, or a tenant before him.''

He nodded.

''You didn't tell the previous owner you had found it?'' She tried to keep condemnation out of her voice, but she was profoundly shocked. She would never have suspected Hugh of dishonesty.

''No.'' That cool, dry English voice again. He showed no sign of embarrassment or regret.

She thought the story over, frowning. ''But obviously someone has found out you've got the box. Or why else are they trying to find it? Have you shown it to someone? Had it valued? Mentioned it to anyone?''

''I haven't told a living soul.''

''Then how does anyone know you've got it?''

He smiled wryly. ''They knew it was there, of course, and found out I've had rebuilding done, so they've guessed I've found the box.''

She nodded slowly. ''Did you buy the villa from Ben's parents?''

Hugh gave her a startled look. ''No. What on earth put that into your head?''

''Then why is Ben after the box?''

He stared down at his desk, frowning. ''If he is.''

That surprised her. ''What do you mean? Why else has he come down here to see you?''

''Never mind. Listen, a week ago somebody threw a stone through one of the little windows in the salon downstairs. Usually Jules fixes things like that, but it was his day off I put a board in the window until he could deal with it. That afternoon, when I was in Cannes at the public library, two men came to the house claiming I had rung them and asked them to replace the glass. Louise stayed with them while they did it. They didn't get a chance to search the house, but they did observe the new fireplace and comment on it, and Louise told them about the storm.''

''So that's how they found out the whole chimney had been replaced? And that you must have found the iron box.'' She gazed at him, mouth parted. ''What did you think when Louise told you?''

His mouth twisted. ''I'd been wondering when or if an interest would be shown, so I wasn't very surprised.''

''Who *did* you buy the villa from, Hugh? I'm worried. They employ some very scary people. You could be in real danger.''

''I know, I'm taking precautions, believe me. But I can't risk telling you anything. The less you know the safer you'll be. Trust me.''

''Of course I do, but I'm worried about you.''

''While I have what they're looking for, they won't dare harm me. They want it back. If they kill me they won't get it back.''

''But if they break in here again and search the house . . .''

''They won't find it. It isn't here. All that concerns me is your safety, Claudia. Be careful. Don't go out alone after dark, and don't let anybody into the villa unless I'm here, and tell you to!''

The phone began to ring and they both jumped. Claudia got up on a reflex action.

''Don't touch it!'' Hugh barked. ''The answering machine will take the call.''

The ringing stopped. When the answering machine buzzed the end of the message, Hugh went over to turn the tape back to the beginning.

Claudia knew the voice at once, the blood flowing out of her face and leaving her icy cold.

"It's Ferret Face!"

"Who?"

"One of the burglars. The one who..." she broke off, reluctant to put into words what the man had done to her.

Hugh watched her shaking hands, his face grim.

"The guy who assaulted you?"

Hugh turned the tape back again, gripped one of her hands tightly as if trying to stop it trembling. They listened without meeting each other's eyes.

"Give it back. Don't be a fool. You can't stay shut up in there for ever. Sooner or later you'll have to come out. And we'll get her. We don't care how long we have to wait. We will get her. And you won't like what we do to her. We're serious people. This isn't a game. You have twenty-four hours. I'll ring again tomorrow."

Hugh walked away from her and looked down into the Chemin de Croe, his face tight and shaken, as though he could see ghosts out there in the twilight.

ENGLAND

30 September 1939

CHAPTER
FIVE

As they drove out of la Croe at dawn he looked back at the shadowy outline of the château and wondered when or if they would ever return. Autumnal trees drooped over the wall, filling him with sadness, although in other years he had been delighted to see the purple figs ripening among leathery, yellowing leaves, glossy brown chestnuts clustering among the branches which almost hid the villa from sight.

He was torn in two ways at once — ached to go home, and yet couldn't stop remembering how happy he had been at la Croe. Happier than he had ever been in his life. For a short while they had had a real home.

She drew the travelling rug up to her chin, shivering. "I can't believe I'm up at this unearthly hour! I'm freezing."

She did not travel well; hated getting up early. But they had a long trip ahead of them, and were not even certain of their destination. He had had orders to stop *en route* to telephone the British Embassy. He would then be told to which port they should proceed.

"Silly cloak and dagger games!" Wallis said. "What do they think they're doing? So childish."

"They're afraid we might be snatched by German

111

agents!''

"More chance of running out of petrol on the way. I hope we have enough cans in the trunk.''

"I made sure of that, darling.''

When they rang the Embassy they were told to make for Cherbourg where Louis Mountbatten would be waiting for them.

Their route took them on roads choked with traffic; convoys of trucks moving at a creeping pace, vans, ambulances, lorries full of troops. It was a depressing sight, reminding him of the Great War, which he had believed would end all wars, but here they were at war with Germany again, tearing his loyalties apart.

Their three cairns were lying on the floor at their feet. Their heavy warmth was soothing; he moved his toe gently to stroke Pookie, who was nearest him.

He had learned a great deal about people during the last three years. A few were faithful and reliable, but most were not. Fair weather friends evaporated if they thought you were in trouble, or had lost the power you once had.

His heart lifted when they reached the docks and saw the *Kelly*'s dogged shape looming through the soft autumnal dusk. As he helped Wallis out of the car, Louis came down the gangplank to meet them with a smile that cut out as he observed the car loaded up with cases, leather hatboxes, cardboard boxes.

"Good God, David, have you brought everything you own in the world? I was hoping for a quick turn-around, but it will take an hour to stow all that. I'm not even sure we have the room unless we put it on deck and then what happens if it rains?''

Bristling at the criticism, he snapped back, ''We weren't leaving everything behind. We may not be able to get back there for years! The villa may be burgled, vandalised. Even if the Germans don't get down there, I don't trust the French. As it was, we only brought what we couldn't replace, especially in wartime.''

Louis had hurriedly apologised, with his usual placatory, soothing charm. He was an odd mixture; arrogant and highhanded at one moment, as gentle as a woman the next ''Sorry, David. Of course. I wasn't thinking.'' He looked at the young officer hovering at his elbow, and his voice bit like a whip. ''Get some men down here at the double.''

''I must lie down,'' Wallis whispered mournfully, cradling one of the cairns in her arms while the other two sniffed around the quayside. Pookie found an old fish head and tentatively picked it up, mumbling it for a second before dropping it in disgust.

Fortunately, a distraction arrived in the shape of Randolph Churchill and Wallis cheered up slightly. His blond, blue-eyed, very English looks attracted her. His youth, too — she enjoyed the company of very young men. Their admiration fed her energy; she laughed more, talked more, when she was surrounded by them.

''What a wonderful uniform, Randy! You look very dashing. I didn't know you were a sailor!''

''He isn't. He's in the Fourth Hussars!'' David said tartly. He never made a mistake about uniform, always having been obsessed with them, a characteristic he had inherited. The men of his family, from Queen Victoria's father downwards, were fanatical about uniforms, loved to wear them and recognised every detail of them.

"Randolph, your spurs are on upside down! Really! What a slovenly soldier you are! If I were your commanding officer I'd put you on a charge."

Unabashed, Randolph laughed, his jaw giving him that Churchill bulldog look and his blue eyes bulging, just as his father's did.

"Sorry, sir. I was in such a hurry to get here to welcome you and her Royal Highness home!"

"You ass, Randolph," he said gratefully, watching Wallis's smile come up like the dawn at hearing Randolph use that title, which was hers by right of marriage, but which Bertie had refused to allow her to use.

If it took him the rest of his life, he was going to get that title for her. As soon as he got Bertie on his own, he would make him see that he could not refuse his wife her right to share his title. He had always been able to talk Bertie round. It was difficult to deal with him on the telephone. Bertie could make excuses and hang up; leaving him frustrated and seething. If he rang back, he was always told in a frosty voice by the operator that "The King has left the Palace". Or "The King is with the Prime Minister". The excuses were paper-thin, a blind man could see through them, and he resented them.

After supper, Louis and Randolph left them alone and Wallis put on a black velvet sleeping mask and lay down on the bunk. He covered her with a couple of blankets, rough, navy-issue, and topped them with her fur coat. He heard her breathing slowing until she finally slept. Then he lay down too but didn't sleep, couldn't, so he got up and went to the porthole to watch for a first glimpse of England.

They arrived at Portsmouth in utter darkness, no lights showing anywhere. As he stared out of the porthole, he caught a glimpse of a painted number and suddenly realised that they were docking at the very same quay from which he had left England on a bleak December night in 1936.

Two years, nine months ago. A short distance in time, a million miles in experience. He had had no idea that day in 1936 what he faced, what might happen to him. Would he have gone through with it if he had known?

Hastily, angrily, he told himself, "Of course! I wouldn't do it any differently now! I would have sacrificed far more if I had had to."

Wallis was washing her face in a basin of warm water brought by the steward. He watched her with the intensity of fascination he always felt at seeing her do these everyday things: put on clothes, take them off, comb her hair, always with such grace and skill. He never tired of the elegant turn of her wrist, the way the light fell on her skin.

As she slowly put on her make-up again she asked, "Is your brother here to meet us, can you see?"

He stared at the Very light which was the only illumination on the quay and by which he had seen the quay number.

"There seems to be nobody here to meet us at all."

She looked up, red mouth a bow of incredulity, her

skin pulled tight over her strong cheekbones. "Nobody?"

"As far as I can see." His throat was raw with anger and pain. "Nobody," he forced out, turning from the porthole. "I'm going up on deck to talk to Louis."

The cairns jumped off the bunk where they had slept with her and ran after him to the door, hopeful of getting back on dry land, but he shut them into the cabin. He didn't want them falling overboard.

The ship danced and rocked as Louis Mountbatten fought to bring it safely alongside. Deciding not to interrupt while Louis had such a job on his hands, he walked down the deck into the bow.

Lights sprang up, making him blink. The band of the Royal Marines loomed out of the darkness. Seeing him they struck up "God Save The King".

His eyes filled with tears.

When they landed some time later, they found a guard of honour waiting on either side of a hastily run-out red carpet. He did a double-take; they instantly took him back to the Great War.

"They look like creatures from out of space," Wallis murmured as they walked between the men in their gas masks and tin hats standing to attention. "Or lines of pigs!"

Behind the masks, the men's eyes stayed rigidly to the front, not meeting theirs.

That was it? This brief, insulting pretence of ceremony. No message of welcome home from the family. No car had been sent from the Palace, he was told. The only people waiting for them were Walter

Monckton, the barrister who was his chief legal representative at home, and Fruity's wife, Alexandra, who had driven here in her own car.

They want me humiliated, as publicly as they dare, he thought. I'm being punished. Taught my place. I walked away from them and what they saw as my duty to the country. Now they're turning their backs on me.

His mother, bitter and stiff-necked, that remote, cold woman who had never loved him, his brother and that prune-mouthed wife of his — the passing of three years had done nothing to soften them.

He had been empty and aching all his life until he met Wallis and found the love he had been denied since he was a child. He needed her. Nothing else mattered.

They stayed in Portsmouth that night, and drove on next day to Fruity's country house, South Hartfield.

As in France, the roads were crowded with vehicles in both directions. They crawled most of the way, sat in traffic jams whenever they got close to a town.

"As for trains, they're even worse!" Alexandra told him. "Full to the roof! When they run! And you often have to wait for hours on the platform. The timetables have been abandoned. You never know when or if a train may arrive, and if you ring the station they claim they don't know either. If you complain, they snap back, 'Don't you know there's a war on?' As if that justifies letting the service collapse altogether!"

"I'm surprised Winston doesn't do something about it. Who's in charge of public transport?"

"Winston has more worrying things on his mind than trains that don't run," Fruity said, shifting his feet as

117

one of the cairns tried to snuggle up to his leg.

Clicking his fingers, David called the dog to him as Alexandra turned off the main road, saying over her shoulder, "Not far now. You must both be very tired. I've ordered a very good dinner, but I hope you will forgive us if our cook serves a very light lunch. There are already shortages, we have to put up with what we find in the shops."

"They're introducing rationing, aren't they?"

The country air was full of the smell of bonfires, and when they drove through Hartfield's gates, the gardens were rich with autumnal scents, white, orange and blood-red chrysanthemums, mauve Michaelmas daisies, pink and blue hydrangeas. The leaves on the great trees surrounding the house were turning yellow, russet, bronze. Autumn was more advanced here than it had been in Antibes. The September wind blew dead leaves in rustling handfuls across the grass and down the drive.

Nature, like England itself was grim, wistful, resigned. The past was ending and the future was grey, uncertain, ominous.

The following day they went up to London, where they were going to use the Metcalfs' London house, 16, Wilton Place, not far from Hyde Park, as a base. Driving into the capital, all sense of a familiar landscape was gone.

While he had been away, busy and happy with his new life, England had gone on into this bleak future, like a ship from which one has embarked full of hope, and then unexpectedly reboarded in some strange, foreign port, to find the ship changed utterly, all the passengers very different in mood.

London's parks had been dug up for trenches, weeks ago, Alexandra told him. "Long before war was declared. They knew there was no real chance of avoiding it. They made the gesture of the ultimatum, but at the same time they were getting arrangements in place ... the evacuation of children from cities, ration and identity cards printed ... oh, they were sure it was coming, long before the rest of us gave up hope of peace, and they weren't going to get caught out. Thank God.''

The blackout curtains were up already; the rooms in Wilton Place dingy with low lighting, whether gas or electric, so that you had to grope your way around like a blind man. Fires burned in grates, but coal shortages had begun, the fires were kept small, rooms were chilly. That was nothing new to him, brought up in houses like Sandringham, or at Windsor, where rooms were iceboxes in winter, and draughts blew down the long, long corridors, freezing your blood, especially at night.

Wallis, used to all the modern comforts of her own country, was appalled. "How dismal everything looks! They're finished, David. This country is on the edge of collapse.''

At least Bertie was going to need him now. Bertie didn't have the backbone for war, they would have to listen to him! His time had come, just as Winston's had.

He went to the Palace next day, expecting to be met with open arms, and ran into a wall of polite stoniness. The King was busy, The King was not free to see him today, His Majesty would be in touch if he found he had any time to spare.

He had to retreat or lose face. Stiff as a martinet, he strode out without meeting any eyes.

"They're freezing me out," he told Fruity over a whisky.

"Don't get too upset, sir. Your brother doesn't quite know how to treat you, I suspect, but they will give you a job, you know."

He stared down into his second whisky, his teeth tight. Bastards. I'll see them in hell for this. Who do they think they are?

He kept busy, day after day, having new uniforms made, which meant fittings, new boots measured, shirts and ties ordered — Fruity's elegant little house was always full of streams of people, coming and going. The knocker sounded every few minutes.

Eventually he saw Bertie, but little was said between them. Bertie had changed beyond recognition. Being King had made a difference in him that was hard to credit. He had grown another skin, spoke with an authoritarian ring to his tone that had never been there before and which David had not expected. This wasn't the shy, hesitant, easily dominated brother he had known all his life.

He brought up the subject of Wallis getting the right to use his title, taking her place in the family at last, and Bertie's face froze. David hurriedly went on, before Bertie could say anything, "You know, if she had her rightful title she could take the load off your wife's shoulders — Wallis would be wonderful at opening hospitals, touring the country, meeting people. That's

120

what she's good at, talking to people. Everyone likes her when they meet her.''

Bertie stayed stiff and hostile.

David burst out, ''Why won't you all give her a chance? You don't know how wonderful she is!''

Talking to Fruity later, he said, ''I got nowhere with him. My family are all against me. Well, I've asked to be sent to Wales as Deputy Regional Commissioner. That should be far enough away for them.''

Fruity looked uneasy. ''They won't like having you based in the British Isles at all, I'm afraid. I think they're terrified you'll attract too much interest in the press.''

A few days later he was told he could not go to Wales.

''They rushed me here from France, now they're sending me back again!'' he told Wallis, a tic jumping under his right eye.

''If they want you to accept this job, make them pay!'' said Wallis. ''Get something in return. Why should you do anything to please them, unless they make it worth your while?''

They sat up half the night working out tactics. Wallis had a hard-edged mind, she was cleverer than most men. He took her advice very seriously. At least he knew he could trust her, whereas he began to distrust most people he met.

In an interview with the Minister for War, Leslie Hore-Belisha, next day, he discovered he was expected to give up the Field Marshal's baton he had been awarded for his service in the First World War and revert to the title of Major General.

Red in the face he snapped, "Why should I?"

Leslie had always been sympathetic to him, had supported him during the long crisis before he had abdicated. A lifelong Liberal, he was eager to see change in Britain; he saw what was wrong with this country, too.

He sighed. "I have never heard of a Field Marshal taking lower rank but it would confuse everybody if you kept the baton."

He had stared down at his shoes, fighting to keep his temper and his dignity.

They wanted to take everything away from him. He had chosen the woman he loved instead of the crown, the country, and them — now they intended that he should have nothing but Wallis.

"Very well," he conceded after a moment. "But if I accept your terms, I want to take my wife to France with me."

That was the primary objective he and Wallis had decided on. She was now terrified of being abandoned among these people who hated her.

Hore-Belisha looked genuinely shocked, staring at him, bolt-eyed. "Soldiers do not take their wives to war, sir. It is unheard of."

"I want Wallis with me." During the months before his abdication, he had discovered the beauty of quiet obstinacy. If you kept repeating something over and over again without budging an inch, sooner or later they gave up and accepted it, however much they opposed you in the beginning.

He would not leave her behind, alone, in this frigid,

hostile country. God knows what they would do to her. He was afraid that if he went to France without her she would go back to America and he would never see her again. She had divorced two other men — he knew by now how iron-hard her mind could be. She was capable of divorcing him if he deserted her now.

"And I want Major Metcalf as my ADC," he told Hore-Belisha, who accepted that without argument.

As soon as they had won their points, they packed up again and set off back to France. Poor darling, she had been as hurt and bitterly disappointed as he had himself during their brief sojourn in London. They had come back to England with such high hopes; all dashed in the most painful fashion within forty-eight hours of arriving.

Fruity was looking disapproving. He thinks he's my conscience, David thought, mouth twitching. Thinks he knows better than I do what I should and should not do. It was beginning to get on his nerves.

Fruity Metcalf had appeared in his life during his visit to India in 1921. He had been surrounded with nagging older diplomats and army officers throughout the visit, as always, telling him what to do and how to behave, trying to stop him reaching out to the people who thronged the streets. Their poverty, their hopelessness, had moved his heart. He had longed to meet some, but when he had expressed that wish he had merely been introduced to rich Indians who had no more in common with the hungry, ragged crowds than he himself.

One day, a young Cavalry officer in uniform had walked into his bedroom during his daily siesta, a local

123

custom he had picked up from his first day in India. The heat of the afternoons was intolerable, especially when you had so many public duties to perform.

He had soon learned to take a cool shower, lie down on his bed almost naked, behind the necessary, enveloping net curtains which were supposed to keep out mosquitoes, although he often found a couple inside. They were easy to swat, however, because there was nowhere for them to go. He didn't want to go back home with malaria, and dosed his gin liberally with quinine.

To be woken up by the arrival of a soldier was even more startling than hearing the ghastly whine of a mosquito. The sudden visitation had made him sit up, alarmed, blinking out of a light doze.

''Who the devil are you?''

Brown as a native, faun-like, with straight tan hair brushed back from a high forehead, the young man had saluted him, his smile lively and full of charm.

''Metcalf, sir. Captain Edward Dudley Metcalf,'' he had said, his accent British but with an Irish lilt to it. ''I've been temporarily attached to your staff.''

''But what the hell are you doing in my room?''

''Sorry to break in on you, but I've been trying to have a chat for ages without managing to get hold of you. I wondered if your Royal Highness would care to play polo?''

''Polo?'' The sheet had fallen off his naked chest, but he was used to being naked in front of servants, and so, of course, was the young officer. It didn't bother either of them.

124

"I've had approaches from some of the maharajas. They're frightfully keen on polo, as you no doubt know, sir."

"Don't think I did. What's that got to do with me?"

"As you'll be touring and meeting some of them, they'd be delighted if you would permit them to lend you some of their best polo ponies, if you would care to play a few chukkas."

He remembered the way his weariness had seemed to drop off. The bright eyes and easy friendliness lifted his spirits.

He had been so sick of being lectured by old men and receiving letters from his father, the King, back in England, full of complaints about the way he was performing his public duties and what he was wearing.

"I think I'll get up," he had said, sliding his legs out of the net-draped bed. "Tell them I'd be happy to accept their very sporting offer, Metcalf. Only thing — will I be able to get some clothes quickly enough? I don't think I have polo gear with me."

"If you don't have the clothes, don't worry. I'll organise a tailor immediately. Great chaps, these Indian tailors. They can run you up an outfit overnight, almost."

"What did you say your first name was?"

"Some people call me The Wild Colonial Boy, but my friends call me Fruity, sir."

"Well, tell me, Fruity, what's life here really like?"

Fruity had told him things he would never have heard from the senior officers, the politicians, who were shepherding him around. He had listened fascinated to tales of life in India; the sport, the gambling, the women, the drinking, the private parties in private rooms in clubs and bars.

Before he left India, Fruity had become his closest friend and aide for years. But that did not give him the right to make judgements, or look censorious. The family did that, for God's sake. He didn't need it from his friends.

Fruity had changed, wasn't the same man he had met in India eighteen years ago. Fruity was married now, to Lord Curzon's daughter, a conventionally minded woman, with whom he had children they both adored. He had a very different lifestyle. Middle-age had crept up on him. Those carefree days in India were forgotten.

"You must report for duty at Vincennes at once, sir," Fruity said when they arrived in France.

"Later. First, we're going to Versailles. I'm going to settle Wallis into her hotel, make certain she will be comfortable. After the last few days, everything we suffered at the hands of my so-called family, we both need a break."

Fruity didn't back down. Stubbornly, he began, "Think how it will look to the general staff if you simply don't turn up at headquarters. This is war, sir, not fun and games."

"The army shouldn't have insisted that my wife and I must live apart."

"Sir, I have had to leave Alex! All the men have left their wives behind. That's war. None of us would have it otherwise. We don't want to put our wives into danger, just because we miss them."

126

The reproof made his temper flare. "How dare you preach at me, damn you! That's enough, I don't want to hear another word from you."

They spent a few all too short days together at Versailles; visiting the exquisite gardens, walking with the dogs under the yellow-leaved trees, eating wonderful French food in good restaurants.

"Fruity seems to me to have turned against us," Wallis sadly suggested. "Maybe I'm imagining things, but why does he keep arguing with you, carping on about every decision you take?"

"We've been friends for so long he believes he has the right to be my conscience!"

"I don't suppose he could have been talked into the enemy camp? I wonder if he went to the Palace while we were in London?"

His heart sank. "He's been my closest friend for years. I can't believe he would betray me."

But the thought, once planted in his mind, would not die. Too many other "friends" had proved disloyal, had deserted him since he had given up the crown. He found it easy to learn distrust.

The little hotel they stayed at, the Trianon Palace, agreed to let Wallis stay on after he had left.

He stroked her face. "Poor darling. It won't be for long. This time next year, with luck, everything will be very different."

But saying goodbye, even for a short while, was as painful as it had been when she had left England before he had abdicated. He was still white and anguished when he reached Vincennes. The first person he ran into was Stevie Morrell. He had forgotten that he would be seeing him. They had not met since that last night in Cap d'Antibes.

As usual, Stevie's uniform was beautifully cut and immaculately pressed. David noticed at once that his rank had risen. "Made up to major already, Stevie! Well done!"

"Thanks, but I did nothing to get it except be around when a war started! They wanted a few more higher ranks, so they made me up. Quite undeserved."

"While you've been moved up the list — I've been moved down. They took my bloody baton away, did you hear?"

Stevie looked up and down the corridor to make sure nobody was in earshot, then said in a low voice, "There's a devil of a flap on — they have been expecting you for days. I was beginning to wonder if you had gone off to Germany!"

"I'm tempted," he said, keeping his own voice low. "No, I simply took Wallis to Versailles for a couple of days, then dropped her at her hotel before coming on here. That package I left with you, Stevie — sure it's okay?"

"Safe as houses, sir." Stevie grinned. "Unless my villa gets a direct hit, but then the safe and everything in it will most likely be blown to bits!"

CAP D'ANTIBES

1999

CHAPTER
SIX

After Louise's powerful cassoulet, Claudia helped her clear the table and put on the dishwasher, before sitting down in the salon with Hugh to drink cups of strong, black coffee and talk quietly. Hugh played a new recording of one of his favourite Mozart piano concertos, the twenty-second, played by a brilliant young French pianist of Chinese descent whom Claudia had seen in concert in Paris that year.

"She's amazing, and only twenty! She made me feel old."

"That's frightening. How will she play in ten years' time? How can someone so young really understand what they're playing?"

"Mozart was playing concerts when he was seven, wasn't he?"

"Mozart was a one-off. You can't judge by him."

"No. Genius makes its own rules, doesn't it?"

Out of the corner of her eye Claudia saw a grey-green lizard around five centimetres long dart up the window and freeze, his feet clamped to the glass, his underbelly pulsing. His mouth was curled up in what looked like a grin, as if he were listening to them, his eyes bulging.

"What are you smiling at?" Hugh asked her.

"The lizard who lives in the wall. I'd forgotten him, but he's still here. I suppose it is the same one? I wonder how long they live?"

"No idea. I must find out. That one has been around for years. One year he lost his tail and grew another one. I recognise the markings on his back and that self-satisfied expression."

"He's sweet. I miss lizards while I'm in Paris. We only have rats and roaches, they're not as pretty or as friendly."

"I'm sure you're more than capable of beating them off. You've become quite a tough young woman."

"I wish I was tougher."

They both knew what they were really talking about.

"You shouldn't need to be — but cities are always full of predators. I suppose these days women have to learn to defend themselves." Sober-faced, Hugh gave her a concerned look. "Did they really scare you, these men?"

"I wouldn't want to face them again. It wasn't so much what they did as what I was afraid they might do."

"That sort of experience can knock you sideways. What you need is some sleep. Off you go to bed while I roll the blinds down and check the security."

"I wish you'd call the police, Hugh. You don't realise the sort of men you're dealing with."

He gave her a dry glance. "Oh, believe me, I do. But the police are the last people I want involved. They ask too many awkward questions."

"If you've told me the truth, how can they ask

132

awkward questions? It may not be very moral to keep property you've found in the house, but it can't be illegal. It was in your house, I'm sure you would be entitled to keep it.''

''It's more complicated than you realise.'' His voice hardened. ''We've talked about it long enough, let's forget it tonight.''

There was no point in arguing any more. He had the obstinate look she recognised all too well. He had made up his mind what to do, and nothing would budge him.

She sighed anxiously, getting up. ''I hope you know what you're doing. Good night, Hugh.''

Her aluminium bedroom shutters were closed, the air-conditioning on a low setting, giving the room a lovely, cool atmosphere which was relaxing after the stresses of the day. She washed, got into a white cotton nightie she had left behind when she had left for Paris, which Louise had laid out on the bed for her. In the hot summer down here it was impossible to wear anything but cotton at night. When you perspired, both nylon and real silk stuck to your body.

Claudia climbed between the immaculately ironed white sheets, put her head with a sigh on the real feather pillows Hugh had brought from England years ago, and lay staring around her bedroom, remembering. It looked smaller; as a child she had thought it enormous. The white paint on the walls, the vivid red and green glass lampshade, the poppy-sprinkled duvet and curtains were all exactly as she remembered, nothing had been changed. Some of her old clothes still hung in the wardrobe, her knickers, slips and bras were neatly laid in tissue scattered with lavender bags in the chest of drawers.

Louise was an old-fashioned, dedicated housekeeper.

The phone rang downstairs. It cut off, she heard Hugh's muffled voice but couldn't hear what he was saying.

He stood stiffly by his desk, face white as paper, his fingers tight around the telephone, his knuckles livid.

After so many years to recognise a voice. Extraordinary. It had never occurred to him that voices stayed the same even though faces and bodies changed with time.

"Hugh? Hugh? Please. Answer me. I know you're there. I can hear you breathing."

He was silent.

"I never really mattered to you. Your work always came first. When I needed you, you were never there. Hugh, say something!"

He couldn't have spoken, even if he had wanted to. That voice. Ice trickled down his spine. He had read once that your hair went on growing after you were dead. Did your voice remain the same until the day you died?

"After all this time, surely you can forgive us? How much revenge do you want?"

He stared at the photos on his walls. Revenge was a kind of wild justice — who had said that? He couldn't remember. It fitted how he felt, though.

"Please, Hugh — please. Do you want me on my knees? OK, I'm on my knees, begging." A silence, then

134

smothered weeping, ragged with bitter feeling.

He put the phone down.

Sweet is revenge — he knew who had written that. Byron. Oh, yes. Byron had understood how love could become hate, and burn into your soul.

He was too restless to settle at his desk now. He could hear Claudia shifting about in her bed. Was she finding it hard to get to sleep? He went down to the kitchen and made hot chocolate, took it up to her.

Before tapping on the door he listened and heard the rustle of a page turning. She was still awake, reading in bed.

''Claudia? OK if I come in? I've brought you some hot chocolate to help you wind down and get to sleep.''

''Oh, marvellous. Just what I need. I'm wide awake, that's the trouble.''

He walked over to put the mug down on her bedside table. ''I don't want you lying awake all night, worrying. I'll deal with this, I promise you. You're quite safe, so long as you don't go out alone at night.''

''I won't, I'm not that stupid. But Louise and I plan to drive into Antibes in the morning to go to the Market Hall. That would be OK, wouldn't it?''

''Of course. They won't dare do anything in daylight, especially if Louise is with you. Could you pop into the English bookshop down by the harbour while you're there? They have a couple of books for me.''

''Sure, I'll collect them.'' She picked up the mug of hot chocolate holding it in both hands, the warmth of it on her palms comforting, and dipped her face towards it. ''Mmm, lovely smell.''

Hugh brushed a hand over her hair in one of his rare tender gestures.

"You look like a little girl again, in that old nightie. It's good to have you home, we've missed you, Louise and I. Good-night."

He was the only father she remembered. Her own father was a shadowy, distant memory. She wasn't even sure if those memories were real. It might be old photographs shown to her during her childhood that she remembered, or anecdotes her mother had told her, to keep his memory alive. Had Hugh not taken his place, she often wondered how different her life might have been. What would have happened to her when her mother had died if Hugh had not been there? Foster parents? A children's home? These days everyone knew the dangers children faced in one of those! She had been lucky, she owed Hugh more than she could ever repay.

She fell asleep within minutes of putting out the light. In her dreams she heard voices out in the garden, shouting, arguing. One was Hugh's, the other was familiar, too, although she wasn't sure whose voice it was.

"You bastard, I'm going to kill you!" Hugh yelled.

"See you in hell first!" The voice choked abruptly as if someone had their hands on the man's throat. Then came a strangled scream, followed at once by a loud splash.

She woke up, sweating, sat up, listening, but there were no sounds outside, just the ripple of wind on the pool, the sigh of the trees. She padded to the window and opened her shutters, but the garden was empty and silent. She closed them and went back to bed, but it took some time before she fell asleep again.

She woke up when Louise opened her shutters to the morning. Claudia flinched as her head stabbed with pain at the invasion of light. "What time is it?"

"Nine o'clock! I wanted to get to the market by this time. You're pale — are you OK? I was getting worried! You were sleeping like the dead, I've been in twice, but you never stirred! Here, I brought your breakfast up. Do you still want to go to Antibes?"

"Yes, please. I've got a headache, I must have slept too heavily."

Her head felt as if a jazz band was playing inside her skull, coloured lights zigzagged in front of her eyes.

Migraine? she thought. But she had slept for over ten hours! She couldn't remember ever sleeping that deeply for so long. Migraines usually meant she hadn't been sleeping well. Of course yesterday had been quite a strain.

Louise frowned, staring at her closely. "Maybe I'd better go to market alone? You can come another day."

"No, I'll be fine when I've drunk my coffee. Give me fifteen minutes." Hugh would be writing all morning, she didn't want to hang around the villa on her own. Her nerves wouldn't stand it.

When Louise had gone she took a headache pill with some water, had a quick shower to wake herself up, put on a towelling robe and sat on her bed to eat a croissant and drink strong, black, coffee.

By the time she got downstairs, in navy blue jeans and a striped blue and white Breton sailor's top which she had worn endlessly in her teens, washed and washed, but which still looked amazingly good, she was wide awake and her headache more or less gone. Hugh was already working in his study. Jules was cleaning out the pool and waved to Claudia as she came down the steps from the house.

"*Ça va?*"

"*Bien, merci, et vous?*"

"*Moi? Comme ci, comme ça!*" he shrugged, his hand held up in a rocking gesture, then put the hand behind him and bent double, groaning. "*Mon dos! C'est affreux.*"

"There he goes again — complaining about his back! Just trying to get out of digging and carrying anything heavy!" muttered Louise, getting into the small red Renault waiting on the drive.

"*Tais–toi, vieille stupide!*"

They squabbled like children every day, but Claudia knew they were deeply fond of each other, underneath.

Jules must have driven the car out of the double garage for them. He was always trying to make Louise's life easier; he grew vegetables for her in a little plot behind the villa, under cloches, to keep off the neighbourhood cats, he carried the dustbin in and out of the gate each morning, took the black plastic bag of rubbish out, cleaned the villa windows upstairs and down. Louise might grumble about him, but she relied on him too.

Claudia got into the driver's seat, zapped the gate, and drove carefully down the slope, took the sharp right-hand turn out into the lane. The shadows of the trees danced and flickered on the tarmac. Behind her the gates automatically closed again.

The brightness of the day made her blink as she turned out of the shadowy lane into the sunlit road at the far end of it.

Louise noticed her screw her eyes up. "Your old sunglasses are still in the glove compartment where you left them."

"Oh, great." Claudia found them, black, elegantly simple. She slid them on to her nose, sighed with relief. "That's better."

Also in the glove compartment was a tape of a singer she had been mad about before she went to Paris, Véronique Sansom. She put it in the tape player and switched it on. The first track was Sansom's best-known song, "*Comme je l'imagine...*" She had loved the sexy melancholy of the voice, singing about remembering how a lover looked. She had been mad about a guy that last year and had always thought of him when she played this tape. Now she couldn't even remember what he had looked like, only knew that when he smiled at her it had made her light-headed.

"I haven't listened to her for ages!"

"I remember you were always playing her music!"

Claudia smiled, touched. This recording had been important to her, but it hadn't occurred to her that anyone else would realise, or remember. What had his name been, that guy she had adored for months? How could you feel so deeply, yet forget so completely in such a short time?

"You remember that? Do you play it?"

Louise made a scornful face. "Me? Not my taste at all.

139

I prefer Piaf, me!''

"I know you play her a lot. And she is wonderful.''

Claudia had driven the Renault every day while she was at college, but it still handled well, although Hugh had bought it secondhand. He had intended both her and Louise to use it, which was why she hadn't taken the car to Paris when she moved up there.

Leaving the car for Louise, she had bought herself a van with some of the money she had inherited from her parents when she was twenty-one.

The van was far more useful, had room to carry her equipment and food in the back, and room for Siegfried and Patti to sit squashed up beside her in the front.

It was fun, though, to drive her little Renault again. It put her in touch with her early self — the girl who had had such dreams, but been afraid she would never realise them. Well, she had. To some extent.

Except that she had never found the dream lover she had believed was waiting for her somewhere, some time. He still hadn't showed.

They parked in one of the harbour car-parks and walked up the narrow, hilly street to the covered Market Hall inside the walls of Antibes. Both of them loved wandering around the stalls, inhaling the smells, looking at the variety of what was sold, from inexpensive, home-made musical instruments — drums made of gourds from Africa with waxed cotton stretched across their mouths, flutes carved out of small branches, small gourds filled with dried beans — to vegetables and fruit, home-made bread from local farms, cheese, meat, and fish caught in the bay.

Louise paused to haggle with a fishmonger over the ingredients for bouillabaisse. Red mullet, monkfish, *rascasse,* langoustine, scallops, prawns, crabs, lobsters, glistened under the bright electric lights. The selection was enormous, the fish probably caught early that morning.

Claudia wandered on to look at the flowers massed in heavenly chaos in metal buckets, wicker baskets and cardboard boxes. The scent of roses, spicy carnations, lavender, almost made the head swim and was certainly preferable to the smell of fish.

''Claudia?''

She looked round in surprise at a very pregnant woman in a tent-like red smock who was smiling at her.

''It's me, Jeanne. Jeanne Fevrier, don't you remember?''

She did remember the name, but she had to look hard before the rather beaky face, that of a predatory bird, nose like a knife, jutting cheekbones, sharp black eyes, with a scalp covered in thick black hair, finally registered. It must be seven years since they had met. The girl she had known had gone, this was a woman confronting her.

''Jeanne! I didn't know you at first. You look so different!''

The woman laughed. ''Of course I do — I'm having a baby!''

''Well, I did notice, but you've changed in other ways, your face is different.'' Softer, less angular, the eyes brighter, the mouth and cheeks warm and full. Jeanne had been bony as a girl. Pregnancy agreed with her.

"I've put on so much weight! Last time we met I had a tiny waist and almost no breasts at all. Look at them now!" Jeanne put a hand up to brush them, grimacing. "I used to long for big boobs, but I never thought of getting them this way!"

They giggled, as they had ten years ago, behind the bicycle sheds at school, and Jeanne was looking more and more familiar with every minute.

"Is this baby your first?"

"Yes. An accident," she said. "Louis and I weren't even married because we didn't want any kids yet, so why bother? But we went to a party, got a bit tipsy, and I woke up a month later up the spout."

"How does Louis feel about the baby?" Claudia remembered him vaguely from their last year at school. He and Jeanne had been together for years; married in all but name. Louis was a rugger player, broad, cheerful, from a large local family, once all fishermen, now all accountants and solicitors.

"Oh, he loved the idea from the word go. His mates patted him on the back and bought him drinks, made him feel he was a big man. And his mother and father are over the moon. It will be their first grandchild! His mother has offered to take care of the baby if I go back to work. What about you? Still cooking?"

"Yes, I have my own business, in Paris, cooking for private parties. I'm doing pretty well."

"Good for you! Are you here on holiday?"

"A few days' break, yes."

"I haven't seen anyone from school for years, most of the old gang moved away. It would be great to have a

142

wallow in nostalgia."

"I'd love to, but I don't know when I'll be free. Give me your number and I'll ring to make a date."

Jeanne wrote her number down. "You won't forget?"

Louise joined them, carrying a heavy plastic bag of fish. "Hallo, Jeanne, I heard you were expecting! Come to La Bastide and eat my bouillabaisse this evening."

"I'd love to eat your bouillabaisse again, Louise, you used to cook it for us when we all came round for a swim and supper, remember? But I have a husband who expects me to be home with his dinner ready when he gets there! Maybe some other time?"

Claudia had a split-second vision of her life — an old-fashioned, spoilt husband brought up French-style to expect his own way by a domineering mother-in-law who tried to run their lives. Poor Jeanne!

"If you don't ring me, I'll ring you, Claudia. I'd better rush, I have an appointment with my doctor in an hour. See you soon, I hope."

Watching her make a stately progress, one hand on her back, towards the Market Hall exit Louise said, "She looks well. When's the baby due? Soon, by the look of her. She wasn't your best friend, was she? That was little Chantal. Wasn't that terrible, the way she died."

Claudia frowned, forced to confront a memory she had kept at bay for a long time, finding it too painful to remember.

"She didn't die, Louise! She was murdered, by that bastard she married. I hope he never gets out of prison."

Claudia had read about the case with horrified disbelief. Louise had sent her several issues of *Nice-*

Matin, which printed the details of the case.

Chantal had been her best friend throughout their school days; a tiny girl with a gentle face and a sweet nature. Claudia still couldn't believe she was dead.

If she had been asked to prophesy futures for her three closest friends, she would have marked Chantal down to marry happily, have lots of children; Jeanne to be a successful career woman; Anne-Marie to be a nun. But none of them had followed any of the paths she had imagined they would. Anne-Marie called herself a dancer, wore a few bright green feathers in strategic places, paraded in front of an audience of men in a nightclub.

At least she had a future. Chantal had died violently, beaten to death by her drunken husband.

Jeanne might talk about going back to work now, but with a husband and mother-in-law like that, she would probably be pregnant again within a couple of years, and once she had several kids, she would be tied hand and foot.

And herself . . . she had never dreamed of being a chef, had she? She had daydreamed about imitating Hugh, becoming a journalist, or a writer.

Yet she loved her life; it had been the right road for her. She made plenty of money and met lots of interesting, even exciting, people, and she was creative, able to improvise, think up new dishes, she was never bored. Maybe one day she might even start writing? She sometimes thought of writing a recipe book; a very different kind, illustrated with watercolours of views of the Côte d'Azur.

144

"I'm going to put this fish into the car, then I want to walk up into town to do some more shopping," Louise said. "Do you want to come?"

"I have to pick up some books from the English bookshop for Hugh. Why don't we meet for coffee later?"

"OK — at the bar next to the bookshop?"

"Fine, how long will you be?"

"Half an hour?"

They walked down the hill in the flickering shadows of the trees, sunlight glinting through new leaves, and separated just before the harbour wall. Louise went through the arch leading to the car-parks. Claudia climbed the steps to an upper pavement above the road to look at a small flea market.

Nothing was worth much — a few pieces of secondhand furniture, an old mirror in a carved wooden frame, a dumb waiter, in the shape of a Renaissance pageboy, whose paint was fading, a pile of yellow and blue china, a cluster of leather-bound antique books.

She bought a dark green china bowl, made to look like a cabbage; it would be perfect for salads. The stallholder wrapped it in sheets of newspaper for her, and she slid it into her basket before going on to the English bookshop. The books Hugh had ordered were waiting below the counter. Putting them underneath the wrapped bowl, Claudia wandered up on to the old walls of Antibes to stare out over the blue, blue sea towards the woody promontory of the Cap where Hugh was working.

How tranquil the world looked this morning. Hard to believe anything could trouble that dreamy view. A faint veil of mist hung over the Îles de Lerins; the horizon could have been smudged in with God's thumb, deep, smoky blue.

White sails on the little yachts were flitting to and fro in the glitter of light, the beaches vivid with coloured umbrellas and young people on sailboards just offshore.

At the villa, Jules would be clipping the cypress hedges into shape, pruning rose trees, sweeping the paths. Hugh would be locked in concentration in his office. Silence would hang over the narrow roads of the Cap.

There were fewer people living there than in other stretches of the coast. Usually all you heard was splashing in someone pool, a magpie scolding in a pine tree, the occasional car passing, or the garbage truck moving from villa to villa in the daily collection of black plastic bags. This was the peaceful life she had grown up in, but today it no longer had the same feel to it, because she knew it was under attack from outside, by these men from Paris.

But who was behind them? What was this all about?

Hugh's refusal to tell her had been almost as worrying as what had happened to her in her aparment the night before last. It brought into question everything she had thought she knew about Hugh, and left her uncertain about him. Hugh — a thief? He was rich, she knew he earned a great deal from his writing, and somehow, although he never talked about the past, she sensed that he came from a wealthy background. Some of his possessions were very old, and from remarks he had let drop she was sure he had inherited them from his family.

146

What exactly had he found in the shattered remains of the chimney? Why had he kept it? Who wanted it back, and how far would they go to get it?

Her head thudded again; she put a hand to her temples, wincing as she remembered dreaming last night about shouting, Hugh threatening to kill someone, then that loud splash, as if a body had landed in the swimming pool.

It had only been a dream. When she had sat up in bed there had been silence outside.

But the dream was a sign of her doubts about Hugh.

Once she had trusted him completely. Now ... did she trust him so implicitly any more? But only children trust without hesitation, and she was no longer a child.

The headache was back. What she needed was some strong coffee. She had to stop worrying, too. She could trust Hugh. He was one of the good guys. Her reason told her so. Or was that simply what she wanted to believe? He was a wealthy man. He wouldn't steal out of greed. He must have a strong reason for keeping whatever he had found the day her mother died.

She had never forgotten her strange feelings that day. The lightning hitting the chimney, the collapse of the roof, followed so soon by her mother's death, had seemed to her to be a stroke of fate. Had she known about the box Hugh had found, she would have believed it to be the working of destiny. Perhaps that was how Hugh saw it?

She walked down the steep slope from the walls back to the café next to the bookshop. There were only a handful of people on the terrace outside. She took an empty table and ordered a black coffee.

Cars kept driving past, going to the harbour, coming the other way to drive up the incline leading to the old walls. From the café the road was one-way only; you could not drive back through the old town of Antibes.

But on this café terrace you could ignore the traffic, separated from it by a pavement, and the wall of the ramp up to the walls. This was a little oasis of calm.

Somebody had left the local paper, *Nice-Matin,* on the table. Just as her coffee arrived, a large photo on the front page caught her eye. Stiffening, she grabbed the paper, stared at Ferret Face's picture. What was he doing on the front page of *Nice-Matin*?

Then she took in the headline. MURDER. That one word stopped her in her tracks, like a horse refusing a fence.

MURDER? Had he killed someone? Who? Her hands turned icy, trembling. She hurriedly read the rest of the headline. MURDER ON BEACH OFF CAP D'ANTIBES. The copy underneath was continued inside to page three.

Her hands shook as she turned the page. The print seemed unreadable. She closed her eyes, opened them again, focusing, read the short columns in a rush, read the whole thing again, more slowly.

His fully clothed body had been found on the Garoupe beach during the night by a fisherman down there for night-fishing. The police were calling it murder, although *Nice-Matin* had not yet found out how he had died. The photo of him came from his plasticised identity card, which the police had found in his inside jacket pocket, in a leather wallet, along with other personal papers.

His name was Jacques Roulet, he was a private detective. Private detective? Her head knocked again with shock and dismay. That must mean that somebody had paid him and his partner to burgle her apartment.

But that didn't answer the questions rushing through her head. How had he died? Who had killed him? And why? Claudia stared at his face with dislike and nervous anxiety.

It had been his voice she had dreamed she had heard screaming in the garden last night. She must have picked that up at the time — why else had she been so upset?

But it had only been a dream. When she had sat up to listen, all she had heard had been the usual night sounds. The distant whisper of the sea, the gurgling of water in the pool, the wind breathing through the leaves, frogs croaking, crickets whirring, the cry of an owl.

Dreams might be disturbing, but they didn't prove anything.

Yet she was afraid. She couldn't deny, or explain, it.

''Hallo.''

She looked up with shock, pupils dilated, face pale.

The last time she had seen the dead man, he had been talking to Ben outside the airport. Had Ben been with him when he died? Had it been Ben who killed him?

His black brows jerked together impatiently. ''No need to look at me as if I were a murderer!''

''Are you?'' She couldn't help the shrill question.

His eyes hardened. ''What are you talking about, for

149

God's sake? I told you I was coming down to Antibes. You didn't tell me you were, did you? How long have you been here? I thought Hugh was just your landlord? Why have you come down here to see him? Did you tell him I have to talk to him? I've rung half a dozen times, without getting a reply. I've been to his villa this morning, but he won't let me in. You've got to make him talk to me. I can't stay here much longer, and I have something important to tell him.''

She didn't really take in what he was saying. Her head was full of what she had just read, and whirling crescents of questions about Ben.

The waiter appeared. *''Vous désirez, M'sieur?''*

''Coffee and a croissant, please.'' Ben sat down at her table, met her dazed stare and lifted an eyebrow. ''Will it kill you if I share your table?''

She didn't answer, just handed him the *Nice-Matin,* watching his face for some reaction to the news, but he waved it away, scowling.

''I don't want to read your newspaper, I want to make you listen to me. I'm sorry I jumped to conclusions yesterday morning. I lost my temper, and I wish to God I hadn't. Can't we forget it happened and start again?''

''I think you'd better read this!'' She tapped the front page.

Ben looked down at her finger, suddenly focused on the photograph, did a double-take, taking the paper from her at last.

''I've seen that guy somewhere before. Can't remember where, but it was down here that I saw him.''

He read the story slowly, frowning. ''Poor chap.

Probably went swimming at night, the water would be icy. Maybe he got cramp and drowned. Easy enough if you don't know the currents off a strange beach.''

''Swimming, fully dressed, at night?''

Her sarcasm made him scowl again. ''Maybe he was drunk!''

''The police are treating it as murder!''

''I know, I just read that in the paper. Doesn't mean the police really believe that. You may not have noticed, but people in my profession often exaggerate. We need a good story the way an addict needs a fix. So if a story isn't strong enough, we pump it up into something bigger. Anyway, why did you want me to look at this? Did you know him?''

''I know *you* did! I saw you with him, yesterday at the airport.''

His eyes narrowed on her face. ''You saw me at the airport? You could have given me a lift to Hugh's villa. That wasn't very friendly of you. If you had taken me there I might have got in to see him there and then.''

''He didn't want to see you.''

''Well, he's going to have to, sooner or later.'' Ben's eyes dropped to the newspaper again. ''The airport? You're right. That *was* where I saw him. He stopped me as I came out of the terminal, and asked me how to get to Cap d'Antibes.''

She gave a short, scornful smile. ''That's an incredible coincidence! Considering he was burgling my apartment the night before, and only a few hours later you pushed your way in and searched my apartment too! Do you really expect me to believe you didn't know him?''

151

Dark red stained those high cheekbones. "What exactly are you accusing me of now? Getting this guy to burgle your apartment? You think I'm a gangster, do you? A killer, too, it seems. You have a very vivid imagination."

"I'm not imagining anything. I'm putting two and two together."

"And making forty-two!"

She ignored that. "You were both at my apartment looking for something. You both came down here. I saw you together at the airport. That man and his partner gave me a threatening message for Hugh, and so did you. You can't expect me to believe it is all pure coincidence. I think the police would be very interested in what I have to tell them, don't you?"

"What do you mean — a threatening message? About what?"

"Don't pretend you don't know what I'm talking about! I know you do. As soon as I mentioned you to Hugh he knew who you were!"

His mouth twisted. "I told you he would. You've got it all wrong, Claudia. I can see it must look like a huge coincidence, but I'm afraid that's what it is. I did not know that guy. I did not kill him. You need a reason for murder, and I had none. You said this man was searching your apartment. What was he looking for?"

She looked away. "I've no idea."

"What was the message he told you to give Hugh?"

"If you don't know, I'm not telling you!"

"It sounds to me as if it was Hugh who had a motive for murder!"

Shock hit her in an icy wave. Shock. Not surprise. Because she had already worked out that Hugh had a motive. But it was disturbing to hear somebody else thought so too.

It couldn't be true. She could not believe he could kill another human being. Hugh was incapable of that.

Yet how well did she really know him? She had thought she did, she would have insisted that he was incapable of dishonesty until yesterday, when he had confessed to having kept whatever he had found in the ruins of the old chimney. That wasn't really theft, though. If you found something, surely you were entitled to keep it. Hugh had been living in the villa for years. Anything he found in it must legally be his, surely?

She shivered, remembering last night's strange, distorted dream. The shouting, the scream, the splash.

But had it been a dream?

Ben was watching her averted face; she felt his eyes physically, her skin heating at their touch, the intimacy sending alarm and panic through her, and with it a strange, bewildering mixture of pleasure and attraction. That morning they had met, on the quayside in the early light, beside the Seine, her response to him had been immediate, sensual, erotic, disturbing. She had never experienced anything like that before. It was strangely familiar, her feeling about him, as though she had met him before, in dreams, many years ago.

Perhaps most girls do dream of the man they will meet one day, their future lover, creating his image out of a favourite film star, or actor, out of their father, or the

153

hero of a book they've read.

She couldn't imagine where her image of Ben had come from, or why she seemed to recognise him on sight. It was bewildering, disturbing.

"You have a gorgeous mouth," he said abruptly, voice deep. "I can't wait to kiss it."

Her lips burned as if he had kissed them. Crazy, half-delirious ideas ran through her head. If he touched her, she would go up in flames. Her body was dry tinder and he could light it with one brush of his finger, she thought, with feverish excitement.

Hot and shaking, she caught sight of Louise advancing towards them down the hill from the upper town. Sick relief hit her.

"Here comes my friend."

He frowned, looking round. "Boyfriend?" His voice was hard and clipped, very English.

She didn't need to answer. Louise arrived, plumped herself down on one of the chairs, sighing.

"*Mes pieds!* My feet are killing me, I'm getting too old for all this walking. Antibes is such a hilly town. I had to go to the post office, then up to a shop by the station, then down here again!" She looked up at the waiter as he strolled over, gave him a friendly smile. "A good milky coffee, M'sieur."

"*Bien sûr, Madame.*"

As he went back into the bar she looked sideways at Ben, her face curious, neutral, uncertain whether to be friendly or not.

"*Bonjour, M'sieur.*"

Claudia could tell she was wondering if she had ever

154

met him before, and if not, who he was and why he was at this table.

He smiled, and Claudia's heart twisted at the charm in his face. How deep did it go, that charm? Did he put it on, one of the many masks he wore? Or was it real?

"*Je m'appelle Ben, enchanté de faire votre connaissance, Madame,*" he said, offering his hand to Louise.

Louise shook it warmly. She immediately picked up on the accent, just as Claudia had. "You're English?"

He nodded, getting up and laying some coins on the table. "It was a pleasure to meet you, Madame. But I'm afraid I have to be on my way." He shot a sideways look at Claudia. "I'll be seeing you."

Was that threat, or promise? His tone gave no clue, yet her nerves jangled.

His tall, graceful body disappeared into the old town; Claudia's eyes stayed on him, wishing she knew more about him, could guess what lay behind his sexy smile.

Her stomach was hollow, ached, with fear, or desire, or both.

"Who is he?" Louise asked eagerly. "He's very handsome. Is he a film star? I'm sure I've seen him somewhere before. Do you know him, or did he try to pick you up?"

Claudia wouldn't have been surprised if her voice had sounded as weird as she felt, but it came out quite normally, if a little husky.

"He's a photographer, I met him the other day, he was taking pictures at Rex Valery's party."

"Did he follow you down here?" Louise looked

155

excited. "Is he after you? I wondered if he might be, the way he was looking at you just before I arrived."

Claudia swallowed. "How was he looking at me?"

"Oh, you know! As if he could eat you!"

Claudia's mouth went dry. "You're imagining it," she said hoarsely.

Louise looked disappointed. "Well, that was how it looked to me. Don't you like him?"

"Here's your coffee," Claudia said with relief. "We ought to get back and start cooking lunch — the bouillabaisse is for tonight, isn't it? What are you planning for *déjeuner*?"

"Something light and quickly cooked, I thought, as it will take so long to prepare the bouillabaisse. I'll cook some of the *moules* in white wine, then serve *salade Niçoise*."

"Sounds great to me. I'll make the salad while you cook the *moules*."

They walked back to the car-park, jostled by the hurrying crowds. Claudia felt somebody fingering her hair and jerked her head away. Turning to give the man behind her an angry stare, she only caught sight of his vanishing back as he ran off.

As she got into the car Louise looked at her sharply. "What on earth has happened to your hair?"

Claudia put a hand to it and felt ragged strands. She leaned forward hurriedly to look into the driving mirror. Horrified, she saw that a big chunk of hair on the right side of her head had gone. It had been cut off. With a razor, from the sharp edges of what was left.

"Who can have done that?" Louise thought aloud.

Dazedly, Claudia told her, "I felt it happen. Just now. Somebody was touching my hair, but when I looked round all I saw was a man running away. I didn't realise he had cut some off. Why on earth would someone do a thing like that?"

"Holy Mother of God, there are some crazy people around! You know, my friend Agnes, who works in a hotel down at the port, told me somebody is always stealing knickers off their washing line!"

Claudia fingered her hair gloomily. "How am I going to disguise the mess he's left? I must make an appointment with a hairdresser at once and see what can be done with it."

As they drove into the Chemin de Croe half an hour later, Claudia recognised Ben's white Citroën parked by the villa gates and drew a shaky breath.

"Now who's that?" muttered Louise, peering into the car as they drove past. It was empty. There was no sign of Ben in the shadowy lane, either.

He must be inside the villa. Fear scraped Claudia's nerves.

CHAPTER
SEVEN

She heard the two men arguing before she reached the house, although she could not make out what they were saying. Their voices carried on the still, summer air; angry, raised voices which made the wood pigeons and gulls fly upwards with a clatter of spread wings. Because Cap d'Antibes was such a quiet backwater, with little traffic passing through the narrow lanes, sound carried a long way. The inhabitants of the other villas, behind their high cypress hedges and stone walls, could probably hear the noise, would be wondering who was shouting, would be irritated and even worried as they sat on their terraces under umbrellas, sipping long cool drinks, reading their newspapers or books. Many of the villas were let to summer visitors from Germany, England, America, who expected peace and quiet as part of their holiday package. Rich people did not wish to be troubled by commotion in a place like this. That was not what they had come here for — they wanted to feel safe as well as pampered.

Louise looked up at the salon windows in surprise.

"Now who can that be shouting at Hugh like that? Do you know who drives that car parked outside, Claudia? I didn't recognise it, but I think it has been parked out there before, although I can't remember when.''

''Yesterday, it arrived just after I got home.''

''I think you're right! You've got a good memory. I can't remember seeing it before. Does it belong to someone we know? He came to see Hugh, who told me not to let him in. It was an Englishman. He definitely had an English accent, but Hugh wouldn't talk to him or see him.''

Louise went round the car to get the shopping out of the boot. Her tabby cat, Belle, streaked across the flowerbeds from the far reaches of the garden and began circling her, rubbing itself against her legs, purring loudly. Louise bent to run an indulgent hand over the silky fur and the cat arched its back.

''Yes, you smell fish, don't you? What a marvellous nose you've got. Well, you'll have to wait until I've made my bouillabaisse. Then you can have some fish heads and the trimmings.''

Claudia hurriedly carried two bags of shopping into the kitchen. She dumped them on the central work counter without unpacking them, and ran up the short flight of stairs to the salon.

The high windows stood open, a cooling breeze blowing in from the sea, which you could glimpse behind the pines and palms; a soft blue backcloth to the view down to Cannes Bay, with white sails moving on it.

Hugh, in a dark blue open-neck shirt and pale blue cotton trousers, had his back to her. Ben confronted him, facing in her direction. Neither of them noticed her for a moment, they were too busy shouting at each other.

"How can you refuse? It will only take a couple of days. Fly over, spend a few minutes with him, then fly straight back. Where's the problem? If you can't afford the fare I'll buy your ticket."

That was a cold sneer, and Hugh reacted as if stung by a hornet. "Don't be so damned insulting!"

Ben grimaced. "OK, I'm sorry, that was childish. But — he's dying. Whatever he did to you, he's dying now and he wants to see you before he dies, he needs your forgiveness."

"Death won't just wash out what he did to me! Wait until someone betrays you, then see how you feel!" A pause, then he said curtly, "I presume you know all about it?"

Ben shook his head. "My mother said it was too personal, very private, she couldn't talk about it."

Hugh laughed harshly. "I bet she did! Helena never faced up to anything without being forced to, she has a wonderful capacity for self-protection!"

"That's enough! I'm not listening to unpleasant remarks about my mother!" Ben's voice was suddenly rough with anger. He had gone dark red. His hands clenched at his side. It was clear that he loved his mother and was protective towards her; Claudia liked that in him, it said so much about him and the people he came from.

Hugh's shoulder muscles bunched with tension as if he were about to hurl more bitter words at the younger man, but none emerged.

"She has had a very bad time these last months, nursing a dying man. She must have lost a stone, and

160

she's always pale, but then she has never looked very strong or had much colour.''

Claudia moved, and Ben saw her for the first time. Something in his face made Hugh turn to look at her too.

"What on earth happened to your hair?'' Ben asked. "You look as if a cow has chewed on it.''

She put a hand up to it, grimacing. "Somebody chopped a bit of it out while I was in Antibes.''

"What?'' both men said together, sounding oddly alike, then scowled at each other.

"Who did it?'' Hugh demanded.

"I don't know, I didn't see. I felt something touch my hair, but when I looked round there was only a man running away, with his back to me. I didn't even realise my hair had been slashed until Louise noticed it.''

Hugh frowned. "I don't like the sound of that.''

"A hair fetishist,'' Ben said. "Some freaky guy who gets off by stealing hair from women. From the look of it, I'd say he used a razor, which makes it even freakier.''

"Dangerous,'' Hugh said curtly. "Men who carry razors around and attack women with them are very dangerous. We'd better ring the police and report this. He may be doing it all over the Riviera.''

"No,'' she protested. "Don't call the police, I'm not hurt, I'm just embarrassed and furious.'' She took a breath then plunged, "What were you two arguing about just now?''

"How long have you been standing there, eavesdropping?'' Hugh snarled.

He made it sound as if she had been spying, as if she

were an enemy he hated. She stared, her eyes full of hurt and shock.

Hugh threw up a hand in bleak apology, closing his eyes briefly. "Sorry. I'm in a filthy mood. Look, show him out, will you? We've finished our conversation, he's just leaving."

"I haven't finished!" Ben protested.

"Well, I have. My family is a door I shut before you were born. I am not opening it again. I have nothing against you, personally, but your father means nothing to me."

"For God's sake, he's dying — where's your humanity?"

Hugh laughed angrily. "Don't be so pious! There was a time when I wanted to kill him, when I prayed he would die of some ghastly disease. Now I simply don't care whether he lives or dies. That's an improvement, isn't it? That shows how humane I am!"

Ben looked stupefied. "I can't believe you hate him that much!"

"You'd better believe it. Because I do. Now, will you get out of my house?"

"Only if you really listen. For the last time, I promise. He told me to tell you how sorry he was, asked me to say he wants to ask your forgiveness, set the books straight before he dies. If you left England before I was born you obviously can't have set eyes on him for twenty-eight years. My God, it's a lifetime — my lifetime, anyway. I never remember seeing you, or even hearing anyone mention your name.

Hugh's voice was sardonic. "Guilty people prefer to

forget what they've done."

"What did he do?"

Hugh shrugged. "It isn't up to me to tell you. Ask him. Ask your mother."

"They're both involved?" Ben's brows lifted suddenly. "Did my father steal her from you? Were you in love with her too, before she married him?"

Hugh did not answer.

Ben slowly said, "He said I should tell you he knows what he did to you and he wants to say sorry to your face. It was all so long ago. You must have got over whatever it was by now."

Hugh shouted at him. "No. No. No."

He turned on his heel and went upstairs at a rush. The door of his office slammed shut.

Ben looked at Claudia with a stunned expression. "What on earth can my father have done to him?"

"Your father?"

"His brother."

She drew a sharp, startled breath. "His brother?"

"Stop repeating everything I say for God's sake!"

"Your father is Hugh's brother?" So that explained the likeness she had picked up the very first time she had seen Ben. It was a family resemblance; colouring, build, temperament.

His eyes were derisive. "Got it at last? Your brain works slowly but it gets there in the end, does it?"

She gave him an angry look. First Hugh insulted her, then Ben does it too. Why did men take that tone with women, like schoolmasters using sarcasm and mockery to slow-witted pupils?

"Don't talk to me like that! It's a shock to discover Hugh has a family — he's never mentioned anyone, I wondered if he was alone in the world. What's your father's name?"

"Rafe."

"Rafe? Sounds French. Is there any French blood in your family? I've often wondered. Hugh's colouring is very French; even his skin has an olive tinge. I thought he might be of French descent, although he never mentioned it."

"My great-grandfather married a French girl he met during the First World War when he was fighting in France. She died long before I was born, but Hugh must have known her when he was a child. My father told me Hugh did a year at the Sorbonne after getting his degree at Oxford. He must have acquired a taste for French life then, but he was probably already interested in France because of his grandmother. He may have learned to speak French from her, in his early childhood."

"He's never mentioned her, either. Or any of his family. You know, whatever your father did to him must have been very serious if he left England and has never gone back. Hugh is so very English, in some ways. He still wears English clothes all the time, and reads the latest English books. What can your father have done to him?"

"You'll have to ask him, my father didn't tell me anything. Just said they had quarrelled before I was born, and Hugh had never spoken to him since. I didn't even know Hugh existed until a week ago, when my father asked me to find him. He knew Hugh's Paris address from the family lawyer, who has been in touch all along, it seems, but Hugh hasn't answered any of the letters my father says he sent once he realised he was seriously ill. I suppose Hugh got them?''

''If they came to the apartment I'd have sent them on. He does get letters from England from time to time, I always forward them. So that's why you didn't know he actually lived here most of the year.''

Ben nodded. ''All I knew was what Benskin — the family lawyer — told me. I even approached Hugh's publishers, but they wouldn't tell me anything at all, just told me to contact Benskin, which I'd already done. Do you think you could talk him into coming to England to see my father?''

She glanced up the stairs, frowning. ''I don't know. I've never seen him so upset. I'll see if he'll talk to me. You'd better go now, though. Ask Louise to let you out of the gate. Where are you staying? If Hugh changes his mind, I'll let you know.''

''I'm staying in Antibes, at the Hôtel Alexandre.''

She knew it vaguely, an old fashioned hotel with fading green paint on the creaking wooden shutters, in the Place de la République. It had rather a good restaurant on the ground floor with an extension out in the square, where she and Hugh had sometimes eaten in the evening, in summer, under the rustling plane trees, by the strange sulphuric yellow glow of glass globe lights. Every few minutes an entertainer appeared among the tables, sometimes a singer, accompanied by an accordion-player, or guitarist; or a white-faced mime artist, dancers, jugglers, or daring flame-eaters.

After they had done their act, they came round with a hat to collect money from their captive audience. Most people gave; being amused while you ate was half the fun of the evening.

"Do you know it?" asked Ben and she nodded.

"I'll ring you there tomorrow."

Ben moved towards the stairs down to the kitchen.

Picking up the copy of *Nice-Matin,* Claudia went up to Hugh's office very quietly, hesitated before knocking on the door.

Normally she would hear the hum of his computer, the soft clatter of the keys as he typed. How often had she stood here, over the years, listening, but never daring to knock, consumed with curiosity about what he was writing, about the solitary life he led in that room?

It had seemed mysterious, glamorous; she had longed to be allowed in, wished she could read his manuscripts before they went off to his editor, before the rest of the world discovered what he had been doing. She ached to be the first to read his work, but had never had the courage to ask.

Her friends at school had been passionate about a quartet of books he had written fifteen years earlier — strange fantasies about another world under the earth where pale goblins lived in a parallel universe to human beings. Hugh had made it all so real, their lives in the caves and tunnels in mountains or under the oceans. As if he knew it, was at home with the cosy kitchens and bedrooms.

His descriptions were down-to-earth and detailed, explaining how they lit their homes with natural gas

166

which gave a fierce white light, or could be turned down low. They had no need for heating; their caves were warm in winter and cool in summer. They hung thick curtains over some entrances, to keep out any draughts, and cooked with the gas. They slept on beds of dried leaves and grass. All vegetarians because they did not believe in taking life, they ate mushrooms, roots, berries, nuts and grains, had special gardens in the sea where they grew kelp, which they made into soup and used for a hundred other purposes.

The title of the first book, *The People of the Labyrinth*, had become the overall title for the series. Children formed labyrinth clubs, wrote eager fan mail to the author, using the language he had invented for the goblins, wore badges which carried the images of the main characters. Adults were just as obsessive.

Last year there had been two academic books devoted to Hugh and his fantasy. At times the writers had seemed to believe that world really existed inside the earth, and Hugh had been there, was possibly a goblin himself, since he never did interviews or had photographs taken. His secrecy was part of the mystique of the quartet.

He had laughed a great deal over the books. "Silly bastards! They need their heads examined!" But both books had sold well and his own sales had climbed again.

None of his other work had had the same impact. Her friends had been desperate to visit her, meet Hugh, ask him questions — but he had solemnly informed them that he was not permitted to talk about the Labyrinth or the people who lived there. She would sometimes let them stand outside this door with her and listen to the tap-tap of his fingers on the computer keys.

Now, though, there was not a sound from the room. Was he in there at all, or had he gone to his bedroom?

Claudia bit her lip. Should she risk knocking? Normally she wouldn't dare. He had once bitten her head off for interrupting him at work and she had never done so again. Hugh in a rage was terrifying.

Tentatively she tried the door handle.

"Go away!" he snarled. "Who's that?"

She swallowed nervously. Her voice when it came was shaky. "Claudia. Hugh, are you OK?"

"Has he gone?"

"Yes. I came up to ask ... I thought you might want to talk."

"Well, I don't. I'm working. My morning has been interrupted and I'm behind with my schedule."

"Hugh, I think you should see *Nice-Matin* ... there's something in it that..."

"I'll look at it later!"

Desperately she said in a rush, "One of the men who broke into the apartment has been murdered! There's a picture of him on the front page."

"What?" The door opened. He took *Nice-Matin* from her, stared down at the photograph, frowning angrily. He was pale; a dark shadow along his jaw suggesting that he hadn't shaved, which struck her forcibly. He normally showered and shaved very early each day. A break in his routine must indicate something serious on his mind.

"He was the one who threatened to rape me! They give his name, see? Hugh, he was a private detective! With an address in Paris. Who do you think hired him? Was it them who killed him? Or someone else?" She was afraid to mention her dream. What if it hadn't been a dream? What if that man had been murdered here, in the garden?

Still holding the paper, he said in a voice that grated, "Tell Louise I'll have lunch later than usual. I've lost too much writing time this morning. I don't want to be disturbed again, is that understood?"

The door slammed shut.

She jumped; damp with nervous perspiration. Hugh was frightening in that mood. She didn't dare knock again.

She went to her room, stood by the window breathing in warm summer air, trying to calm her nerves, looking down to see if Ben had gone. There was no sign of him, and his car was no longer parked outside.

Sunlight glimmered on the blue pool, beckoning seductively. She suddenly longed to get into the water. That was what she needed.

She stripped off hurriedly, dropping her clothes into the wicker washing basket, put on a plain black swimsuit, slid her feet into black beach sandals. The path down to the pool was rocky; she had cut her feet too often in the past to risk going barefoot any more.

Standing in front of the long mirror she wryly flicked a finger over the shorn ends of hair. She really must tidy that up. She found some scissors and carefully trimmed the hair, combing uncut strands over the place until the razored edges didn't show. It would grow in time, but it was going to be a problem for months.

Damn it! she thought, turning away.

She went downstairs with a black towelling robe and a vividly coloured beach towel over her arm.

Outside Hugh's office door she paused, hearing him walking to and fro. Was he thinking about the murder? Or had he shed memories of that in order to concentrate on his new book? He was a man of habit; he wrote every day and seemed able to forget everything else. She envied him. Her mind was not so biddable. She couldn't force it to forget anything.

"I'm going down for a swim, Louise," she called as she headed across the salon to the French windows which opened out on to the terrace.

No reply. Louise must be absorbed in dealing with all that fish; chopping off heads and tails, gutting, cleaning the interiors. She would use most of the trimmings in her stock and the cat would get them afterwards. Louise was a careful, thrifty French housewife of the old school; she didn't go to supermarkets to buy pre-prepared food. She bought fresh produce, the cheaper the better, and cooked it herself. A brilliant cook, she loved trying new recipes, but had many favourite old ones.

Dropping her robe and towel on a lounger, Claudia kicked off her beach sandals and slowly went down the marble steps into the water.

It was always chilly around dawn, but the sun had warmed it slowly during the hours since. The blue water was cool and delicious on her overheated skin.

She had swum a slow, leisurely length and was turning back when she heard another splash. Someone else had dived into the deeper end of the pool. A spray of spume clouded her sight for a second, then she saw black hair, a gleam of golden skin, wide, bare shoulders, and her mouth dried.

As soon as she could speak, she trod water. "I told you to go nearly a quarter of an hour ago! What are you doing, still here?"

He was floating on his back next to her, his long body calmly relaxed. "I was going when I noticed a strange brown squirrel running along the electric wires up there, and stopped to watch it. I've never seen one that colour before. In England they're grey or, very rarely now, red. Your local ones are bigger, too. I was about to go when I heard a splash and saw you in the pool. The sight of you in the water was so tempting, I had to join you."

Flushed, angry, stupidly aroused by what he had said, she could barely speak. "You … you … had no right, this is private property. Get out!"

His long body uncoiled, she shivered helplessly as his legs brushed past hers, wet skin on wet skin, his hips sliding along hers. That was when she realised he wasn't wearing anything. He had simply stripped off all his clothes before diving into the pool. Her heart almost seemed to stop in shock.

"I'll go, don't worry — when I've had my swim!" Ben swam away towards the far end of the pool.

She was so shaken by the realisation that he was naked, that it was a minute or so before she swam after him.

171

"If you don't get out of the pool and leave, I'll call the police!" she threatened.

He turned suddenly with the graceful carelessness of some great fish. Their bodies collided in the water. Off balance and gasping, she grabbed at his shoulders to steady herself. His arms went round her, his legs entwined hers. Like some smooth-skinned crocodile he took her down into the deep, sunlit, blue water as if for a death roll. Over and over their bodies tumbled before they broke free of the surface again, coming up in a fountain of spray.

Clinging to him, her arms round his neck now, passionately aware of his body touching hers from their shoulders to their feet, Claudia looked up, blinded by light, and saw his face moving down towards her.

Their mouths met.

She forgot everything but the blinding erotic pleasure of that kiss, the deep, hot pressure of his lips, the taste of his tongue in her mouth. Her eyes shut. Behind her lids the sun pierced her cerebral cortex, colour exploded in her brain, orange, bright yellow, red. Her body trembled, shivered with sensual excitement. His hands were moving. Touching her everywhere. Her overheated blood seemed to follow the stroke of his fingers. Her breasts ached, her nipples hard, pushing against the tight-fitting swimsuit. She was weak with surrender and desire. She wanted him so badly it hurt.

He lifted his mouth. Her lids flickered up; they stared at each other.

"Now you know how much I want you," he said in a voice hoarse with passion. "You can see it."

She looked down, face burning, then hurriedly looked away from his aroused flesh.

"They can see us from the house!"

She glanced up at Hugh's window. There was a movement behind the glass as if someone had just stepped back.

Claudia bit her lip.

"I think he was watching!"

Ben's voice was scornful. "What if he was? You're an adult, not a child. Does it matter what he thinks? I'm beginning to wonder what sort of relationship you have with him! He isn't a blood relative. Why is he so important to you?"

"The problem is your relationship with him, not mine!"

She pushed him away and swam to the side, heaved herself out, put on her towelling robe. Ben climbed out too. She averted her eyes from his dripping nakedness.

"You can use my towel!" she told him offhandedly, holding it out.

"Thanks." He stood there, water running off his legs to form pools on the tiles, dried his hair roughly, towelled his body, then wrapped the towel round his waist, pleating it into something like a sarong.

"Where are your clothes?" She looked away, fighting the desire to touch him again. His damp shoulders glistened like liquid gold in the sunlight.

"Over there, under that pine tree."

"Well, please get dressed then. But before you put your clothes on, you had better check you haven't acquired a few ants as passengers. The garden's overrun with them; the soil around here is very sandy, this was all forest at one time. Some of the bigger ants have a very nasty bite.''

Instead of going to collect his clothes and get dressed again, he lay down on one of the loungers, stretching himself with a yawn, his waist slim, his chest powerful, his long legs muscular under dark hairs.

''You aren't a virgin, are you?''

She felt herself turn hot. Her voice flustered, she threw back, ''What's that got to do with you? I want you to go. Now!''

He closed his eyes, smiling.

She stared at him, could not stop; he was the sexiest man she had ever seen.

''How long ago?'' he drawled without looking at her.

''What?''

''How old were you when you first had sex? I was fifteen. I was given my first lesson by my best friend's mother. She was a nymphomaniac. All the other boys told me so, but I didn't believe them. Mothers weren't like that, I thought. Mine wasn't. In fact, mine is very old fashioned. She is not what you would call a party animal. She and my father were always together. But this woman was different. I spent most of one summer at their place in the country and she seduced me the very first night. We did it for the whole of August, in the woods, in fields, in the house.''

She was shocked and couldn't keep her reaction out of her voice. ''What about her husband?''

''In the army and thousands of miles away all that year.''

"Did your friend know what was going on?"

"Of course he did. He barely spoke to me for the last two years at school, and if I see him now he pretends he doesn't know me. But other friends who had stayed with them asked me if I'd done it with her, said she had seduced them, too. So he can't have been surprised. He must have known just what she was."

"How terrible for him, poor boy. It may have put him off sex for life."

"Well, sex with women, anyway. He's gay."

"No wonder! How would you have felt if your mother..."

"I know, I've thought about that. I often wondered if she had seduced him too."

Claudia shuddered. "You can't be serious?"

"I wish I wasn't. What about you? Come on, I've told you my secret. It's your turn. What was your first time like? Were you in love?"

"I was dazzled, anyway," she admitted wryly. "I was nearly seventeen and he was a boy a year older. The school rugger captain, six feet tall and as strong as an ox. He could have had any girl in my class. I was overwhelmed when he picked me. One day we were at a birthday party at Juan-les-Pins. We sneaked out of the house and made love under an umbrella pine the moonlight."

"It sounds wonderfully romantic."

"It hurt like hell. I was the one lying on pine needles, for a start, and then, well ... I could barely walk for days. I told you he was an ox, in the head as well as the body. It never occurred to him that as I was a virgin he should go gently at first. I was too proud to scream. I just suffered. And he boasted to all his friends next day. I was mortified.''

''Poor you. I hope you dumped him.''

''He dumped me. Once he had had me he went on to someone else.'' She turned away. ''I'm going in to get dressed! I want you gone in ten minutes.''

He flapped a hand. ''Bye, bye,'' he said in English.

''Hugh will have the gardener put you out if you aren't gone by then!''

His mouth curled in amusement. ''He'll find me here when he comes looking for me!''

She looked at him helplessly, from his long, slim, bare brown feet up to his damp black hair. He was muscular, very fit. Jules was far bigger, but she had an idea Ben was quicker on his feet, and probably ruthless in a fight. He had that sort of mouth and jawline. Like Hugh's.

''Why are you so annoying?'' she asked rhetorically, and he laughed.

''Just my nature, I guess,'' he said, still in English, sounding self-satisfied.

''Speak French!''

''Why should I? You know what I'm saying. I'm sure you speak English well enough. Living with him all these years you must have learned to speak his language pretty well. Typical of the French! They always try to pretend they don't speak English when they do. It's one of their ways of protesting about the world dominance of the English language.''

''The American language, I think you'll find!'' she snapped in French. ''The English aren't a colonial world

176

power any more. They're just lucky that they planted their language in so many other countries. If they hadn't, nobody would remember who they are!''

''What a typical French reaction! You seem to love Hugh, and he's English. Did you show him *Nice-Matin*?''

The soft question made her feel sick. He didn't know what she had dreamed she had heard in the night, and she would never tell him, tell anyone. It might really have been a dream, after all. Or maybe she had heard what she thought she had heard, but that would prove nothing. She hadn't seen what had happened.

''Did you?'' he pressed, and she wondered if he suspected something. But he couldn't read her mind, nor could he know anything about the iron box, unless he had owned the villa before Hugh. That couldn't be.

If that were true, it would mean it had been he who had hired the dead man. She couldn't believe that.

She didn't want to believe it, that was the truth.

Maybe he knew more about Hugh than she did — why Hugh had left England, for a start. Ben's father might have told him.

There had to be a good reason why Hugh would not go back. And how could it be a coincidence that Ben had appeared in Paris the very same day that her apartment was burgled.

''How did he react?'' Ben asked.

''I have no idea! I handed him the newspaper and he went into his room without a word.'' At that instant her memory brought up words she had learned at school. '*Il est parti, sans une parole, sans me regarder.*' ''

"What did you say?" Ben asked.

"Nothing."

"Of course you did. It didn't make much sense, but you said something."

"It was just a few words from Jacques Prevert."

"Who?"

"Don't you know his work? He was an important French poet around the middle of this century. I was quoting one of his best-known poems; *'Déjeuner du matin'*. He wrote it entirely in the *passé composé* – the French past tense, so it's used a lot in schools. It's part of our childhood, as familiar as the ABC."

"Say it again."

" 'He went without a word, without looking at me, and I put my head in my hands and cried.' It's a poem about a quarrel over the breakfast table. Very simple, but very moving."

Ben's eyes probed her face. "And did you?"

She stared blankly. "Did I what?"

"Cry."

"Don't be ridiculous. Those are just the final words of the poem. You asked me how Hugh reacted when I showed him *Nice-Matin*. I was explaining that he just took the paper without a word and went back into his office. He doesn't allow anything to interrupt his morning's work. He'll read the paper later."

Ben went on staring. Suddenly he said, "You're scared of him, aren't you?"

"No, I'm not!" she said indignantly, then sighed. "Of course he's not an easy man to deal with, but I'm very fond of him. He's been very kind to me."

"He wasn't kind to his own family."

"He must have a reason for..."

"What reason can excuse a silence of nearly thirty years? His parents, my parents — none of them have seen or heard from him in all that time."

She couldn't deny that it was strange. "I wonder what's behind it all?"

"Ask him." Ben eyed her coolly. "But you wouldn't dare, would you?"

She lifted her chin, her eyes bright with defiance. "Oh, yes, I would! In fact, I'll ask him today."

"Have lunch with me tomorrow and tell me what he says."

She got up. "I must go in and help Louise."

He caught her wrist, lay smiling up at her, that beautiful body of his making it hard to look away. "Will you meet me tomorrow?"

"Where? What time?"

"I'll pick you up here at noon. I thought we could have lunch at Valbonne. I'm told the old medieval centre is charming, and there are some good restaurants."

"Yes, there are, several very good ones." She hesitated, then nodded. "OK, I'll see you tomorrow."

She pulled her hand free and walked back up to the house. When she looked out from her bedroom, after showering and dressing, she saw that Ben had gone, the garden was empty.

"You knew he hadn't gone, didn't you?" she accused Louise when she found her in the kitchen.

"The nephew?" Louise opened innocent eyes at her.

"He said he wanted to look at the garden, I couldn't see the harm in that, as he's family."

Ben had quickly realised how to talk her round! To Louise, as to most French people, family was sacred, the home a vital stronghold into which few outsiders were ever invited.

"If he's telling the truth and is who he says he is! How would we know?"

"He showed me his passport. I'm not stupid. I asked to see it, and he has the same surname as Hugh. Looks like him, too. Why didn't you tell me this morning, in Antibes? You were sitting there talking away to him. I could see you knew him really well. You must have known who he was!"

"I didn't! I only just found out!"

"Surprised you didn't pick up the resemblance."

"You didn't either!"

"I thought he looked familiar."

Louise turned towards the stove. "I must get the *moules* on! Hand me the board, I've already chopped the onions, garlic and herbs." She pushed them into a large pan, adding white wine and some water to cover the vegetables; turned the heat up a fraction.

A wonderful smell began to fill the air. Louise then turned the heat down and the contents of the pan settled to a steady simmer. There was a large bowl of cleaned mussels on the table. Louise leaned across to bring it over to the stove. "I'll be adding the mussels in ten minutes. Are you going to make the salad or not?"

"I'll do it now." Claudia rubbed garlic around the large blue and yellow earthenware bowl, tore up lettuce and laid it as a base, tossed on top broken sticks of *haricots verts*, quartered tomatoes, radishes, a few black olives, hardboiled eggs which Louise had cooked earlier, thinly sliced onion, opened a tin of tuna and scattered that over the top, with some anchovies, red peppers and cress, then trickled over it a dressing of wine vinegar and olive oil lightly beaten with pepper and herbs.

"How's that?"

"Looks great," Louise said. "Now go and brush your hair, you look as if you've been dragged through a hedge backwards. Those razored ends are sticking up in the air now."

Claudia groaned, feeling them. "I must make an appointment with a hairdresser."

"Before you do, tell Hugh to come down for lunch."

Claudia looked at her unruly hair with disfavour, quickly brushed it into some sort of tidiness. She didn't need to call Hugh, he was coming downstairs as she went into the salon. His face was set and grim. She wondered if he had seen her and Ben in the pool.

A flush grew in her face, but she forced herself to plunge into the question she had promised Ben she would ask.

"Hugh, what happened to make you leave England and never go back?"

Hugh walked out on to the terrace and stood staring over the other gardens which could be glimpsed beyond the hedges, and through pine trees and cypresses, down past the sea road, to the blue bay where the white-sailed yachts still tacked to and fro.

"I don't want to talk about it, Claudia, so change the subject."

She saw his hands gripping the stone balustrade, the knuckles white through his brown skin. From the kitchen the smell of cooking mussels drifted out to them, redolent of so many meals on summer days like this, the scent of the sea, of wine, of garlic, which peasants in the mountains still put under the tongues of the newborn to give them strength and make sure they will grow up liking it.

"Surely you won't let your brother die without..."

"I don't want to talk about it!"

She could not ask any more questions; he was too scary in this mood.

Instead she told him, "We're having a light lunch, just *moules marinières* and then a *salade Niçoise*. Are you hungry?"

He shook his head. She wasn't surprised. Neither was she.

Louise began bringing the food out to the table on the terrace, which she had already laid with straw place mats and cutlery, wine glasses, a bottle cooling in an ice bucket.

"Sit down, sit down!" she scolded, placing the great pot of mussels in the centre.

They obeyed. The *moules* were easy to swallow, it wasn't like eating, you just opened your mouth, tipped the shell towards you, and they slid down your throat, scented with wine and garlic and parsley. They finished the whole dish. Hugh might not be hungry, but, like her, he ate the "soup" in which the mussels had cooked, drinking a glass of very dry Sancerre with it. They had a small plateful of the salad after that, enough to placate Louise who, like most good cooks, was resentful if you did not eat the meal she had prepared for you.

"Chocolate mousse or apple flan?" she asked, but neither of them wanted dessert.

While they were drinking coffee, they heard the sound of a car pulling up outside. From the terrace they could see the top of the vehicle.

Claudia's breath caught.

"What on earth are the police doing here?" Louise exclaimed.

"You'd better go and let them in, and find out," Hugh ordered flatly.

Louise hurried away.

CHAPTER
EIGHT

"Go up to your room and stay there unless I call you down."

She hesitated, and Hugh gave her one of his direct, insistent, commanding looks, brows low.

"Claudia, go upstairs. Now!"

He still thought of her as a child; she resented his tone, but decided not to argue. She was anxious and curious about the police coming here, but she didn't want to face their questions. Before she reached the top of the stairs she heard his voice below. "Inspector Bourrier? You're looking well. Married life agrees with you obviously."

Claudia stood on the landing, hovering just out of sight. Apart from the holiday-makers, who came and went, and the foreign residents who were often absent for most of the year, the local population was small. Most people knew the local police by sight if not name.

The policeman's voice was deep and warm. "Married life is just fine, thank you, M'sieur. It's good to come home to a cooked meal and a warm welcome from your own woman. I'm spending a lot less time in bars."

Hugh laughed. "Good for you. Marie's a nice woman, a very good cook, I used to eat in that café of hers now and then, and I remember her omelettes with affection. She's pretty, too, luckily for you! Give her my best wishes."

"I will, thank you. What about you, sir? I hope you're well. I read your latest book, a very good read. I'm very into science fantasy. You make everything come alive, a great gift."

"Thank you, *mon ami*. Glad you enjoyed it. Can I tempt you with a little cognac?"

"No, no. I've a lot of other visits to make. Must keep a clear head. Another time, perhaps. You've heard about the murder we've had?"

"The body on the beach? Of course, the whole town has been talking about it. Is it your case? Congratulations."

"Oh, I'm just doing the legwork. The examining magistrate came up with certain theories. The victim isn't local and our M'sieur Carnac thinks all Parisians are villains. If they turn up dead, it's bound to be a gangland killing. We aren't supposed to do any thinking, you know; just proceed with his instructions. He asked me to call on you. The thing is ... well, you see we found a notebook in the dead man's pocket. Your name and address were in it."

Hugh sounded amazed. "You're kidding! My name? Why? I didn't know him. I saw the photo in the newspaper and didn't recognise the face at all."

He sounded so natural, so spontaneous. You would never suspect he might be lying. But he had told her the dead man had never visited this house, that he had never set eyes on him, so he was telling the exact truth.

"Sure?" The policeman had a disappointed note in his voice. "Could you take a close look at this photograph of him? You're certain you've never seen him?"

A little silence, then Hugh calmly, almost regretfully, said, "Sorry, no, he's a complete stranger, I can't help you. I wonder why he had my name and address in his notebook?"

"To be frank, there was a whole string of names — yours was the only local address. He was a private detective from Paris and down here on business. We asked his partner if he knew you, and he claimed he didn't."

"His partner? Do you think he might have a hand in the murder?"

"Wouldn't be surprised. Now, if the body had turned up in Nice, it might well have been a local gang. But on Cap d'Antibes? Not very likely. We get plenty of robberies, villas burgled. But murders? No. So maybe the partner is involved somewhere, or this is linked to whatever they were investigating. Well, thank you. If you think of anything, could you give me a ring at the local station?"

"Of course. But, you know, he could be a fan of mine. I get lots of letters from readers. And then..."

The voices moved away. Claudia walked to her bedroom and lay down on the bed, staring at the ceiling. Sunlight dazzled across it, blinding her. From outside she heard an engine flare, the grate of tyres on the road. The policeman was going. Had he believed Hugh? Or would he be back? She wished she knew whether Hugh had had any hand in the death of that horrible little man.

Yet dreaded knowing.

She fell asleep and dreamed of Paris; moved through familiar streets, along the quays, by the grey Seine, a constantly shifting scene through which she ran in a panic, knowing someone was following her, meant to kill her.

Heart thumping, sweat trickling down her body, she woke in twilight in a state of terror.

It was raining, streaming down the windows, splashing into gutters, soaking into the baked earth outside. She found the sounds comforting and lay listening to them, trying to remember the details of her dream, but could only summon up disturbing fragments. The sound of heels on pavements. Breathing. Ben's voice.

Hurriedly, she got off the bed, went into the bathroom, showered and put on a short white skirt and a T-shirt. Before she got downstairs she could smell the strong aroma of bouillabaisse; as if the sea itself had invaded the house, a scent loaded with garlic and rich with saffron.

Louise looked up as she appeared, gave her a searching glance. ''You slept well? I came up once and could hear you through the door.''

''Was I snoring?''

''Not exactly. Just breathing as if you were dead to the world.''

She had been having bad dreams about Ben, but she wouldn't tell Louise that. Instead she lifted the lid of the huge pan and inhaled the fragrance of the fish. ''Where's Hugh? This is almost ready, isn't it? Mmm ... smells gorgeous.''

187

"I haven't seen him, either. I don't think he's been having a siesta, though. I've heard him moving about, the floor creaking, in his office. Give him a shout."

Hugh came down at once. His face had that hard, clenched look she hated; it meant he was going to be difficult to talk to, and she needed to talk to him. When he looked that way he scared her. Had he always been this tough, or had he hardened over the years because of the rift between him and his family?

They ate inside because of the rain. Hugh hardly said a word, eating with concentration, head bent over his soup plate. Afterwards they drank their coffee listening to Mozart. The rain had died away; the cicadas began again, and above their strange chirping sounds she heard the waves crashing up on to the rocks edging the Garoupe beach, as if the storm had moved further out to sea.

The silence between her and Hugh dragged, and she was afraid to break it although she was eaten up with questions she longed to ask. At ten she went to bed, although she wasn't sleepy after her long siesta that afternoon. She read for several hours, listening to the sighing of the pine trees in the wind, the distant murmur of the sea. The storm had moved away, although when she peered through the slats of the shutters she caught a flicker of lightning miles away.

In the morning she came downstairs for breakfast and was surprised to see Hugh out on the terrace drinking coffee and eating croissants. He had usually eaten his *petit déjeuner* and gone to his desk by this time of day.

He poured her coffee and pushed the wicker basket of

croissants over to her. She took one, but before she ate it she took an orange from a bowl of fruit, segmented it, juice spurting, put a piece in her mouth. A fat brown squirrel leaped from tree to tree across the garden, bushy tail balancing him so that he seemed to fly, until his body crashed down through branches. He recovered his balance to sit in a low branch, chattering angrily. From other gardens she heard children laughing. A splashing in somebody's pool. Wagner blaring from the villa where a group of Germans were staying.

They heard the pop-pop of the postman's bike and saw him wave a hand as he put Hugh's mail into the box in the wall.

Hugh waved back, then asked Claudia, "So, what are you planning to do today?"

She contemplated telling him that she had agreed to have lunch with Ben, but wasn't sure how he would react. It was such a peaceful morning; she didn't want to spoil the atmosphere.

Louise walked down to collect the mail from the box. There was always a pile of stuff for Hugh. His fan mail was constant; often letters from teenagers and even children.

Handing them to him, Louise asked, "More coffee?"

They both shook their heads. Hugh flicked through his letters; most of them had English postmarks, some had American stamps on them, only one or two were French.

Hugh opened those first, grimacing. "The electricity bill!" The second letter rustled as he slit it open.

He looked inside the plain white envelope. Claudia heard the intake of his breath and was immediately alert.

"What's wrong?"

He turned the envelope upside down and shook the contents into his palm. First a piece of folded paper, then hair.

Curls of bronze which shone almost gold in the sunlight.

Claudia's stomach turned over. Until that moment she had supposed that her hair had been cut by some freak who just happened to hit on her. She had been wrong. He had known who she was and where she lived.

"Hell. Hell," Hugh grated.

One curl was darkened and sticky.

Hugh pushed it with a long forefinger, picked it up and sniffed it. "Blood. He spilled blood on it. God, this is a sick bastard."

He picked up the folded piece of paper. She saw large, black capital letters printed in the centre. Even upside down she could read them.

IT COULD HAVE BEEN HER THROAT

It could have been.

To look as if she was quite calm, she picked up her cup, but her hand shook so much that hot coffee washed over the side of the cup and hit her bare arm.

She put the cup down with a clatter; automatically rubbed at the wet place on her skin.

"Don't you think we should call the police now?" she whispered.

Hugh was curt. "Did you see his face?"

She shook her head.

"What he wore?"

"A T-shirt, jeans."

Hugh gave her a pitying look. "That description could fit a thousand men. Where's the point in calling the police? These people are acting for someone. We'll wait until he shows up in person.

"Who? Who is it? You obviously know who's behind it." Her voice shook, she was close to hysteria, but fought to control herself. "If you know who it is, can't you get in touch with them?"

"I'm waiting for him to appear. For now, I'm going up to work. See you later. Just don't go out alone and you'll be fine."

She didn't tell him Ben was coming at noon. He might order her not to see him.

And she wanted to — no, it was more than that. She needed to.

"I won't be in for lunch," she told Louise after Hugh had gone upstairs. "Can I help you get Hugh's lunch ready? What is he having?"

"Melon and then lamb chop with redcurrant sauce. It's the English way of serving it, he tells me. Very plain. No herbs, no garlic or rosemary, just this sweet sauce. I won't need any help; it's a very simple meal. You go and get ready for that nice young man."

Claudia went pink under Louise's amused gaze, but pretended to be cool.

"What makes you think I'm seeing him?"

Louise simply grinned at her.

Claudia laughed ruefully. "Oh, OK, I am. He is Hugh's nephew, after all. I'm going to try to talk Hugh into having him here for dinner. Time they got to know each other properly."

"Family is family," agreed Louise. "There's nothing more important. It's funny that Hugh has never mentioned them, not once, in all the years I've known him. Did his nephew tell you what the family quarrel was about?"

"He doesn't know either, he says."

"Do you think he's telling the truth?"

"Yes. He wants me to ask Hugh, but I don't quite dare. I'll go and get ready, then I'll sunbathe in the garden until he arrives."

Louise gave her a knowing look. "So as to be able to answer the bell and leave with your young man before Hugh sees him?"

Claudia went off without answering. Louise knew her too well.

She decided to wear a dress instead of jeans — a silky green dress with tiny cap sleeves and a scooped neckline. It was lined so that it did not cling to her, rustling coolly as she walked.

With it she wore fine white leather sandals; just a few frail straps crossing her feet. The heels were high enough to be elegant, but not impractical or hard to walk in. Claudia spent some time on her hair, trimming the cut strands and hiding them behind others which she kept in place with a diamanté-studded clip.

Louise whistled when she saw her. "You look lovely, darling. That's a pretty dress, I've never seen that before!"

"Of course you have. I bought it last summer. And wore it several times, to parties. If Hugh asks where I am, tell him the truth — say I've gone to lunch with Ben at Valbonne.''

''Valbonne? Ah, he'll take you to the *Caudron Soleil*, I bet! Not too expensive, but the food is terrific.''

Claudia laughed. ''You mean, you love it! Well, if he asks me where we should eat, I'll suggest it. I love their salads.''

The telephone began to ring, then cut out as the answerphone took over. Was Ben calling to say he could not come after all? Claudia went into the salon to listen to the recording.

''Claudia, this is Rex, Rex Valery.''

Louise exclaimed behind her, going pink with excitement.

''Darling, my run in this play is coming to an end and I have a few weeks off before I go into rehearsal with the new piece. I'm due a holiday, way overdue. So Yuan and I are coming down to my villa in Cannes for a couple of weeks. I saw that gorgeous boy, Siegfried, waiting tables at a dinner party last night, and he said you were at Cap d'Antibes for a while. I wondered if you would cater for a party for us while we're there — a summer garden party, I thought. Delicious food, as we're on holiday — artichokes stuffed with truffle and peas, lobster thermidor, lots of pink champagne. You will try, won't you? And bring your staff down for the weekend; we all adore Siegfried, even if he is boringly straight. Oh, and invite a partner for yourself darling.''

The message ended with a series of clicks.

''You'll go, won't you?'' Louise asked eagerly. ''You must! Anybody could be there, absolutely anybody. You could take Ben.''

"If he's still here."

They heard a car engine outside; Claudia hurried to look out. "He's early. I must go."

As she opened the gate she glanced up at the villa and saw Hugh at the window, his face grim.

She looked away again, went out and closed the gate behind her in case he signalled to her not to go.

Ben was far more casually dressed; in white jeans and a pale blue T-shirt. Her mouth dried in sexual tension as she climbed into his car. Every time she saw him she wanted him more. It was worrying. She had never felt this piercing hunger. Her body seemed to burn just looking at him.

"Does Hugh know I'm taking you out?" he asked as she fastened her safety belt.

She shook her head.

"So that's why he's scowling! And you say you aren't scared of him?"

"He has too much on his mind at the moment. I don't want to upset him even more."

They drove away and took the road leading up to Grasse, the old *Route Napoléon,* along which the Emperor had marched with his army after landing on the coast when he escaped from Elba and tried to recover his throne. Claudia pointed out to Ben the slabs of concrete on either side of the road, embossed with huge bees, the symbol of Bonaparte.

"What would he think, if he came back and saw them?" Ben said derisively. "They're rather vulgar, aren't they?"

"He would probably be gratified because the French

are still proud of him.''

''But he was not French, was he? He was Corsican.''

''He loved France, though — and to the French that is what matters.'' As they climbed the hill towards Valbonne she asked, ''Where were you thinking of having lunch?''

''I've already booked at a place recommended by the hotel. The *Chandellerie*.''

''Oh, I know it, it is good.''

They parked outside the old town, but walked up into the ancient streets of high, narrow houses, and found the restaurant a stone's throw from the town square. It was crowded with market stalls and bustling people buying organic local vegetables, *chèvre* made on nearby farms, flavoured with garlic or herbs, wonderful home-made bread full of olives or walnuts, honeycombs and lavender soap. The smells made your head spin and there was a chatty, lively atmosphere, with the café tables all full, and English voices everywhere. This old town was surrounded now with rings of modern villas in which the English lived.

Over lunch she asked Ben how long he would be staying. ''Rex Valery is coming down here in a couple of weeks, and wants me to cater for one of his parties, Rex told me to bring someone — if you would be interested.''

''Thanks, but I doubt if I'll be here in a couple of weeks.''

Her heart sank. But she smiled brightly. ''No, of course, you'll be back in England by then.''

He gave her a sideways glance. ''I could always fly

back, though.''

She tried not to look as delighted as she felt. ''I'll let you know the date when Rex gives me the details.''

They took hours over lunch, laughing and talking, eating slowly. The restaurant was small; you could either eat outside, or go down steps into the shadowy little interior which had the feel of a cave. The deep stone walls were cool after the heat of the sun outside in the narrow street. The table was laid with a lace cloth; flowers in the centre, several red rosebuds and a spray of vivid, yellow iris.

They drank Beaumes de Venise, a sweet white wine from the Rhône, which was perfect with their lunch — rabbit cooked with honey and mustard, served with *pommes dauphinoises* and peas flavoured with mint and thickened with lettuce. Footsteps and voices drifted in from the town. Someone was playing music.

''Mozart,'' identified Ben. ''Don't tell me you don't love him or I shall have to reconsider falling in love with you.''

''I love Mozart,'' she promised.

He put a hand across the table, stroked a finger down her arm, sending a shudder of pleasure through her. ''Your skin looks like honey in this dim light.''

''I'm getting my tan back. I lose it when I'm in Paris.''

''I want to photograph you — I brought my cameras and tripod, they're locked in the boot.''

It was nearly four before they started taking pictures, and Claudia was drowsy with heat and wine and marvellous food. Hugh bought her a cream straw hat and a pleated cream paper Japanese sunshade. He posed her on a stone step beside an old stone horse trough, in the town; took pictures of her half asleep under the sunshade. When they passed a flower shop he rushed in and bought her an armful of flowers, twined them into the brim of her hat, made her hold them in the crook of her arm.

"Now you look like a shepherdess."

Click, click, click, went his shutter.

Claudia yawned, her eyes half closing. A dog came and sat with her. She stroked him, Ben took pictures of them both and she laughed at him.

"What an opportunist you are! You snatch at anything going past, to help make a picture!"

He took off her hat to rearrange her hair, and she suddenly remembered the envelope that had arrived that morning.

When she told him about it, Ben turned white with rage. "Jesus! That bastard! Claudia, don't let him scare you."

She shivered. "Easy for you to say! It freaks me out to have him steal bits of my hair — and send them back covered in blood."

He stared at her, frowning, and suddenly said, "Can't say I blame you. I don't like it. There's something crazy about this guy. Why the hell doesn't Hugh call the police? Maybe I should? If he won't. The police ought to know what's going on."

"Hugh seems to know who it is — and he's not ready to call the police. He's waiting for something."

"For what?" Ben asked angrily. "For you to get your throat cut?"

"Don't!" She shuddered, remembering the blood on those strands of her hair.

They walked on in silence, in a different mood. A car driving up far too fast through the great stone arch in the town wall almost hit them and they sprang apart.

Claudia fell against the wall, her face white, her hair wild. Ben turned and saw her face; brought up his camera to frame her between the stones with their carved coat-of-arms.

"You look like a ghost," Ben said, snapping away.

She felt like one, there in the shadows with the sunlight outside. She ran out, shivering, needing the touch of the sun on her icy skin.

"Where are you going? That's the wrong way," Ben said, and as she turned to look at him he took another picture, beside the faded wooden shutters of a crumbling old house with ivy climbing up its walls.

"I'm tired," she complained. "Can we stop? My feet ache and so does my back."

"OK, we'll go," Ben agreed reluctantly, putting his equipment back into its bags.

Claudia climbed into the parked car and immediately fell asleep, while Ben put his equipment into the boot.

She woke up as he piled rustling paper bags of cherries and peaches into her lap.

"Here you are — this is your fee for posing."

The delicious, summer smell of the fruit woke her up. "Where did you get them?"

"At that stall over there."

They ate the sweet pink and white cherries as they drove. She fed him; her fingers pushing fruit into his

198

mouth. Ben nibbled at her fingertips, too, kissing and licking them before he ate the cherries.

When he parked outside the villa he turned to look down into her drowsy eyes, then bent his head to kiss her.

She tasted the cherries on his lips.

"Sweet," he whispered. "You're so sweet. I could eat you."

His tongue slid inside her mouth. Moaning, her body melting, she put her arms round his neck and kissed him back passionately.

"I need to make love to you," he whispered.

"Me, too." She had never felt such heat, such need. She was so desperate for him she would have made love there and then, in his car, in the street, in broad daylight.

He groaned, lifting his head. "We could go to my room, at the hotel. Come on, Claudia, come back with me."

Before she could decide, they heard the gate opening. Hugh glared at them, from a few feet away.

"Where the hell have you been? I was just on the point of ringing the police! You've been gone for hours."

She hurriedly got out of the car and stumbled towards him carrying her hat; her hair tousled, flowers still thrust into it, her dress crumpled, stained with fruit, her face sun-flushed.

"Bye," she muttered to Ben without looking at him.

"I'll ring you," he called after her, and she nodded.

To Hugh she said, "We had lunch at Valbonne, didn't Louise tell you we were going there?"

"All this time for lunch?"

"Ben took some photos of me afterwards."

Hugh slammed the gate shut behind them. She heard the car driving away, very fast, with a squeal of brakes.

Back in the house, she lay down on a sofa, yawning. "The sun was so hot, and I think I drank too much wine."

"You should not have gone out at all."

"Ben is your nephew, you surely can't suspect him?"

"Why not? The worst betrayals are always inside the family. They're the ones that hurt most, and they happen every day. His father stole my wife."

She sat up, staring, incredulous, stunned.

"Your ... wife? But ... I never knew you had been married. When was this? I mean ... she isn't Ben's mother, obviously."

"Yes, she's Ben's mother."

Like a pebble flung into a quiet pool the ripples spread out inside her mind, circles of meaning, of emotion. Hugh had been married to Ben's mother, who had left him for his brother? The betrayal was far deeper than she had imagined.

"Ben's mother," she said again, struggling to take it in.

"Helena," he said, as if handling her name with tongs, holding it far away from him in case it burned him. That told her a great deal, spoke of a pain that had not faded with time.

"But ... when were you married to her?"

"Before Ben was born. Helena and I had known each other all our lives. She was the same age as Rafe, my brother, three years younger than me. Our families knew

200

each other pretty well. We grew up in a fairly remote country area. Northumbria. Right up at the northern edge of England, close to the Scottish border. Life is organised around social gatherings up there. Fairs and markets and big parties. That's how it was in the Middle Ages, how it is now, except that today people meet far more often than they did once.''

''Like parts of rural France, as it used to be,'' she thought aloud. ''Before tourism spoiled it.''

''You can't remember those days! You're not old enough.''

''No, but Louise has often talked about it. She's very nostalgic for the old days.''

His eyes softened. ''You're very fond of her, aren't you?''

''She wasn't my mother, any more than you were my father, but, I suppose because she had no child she treated me as if I were her own, and because there was just me, no other children, she spoiled me, and I loved her.''

''Helena was a spoilt only child. Her father adored her. They were an important local family, still are. The Morrells own a huge chunk of the region. For generations they have dominated local life. Ran the county. Sat as magistrates, organised local institutions — some were in the church, some in the army. There were very few areas of life in our part of the world that didn't have a Morrell involved. The head of the family owns a famous house and is very rich. Helena came from a cadet branch of the family. Her father was well-to-do, not rich.''

"What did he do?"

"He farmed a few hundred acres; good arable land mostly, cereal in the lower meadows, and he ran sheep on his rough pastures. He had a comfortable income. And he was a Morrell, he was related to our most powerful local family. He wanted his precious daughter to marry well, and I was not the sort of son-in-law he was looking for."

"Your family weren't rich or powerful?"

He laughed curtly. "No. My father had a farm, too, but we had very little money and no influence."

"That was his objection to you? That you weren't rich?"

"I wasn't good enough for his Helena. My family wasn't poor, we owned our farm, but the land was rough, hilly ground. We ran sheep, too. But our house was half the size of Helena's. She lived in a Georgian manor house. Ours was older and smaller. A late sixteenth-century farmhouse, very cold in winter, with creaky old floors and stairs."

"And you hadn't started writing yet, I suppose?"

"No. I was up at Oxford. I asked Helena to marry me in my final year. I was just twenty-one, but I'd been offered a job on a London paper. I thought I was going to be rich and famous; I had the sort of crazy certainty you only have at that age."

She could just imagine him, glittering with confidence, a beautiful boy with a great future in front of him. How could any girl have resisted? Very few students looked like Hugh or had his amazing charisma.

"Was she pretty?"

"Pretty? Too tame a word. She was breathtaking. At eighteen she had a face like a cameo, oval, every feature in proportion, and the creamiest, most perfect skin I'd ever seen. But above all a smile to break your heart."

"Was she a student at Oxford, too?"

"Good heavens no. She wasn't academic. She did a secretarial course and stayed at home, playing at being her father's secretary."

It sounded very dull. However beautiful she may have been, this woman couldn't have been a match for Hugh's charm and powerful intelligence.

Hugh read her expression and smiled ironically. "But her social life was hectic. Men queued up to take her out. I was afraid that if I didn't marry her soon somebody else would get her. So I proposed one night, after a summer ball, in the moonlight, in the college gardens. I planned it like a military campaign. The most romantic, most glamorous setting I could imagine. Music coming from the open French windows, a full moon turning the gardens silver. I took out a bottle of champagne and two glasses. We danced, I kissed her, then proposed."

"And swept her off her feet!" He might have planned it, but the girl must have been bemused by champagne and moonlight. At eighteen you could imagine yourself in love so easily. You played at love at that age; it was the most marvellous, enthralling, exciting game you had ever discovered. You had no idea of consequences, of what came after. The moment was all that mattered. Tomorrow meant nothing.

"She said yes, anyway. I was so mad about her, so

much in love, it never occurred to me that she might not love me the same way.''

How could his wife not have been crazy about him? thought Claudia, but didn't say a word.

''I think now that she was excited by the idea of getting married. But her father hit the roof. He refused his permission, at first, but somehow she talked him round.''

''Was it a wonderful wedding?''

''It was a big, society wedding, with hundreds of guests. She was nineteen and looked like a fairy princess. She wore a Victorian dress, made for her great-grandmother, at the turn of the century — ivory satin and lace, a gold coronet over her veil. A vision, believe me.''

''It sounds marvellous.''

''But it was all an illusion. Everything went downhill after the wedding. My job meant we had to live in London, and Helena hated city life. I thought she was happy, because I was. It's so easy to deceive yourself.''

''Did you start quarrelling?''

''Helena wasn't the type. She just went silent. But I never noticed at the time — it was only when I looked back that I saw what had happened. We drifted apart day by day. We didn't even see much of each other.''

''Did she have a job?''

''Yes, in an office, which she hated so much she walked out after a month. I was irritated by that. We needed the money. She got another job, but then she had flu and was quite ill. It almost turned into pneumonia. After she got better she went home to convalesce because the doctor told her she needed country air. She never came back. That was when she saw a lot of my brother. After all, they were family.'' His mouth twisted cynically.

She watched him with sympathy. ''And you had no idea?''

''None at all. I was too busy; totally absorbed in my job, going abroad for weeks at a time. I was a foreign correspondent by then.''

''When did you find out?''

''When they told me. I think my parents knew what was going on, but he was always their favourite. They took his side.''

''Oh, no, surely . . .'' she protested.

''Oh, yes. Since the day he was born they had given him everything he cried for, and that included my wife.'' There was bitterness in his voice, in the skin stretched over his cheekbones, the taut drag of his mouth. He had never mentioned his family to her before, she didn't know about his parents — would they have encouraged his brother in such treachery? How could his brother have done it? Adultery was always painful, but when the man involved is your own brother it must be ten times worse.

''He was very like my father. They had a lot in common. He loved farming and country life. I was bored by it. Because he was the youngest, my mother doted on him. He was her baby, even when he was a man. I was an outsider in that cosy little threesome.''

''How did your wife finally tell you?''

''I got a letter out of the blue. A very short letter.

Brutal, in fact. Helena told me she was expecting his baby and wanted a divorce so that they could get married.''

Claudia bit her lip, distressed by the harshness in his face and voice. ''Oh ... Hugh ...''

''I can't claim to have been a very good husband. I had neglected her, been selfish and thoughtless. I was obsessed with being a foreign correspondent, it was an exciting, glamorous life to a boy of my age, but I still loved her, I had been totally faithful to her, although I'd had plenty of opportunities to sleep around. She said she was sorry, she didn't want to hurt me — but she was sure I had realised by now that we weren't suited, we were too different, our marriage had been a terrible mistake.''

Claudia didn't know what to say to him. She had a feeling he hadn't reached the end of his story.

''When I had got my breath back I rang her, but she wouldn't come to the phone. Her father said she was too upset. I raged at him, said she was going to have to face me, I was coming up north on the next train. When I got there, I found they had fled, gone away.

She could understand their fear; Hugh in a temper could be terrifying. He was never an easy man, but when he was angry he made your knees shake.

''Where did they go? Did you find them?''

''No, I stopped looking almost at once. They rented a cottage in Provence, not that I knew that at the time. I divorced her — what else could I do when my wife was carrying my brother's child and had run away from me? I'd have looked ridiculous if I had refused. They got married the day after the divorce was made final, and the baby — Ben — was born a few days later.''

Ben had insisted that he had no idea what lay behind the quarrel between the two brothers. When he found out the truth it would be as much a shock to him as it was to her.

''And you've never seen them since?'' All these years Hugh had been brooding over what his brother had done, never relenting, never forgiving? It made her shiver.

''No. I came to France as a foreign correspondent for an English newspaper and have lived here ever since.''

''Shouldn't you tell Ben what you just told me?'' She watched him, seeing the physical symptoms of his pain. The bones and muscles in his face and neck were rigid, as if he could not relax or he might fall apart. Did he still love Helena? But how could he go on loving someone he hadn't seen for nearly thirty years? No, it must be hatred that was eating him up, not love.

He looked at her blankly. ''Certainly not. His parents can do that.''

''He says his father is very ill, dying — couldn't you forgive him now? After all these years surely you could agree to see him for the last time.''

''No. The past can't be changed. My life is here now. My family mean nothing to me. His death will make no difference.''

How could she judge him when she had never been through the experience he had?

He looked at his watch. ''Sorry, I have to go out — Louise and I are going to a party — the Mayor's twentieth wedding anniversary. Would you like to come?''

She shook her head. ''I'm too sleepy and tired.''

''Well, we shouldn't be long, it is only a dessert and a glass of champagne or two, nothing elaborate. But dinner will be late — around eight-thirty, I expect. Louise has planned a salad and a cold pudding, is that OK for you?''

''I'm not hungry now, anyway; we had such a big lunch. I'll have a nap, then a nice, long bath while I'm waiting for you.''

Hugh and Louise left at six o'clock. Claudia lay down on her bed and fell asleep at once. Half an hour later the phone woke her up so she went downstairs feeling shaky, hesitating before picking up the receiver.

But it was only Patti.

''Are you all right? You sound weird.''

''I was asleep.''

''Hell, sorry. That never occurred to me, it's only half-past six. I just rang to ask when you were coming back.''

''I don't know yet.''

''We're getting lots of bookings, and I have to turn down half of them,'' Patti complained. ''We're earning more than ever before, though, so we don't need any more work, we just about manage as it is.''

''Don't overwork, Patti. Take it easy. Only take a booking if you're sure you can cope. I'll be in touch again soon.''

It was twilight, the bewitching hour when colour soaks into the sky and the world turns blue and silver. Claudia ran her bath and stripped off. She found a box of scented candles Hugh had given her last Christmas and set them around the bathroom. She closed the shutters before getting into the bath, but did not put on the electric light.

She was about to step into the warm water when somebody rang the bell on the gate.

She tensed, stood still, listening.

It couldn't be Hugh and Louise coming back early. They wouldn't ring the bell, Hugh would use his key.

She wrapped a dry towel around her breasts, sarong fashion, and went into her bedroom to peer through the closed shutters.

Ben's car was parked outside. As she watched, she saw him get back inside. The engine flared. She saw the car move and turned away.

Going back to the bathroom she climbed into the warm water and lay down, her head on a folded hand towel arranged the back of the bath. She closed her eyes to visualise that afternoon, the most romantic, most memorable of her life; Valbonne, flowers, wine, Ben's kisses. It had been wonderful.

But ... oh, God ... how could she allow herself to go on seeing him when his parents had hurt Hugh so badly? She could not choose between him and Hugh, to whom she owed so much.

Her eyes crystalised with grief. The room danced with the blur and dazzle of the candle flames, and their scent drenched the air — lavender, rose, lily of the valley. She moved to reach for the soap, and water dripped off her bare limbs; the candle flames giving her skin a pearly wet shimmer.

She could not bear never to see Ben again, either.

She soaped herself slowly, rinsed the lather off, and as she did so heard a strange scratching noise, as if a squirrel were gnawing at the house.

Or a rat? she thought, shuddering with repulsion. She hated them, those long, snakelike tails slithering behind them, their eyes shining red in the light of cars.

The rasping sound went on rhythmically. Claudia sat up, water splashing around her.

That wasn't a squirrel. Or a rat.

She stepped naked out of the bath, her skin gleaming in the candlelight, grabbed the white bath robe from its hook on the door, slid into it. She was in such a hurry she didn't stop to blow out the candles or put on the lights.

She began to go downstairs then halted, staring down into the salon. When she had gone up to bed an hour ago, she had locked the glass doors, but forgotten to close the electronically operated shutters because it was not yet dark then.

Night had fallen since.

A black shadow stood outside on the terrace, clearly visible through the glass door.

She couldn't see his face, he was wearing a hood which hid his features. The hood of a black tracksuit, she realised with a shock.

His gloved hand moved slowly, carefully, each movement making that scratching sound.

He was cutting a circle in the glass. While she watched, he finished it and the glass fell inwards, shattering.

He put his hand through the hole and turned the handle, opening the door.

Panic rose up in her throat. She turned and ran back upstairs, her heart beating too quickly.

He came after her, fast, leaping up the treads, like some great black cat.

He caught up with her on the landing.

As his heavy body crashed into hers she began to scream, too late. She went down with him on top of her.

CHAPTER
NINE

She heaved her body up, trying to throw him off. In the struggle he turned her round and pinned her shoulders to the floor, his knees forcing her legs apart. Her robe came undone. She saw the glitter of his eyes in the dark. He was staring down at her damp, naked body.

A musky wave of heat came from him. He was suddenly aroused.

No! she wanted to scream. She fought him angrily, hitting his face, his chest.

He dropped his head. His wet mouth sucked at her nipples.

Panic seared her. In her terror she acted instinctively. She reached up for him each of her thumbs sinking into one of his eyes.

He yelled. "Bitch! You fucking bitch! That hurts."

He hit her round the face so hard her head rolled from one side to the other. She was deafened by the force of the blow and let go of him. He grabbed her wrists and held them together, up above her head.

She wrenched and tugged, but could not get her hands free.

He laughed, watching her useless struggle. His head went down again, but this time he did not suck at her.

He bit her breast. She shrieked in pain.

She felt him pulling his tracksuit bottoms down with one hand. He was between her thighs, his other hand fondling the warm softness between her parted legs.

She retched, shuddering, but before he could enter her they both heard a crash downstairs. Feet thudded on the stairs.

The man on top of her pulled up his tracksuit bottoms again and got to his feet, whirling to meet the newcomer.

Claudia dragged herself up too, clumsily pulling the robe around her body. Even in the dark she recognised the set of Ben's broad shoulders as he launched himself at the intruder.

He only got in one punch before the other man grabbed a polished copper vase from a small table nearby. He smashed it down on Ben's head. Ben crumpled up without a sound.

Claudia got to the light switch and blinked in the dazzle of electricity.

Keeping his face averted from her, the intruder leaped over Ben's body and ran down the stairs, out of the open door into the garden.

Claudia kneeled down beside Ben, tears running down her face. "Ben ... oh, Ben ..."

He stirred and half sat up, looked around. "Where is he?"

"Gone."

Ben felt his head gingerly. "What the hell did he hit me with?"

"That," she said, pointing to the vase which lay on the

floor. "I'm sorry, Ben — does your head hurt much?"

"I'll live." He began to get up and she helped him, an arm round his waist. "What about you?" he asked, looking down at her. "What ... what did he do to you?"

She saw the expression in his eyes. "He was trying to rape me when you turned up."

She heard his sigh of relief "But he hadn't?"

She shook her head. "No, he had just hit me a couple of times." She forced a laugh. "To soften me up." She didn't tell him about the details; the vicious bites or the hot, intrusive hand between her legs.

"You're trembling," Ben said abruptly, his arm around her. "And no wonder. Christ, this has gone on long enough. This time I am going to call the police."

Anxiously she argued. "No, don't, Ben! I don't want to talk to them. Wait until Hugh gets back."

"Hugh won't call them, will he? I don't know exactly what's going on here, but it has got to stop."

He went back down the stairs, walked over to the open glass door, closed it, pressed the button which operated the electric shutters. They glided down outside.

Claudia's legs were shaking so much she couldn't stand up any more. She sat down on the top stair and pleaded with Ben.

"Don't call the police, Ben! Please! Hugh will be very angry if you do."

"I'm really scared of him," Ben mocked furiously, picking up the telephone. He dialled just three digits. The emergency number, she recognised.

"Police, please."

Claudia listened to him for a moment, then stood up

and ran into her bedroom, slamming the door behind her. She was still shaking.

She switched on the light, then sat down on her bed, staring at the wall.

She felt dirty. Although she had only just had a bath, she would give anything to take a shower, wash the marks of that man's hands off her skin, off her breast, from between her legs.

She opened her robe slightly and stared at her reflection in the dressing-table mirror. She could see the red indentations around her nipple where he had bitten her.

The door opened and she jumped, angrily pulled her lapels shut again.

"Knock before you walk in on me!"

Ben was frowning. "Sorry, I didn't think." He stood there, watching her. "What the hell were those marks?"

She turned her head aside and asked, "How soon will the police get here?"

"Tomorrow."

Her head jerked round again sharply. "Tomorrow?"

"They did not think it sounded urgent and they're very busy. Apparently there have been several burglaries and a man has been killed in a fight in a bar, so they can't spare anyone tonight, it will have to be tomorrow. We're low down on their urgent list — nothing was stolen, nobody was injured."

"You didn't tell them he tried to . . ."

"No, I could see you wouldn't want to talk about that."

She gave him a grateful smile. "Thank you, Ben."

"You should, of course. But I can see why you wouldn't."

"Well, he didn't ... so there wouldn't be DNA, or anything, to help catch him."

"No, I suppose not. And I gathered that an attempted burglary which was foiled does not rate too highly, especially after I told them he was wearing gloves. But they told me not to touch the point of entry, or sweep up the glass. They didn't seem too optimistic about catching him as I didn't see his face or even hear him speak. Did you?"

She shook her head.

"He didn't say anything?"

"I don't know, I can't remember..." She was confused, uncertain. "Maybe he did say something, but I can't even remember ... oh, yes, he swore at me. I didn't recognise his voice though, except that he was definitely French. I never saw his face. It was dark, he had a hood over his head. Oh I can't remember! I can't ... think..."

Ben came over and sat beside her on the bed, put his arm around her. "Are you OK? Did he hurt you much?"

She shook her head.

"Tell me about the marks ... I saw them, Claudia." She didn't answer.

"They looked like teethmarks."

She nodded, not wanting to meet his gaze.

"He *bit* you?" Ben sounded as if he could not believe it. He bit you ... there?"

"Oh, shut up, shut up," she raged, shaking as if she were about to fall apart.

216

Ben put his arms round her and held her tightly, making the shushing noises you make to calm hurt children.

"It's all right, Claudia, you're safe now ... I'm here ... he's gone. Ssh ... ssh ..."

She turned her face into him, inhaling the warmth of his body. "Oh, Ben ... Ben, I thought ... he was ... going to ... I couldn't bear it, I was so terrified ..."

He rocked her, murmuring wordlessly, stroking her hair.

She pushed her tear-stained face into his neck. The touch of his skin under her mouth was soothing. "Ben, oh, Ben. I was so scared." She needed him, wanted to sink into him, be held, be safe the way she had as a child when she had a nightmare and her mother came and comforted her.

"I'm here, nobody will hurt you again," he whispered, and she turned her face up to him, her lips parted, trembling.

He gently kissed them and she put her arms around his neck to hold him tightly, her fingertips running up into his hair.

"Hold me tight. Don't let me go."

Their mouths clung; heat sprang between them. She moved even closer, and he overbalanced, fell back on the bed. She fell with him, laughing wildly, and lay on top of him, looking down into his eyes.

Nobody had ever looked at her like that before. She could barely breathe.

In the fall, her robe had parted again; Ben pushed his hand very slowly inside and caressed her midriff, ran his fingers down the curve of her belly with a sensitivity that made her breathe faster and faster.

"You're beautiftil, I'm crazy about you. You know that, don't you?"

"You're beautiful, too, Ben. But ... there's Hugh ... do you know yet why he hates your parents?"

"Forget Hugh."

"It isn't something that will just go away, Ben — they hurt him badly. I don't think he'll ever forgive them."

He frowned. "Whatever happened thirty years ago is nothing to do with us."

"No, but they are your parents, and Hugh is the closest thing to a father I have, and ..."

Ben pushed her down on the bed, kneeled above her, kissed her gently, softly, his mouth brushing over hers again and again until she stopped thinking about anything else, her body melting, her mouth quivering as she kissed him back.

He slid his mouth down her neck and kissed her shoulder, then he very lightly put his lips to her naked breast, where the dark red marks showed.

"I wish I could kiss the pain away. Poor darling. I'm not hurting you, am I? Tell me when you want me to stop, you only have to say one word. Mmm ... your skin smells like honey ... you've had a bath, haven't you? I can smell it on your skin."

She breathed thickly as his hand travelled down her smooth skin to the short curly hairs above her thighs.

"Tell me to stop if you don't want me to do this," he breathed, his mouth following the path of his fingers while at the same time he shed his own clothes in a

218

wriggling movement.

She moaned as his tongue probed up inside her, the licking flames of desire following.

Making love to him would alter the way she remembered what had happened tonight; overlay bad memories with the remembrance of shared sweetness, of pleasure given and taken.

She had been wanting to make love with him ever since she first saw him.

She cried out in agonised delight at what he was doing.

"Last chance to decide," he whispered, naked above her. "No? Or yes?"

"Yes. Oh, yes."

She arched to enfold his flesh as it came slowly, slowly into her. This was what she had to have, the emptiness inside her filled. They merged, completed, lay still for a second, one body, their arms around each other, their mouths touching.

"We've known each other just a few days, but I think I'm in love with you," he said, sounding as surprised and bewildered as she felt. "Is that crazy?"

"It's wonderful — I love you, too." She stroked his nape, his long, powerful back, feeling the short hairs bristle under her fingers, following the indentation of the spine to where it disappeared into his firm, smooth buttocks.

"Darling ... oh, I want you so badly," he muttered huskily, and then began to move again. Her mind stopped working. She was just her body; their limbs driving against each other, the hot thrust of his penis clutched by her moist flesh, their breathing ragged. The

219

rhythm grew wild; they sobbed and shuddered, still holding each other, their skin damp with perspiration.

Her cheek was burning against his, her facial bones clenched in a rictus of erotic desire, mouth open.

"Faster, faster," she pleaded, riding up and down under him, needing to reach the peak of orgasm. Sweat ran down her back, trickled between her breasts. In this fierce race she could forget everything that had happened before. There was just a desperate urgency rising inside her.

Suddenly she was there. She cried out ecstatically, the pleasure so intense she was afraid her temperature would explode and blow her skull apart.

Ben sobbed with pleasure on top of her a moment later, his whole body jerking and shaking.

"Claudia . . . God, oh, God," he moaned.

Only afterwards did she realise how much noise they had been making.

Ben collapsed on top of her, his hot face buried on her shoulder. They didn't move or speak, too exhausted, breathing too desperately, chests heaving.

Around them the house was utterly silent, but just as their hearts were slowing down a little they heard voices downstairs.

Ben rolled off her, sat up. "They're back." He swore. "Why couldn't they stay out longer?"

"Quick, bolt the door!" She was terrified of Hugh or Louise coming up here.

He got off the bed and loped naked to the door, bolted it.

Claudia put a hand over her mouth, giggling, then got

off the bed and began to look for clothes. Ben was already dressing in a hurry.

"I'm all fingers and thumbs. What do we do if Hugh comes up and asks you to open the door?"

"Pray he doesn't."

She stood in front of the dressing table, brushing her hair. Ben came up behind her and kissed her neck.

"I love you."

Their eyes met in the mirror. She leaned back against him. "Oh, me, too, Ben."

"Are we out of our skulls?"

"Who cares?"

From downstairs they heard Hugh's voice raised angrily. "What the hell happened here? There's glass all over the floor."

Claudia thought fast. "Stay in here, I'm going down to explain."

"No, I'm not skulking about in here while you get bellowed at by him!"

"He'll wonder what we were doing up here!"

"Let him. We're adults. It's no business of his." Ben opened the door and went out, and she could only follow him.

Hugh was shouting her name while coming up the stairs.

He stopped dead as he saw Ben with her.

"Are you responsible for breaking into the house?" he snarled, body stiff with aggression.

"No. You had a burglary here tonight."

Louise gave a gasp of horror. "No! I had a bad feeling as soon as I saw that glass on the floor. What happened?

What did they take?''

Hugh was looking anxiously at Claudia. "Are you OK?''

She nodded reassurance. "Luckily Ben heard me scream.''

"You were here when this guy broke in, then?'' His voice roughened. "For God's sake, how many times have I told you to close the shutters as soon as it starts to get dark? You know how dangerous it is to leave these bastards any way into the house!''

"I'm sorry, I forgot.''

"You forgot? How could you be so stupid?''

"Anyone can forget to do something,'' Ben interrupted impatiently.

"I suppose you were here and distracted her?'' Hugh snapped, glaring at him.

"No, he wasn't! I went to have a bath and ... I simply forgot, Hugh. I'm sorry, it was stupid of me.''

He sighed. "All right.'' But then he turned that scowl on Ben again. "What are you doing here, then?''

"I was parked outside. I thought you were all out, nobody answered when I rang the bell. Then I heard her scream, so I climbed on top of my car and over the wall. The guy must have come in over the back wall or I'd have seen him.''

Hugh was watching her with a concerned expression. "So what happened, Claudia? Were you still in the bath?''

"I heard him breaking in and started to come downstairs, then he got his hand inside and opened the door, and I ran back up the stairs. I suppose that was

222

when I started screaming.''

''I heard her, and climbed over, but by the time I got in here he had knocked her to the floor and was ... was attacking her.''

Louise had come upstairs and was standing behind Hugh. She gave a sharp cry, then put her hand to her mouth.

Hugh asked sharply, ''Attacking her?''

''He tried to rape me,'' Claudia said, because she would rather say it herself than have Ben say it.

Louise hurried over and put her arms around Claudia, muttering comfort. ''Poor girl, oh, you poor girl.''

''I pulled the bastard off her, we had a fight, but he hit me with a copper vase — it's there, on the floor, and you mustn't touch it. I called the police ...''

''You did what?'' snarled Hugh.

Ben ignored that. ''But they were too busy, they'll be here tomorrow, and they don't want any evidence touched before they can fingerprint it. Not that there will be any prints — he was wearing gloves. Obviously a professional.''

''You had no right to ring the police, this is my home and ...''

Ben gave him a cold, contemptuous look. ''Somebody had to. If I hadn't been here, I hate to think what would have happened to Claudia. I got here just in time.''

Louise turned pale. ''Are you sure you're OK, *chérie?* He didn't hurt you?''

''Ben stopped him in time.'' She didn't want to talk about it. She didn't want to think about it. She was trying to wipe it out of her memory, only remember those moments with Ben.

Hugh ran a hand through his hair, perspiration on his temples. "You're right, I suppose. I was trying to keep the police out of this. But they know Claudia is my weak spot. They keep trying to get at me through you, Claudia. I think you should go away, until this is over. You need a holiday. You often say you'd like to go to Greece. This is your chance. I'll pay."

Her face stubborn, she shook her head. "No. I'm not going away — you might be killed while I'm gone. I'm staying right here, with you."

Ben said curtly, "Who are they? What are they after, anyway? Can't you just give them whatever they want?"

At that second there was a trilling sound. All of them looked around in surprise and bewilderment.

"My mobile!" Ben said, pulling it out of his jacket pocket. He flipped it open, lifted it to his ear. "Hallo?"

"I'll make some hot chocolate, shall I?" offered Louise.

"Oh, would you? I'd love some, thanks," Claudia whispered.

Louise trotted off down the stairs.

Ben had turned pale, his features drawn.

"I see. Yes. No, he won't. I'm sorry, I did my damnedest, but I've got nowhere."

Claudia felt her heart turn over. What was he talking about? Was he, after all, part of what was going on?

Then he said, "Yes, I'll leave at once. I'll get the next flight, tomorrow morning, probably."

Claudia turned cold; depression seeping into her. He

was leaving. After what had happened between them tonight, he was going away, abandoning her.

So much for his talk of love. Had that merely been the bait to get her into bed?

She held back tears. She wouldn't cry over him. He wasn't worth it.

He closed the phone and looked at Hugh. "That was my mother. The doctors just told her my father is worse; he only has a few hours to live, may die at any minute."

Claudia bit her lip, shamed by what she had been thinking. She put her hand on Ben's arm.

"Oh, I'm so sorry, Ben."

"Thanks." He covered her hand with his.

Hugh's face was icily blank.

Bitterly, Ben demanded, "Haven't you got anything to say? He's dying — doesn't that mean a thing to you?"

Hugh walked away without answering and went to his office, slamming the door behind him.

Ben stared after him, looking ill, his face white, shadows under his eyes.

She remembered how it felt to have a parent die; like an amputation, part of your own body gone, leaving that shadow of themselves on your soul, making you aware of your own mortality, making you feel older, incomplete for ever now.

"I have to go," he murmured abstractedly.

"Of course, your mother will need you."

He kissed her fiercely. "Why don't you come with me? Hugh's right, you should get away from here for a while. Come with me, meet my family. I want them to get to know you.

"This isn't the time, Ben. Later, I'd love to meet them, but I can't intrude on their grief. Your mother will want you to herself. And I can't leave Hugh just now, either. I'm worried about him, afraid something may happen to him at any minute."

He sighed. "Well, talk to him, try to persuade him to come to England, or at least to ring my mother, tell her he forgives my father. Will you try?"

She nodded, knowing there was no chance of Hugh agreeing, or even listening. And this was not the time to tell Ben why.

Ben looked at his watch. "I must go and try to book myself on to the next plane. I'll be in touch."

She went with him to the gate. They kissed in the shadows, then she watched him drive away, wondering miserably if she would ever see him again.

PARIS

1940

CHAPTER
TEN

It seemed to him the longest, coldest, most boring, winter of his life. "How I hate all this waiting about," he told Wallis. "I wish the fighting would start tomorrow. Maybe then they would give me something to do. I'm so sick of sitting about behind a desk or driving around on inspections, then writing reports nobody seems to read."

She was lying full-length on a *chaise-longue*, her head on a pile of silk cushions, reading an American newspaper and didn't look at him. How wonderful she looked, arranged as if for a photo in spite of being alone with him, everything perfect, hair, face, body. She never had a hair out of place, at any hour of the night or day. In that, she reminded him of his mother, who had always been perfectly coiffeured, cool, dressed to perfection. Wallis would not like it if he told her she reminded him of Mama, in any way. She disliked Mama, not surprisingly, since Mama had always refused to meet her.

He had asked her once, belligerently, "But why? Why won't you at least meet her? How can you know what she is like until you see her?"

"I know what she is, David. A cheap adventuress. If

229

you do marry her, you will be her third living husband.''

That had hurt so much he had not gone on arguing and pleading. He had left, trembling with rage so much he had hardly been able to walk straight.

She yawned and looked at her watch. ''Talking about headquarters, don't you have to be there in half an hour?''

''I'm just going.'' He went over to kiss her and she moved her head aside with a petulant shrug.

''David, I've only just done my mouth! How many times must I tell you not to smear my lipstick?''

''I'm sorry, darling, I forgot.'' He dropped a kiss on the top of her head and left like a scolded schoolboy. His mother had always made him feel like that — clumsy and awkward. It depressed him for the rest of the day when Wallis was cold to him.

He was to visit British GHQ that day. Lord Gort introduced him to many of the commanding officers and their staff. Harry, his brother, the Duke of Gloucester, was also touring the camp.

Always short of words and short of warmth, too, Harry had never been as close to him as either Bertie or George. Of all the brothers, Harry took after their father most. He was stocky, heavily built, with protuberant blue eyes, a large nose, big ears, and a moustache that made him look older.

Their father had believed in army treatment for the boys — bullied them, demanded unquestioning obedience to his slightest word, played practical jokes on them and teased them mercilessly.

They had all been terrified of his rages, of those

bulging blue eyes, that rough, roaring voice, but Harry had modelled himself on Papa. He loved being in the army, was a martinet, obsessed with detail and his own status. They said very little to each other as they went around the billets with a senior escort of officers, who explained anything they saw and didn't understand.

Harry stopped to talk to an old friend. David walked on with the commanding officer, who was telling him that his men had played a football match with a French army team the previous week.

Some guardsmen on duty presented arms, and without thinking David returned their salute. It was second nature; years of being in the army, let alone being King, or Prince of Wales before that, had taught him to salute back when he was saluted.

He noticed his brother's frostiness of manner as they met up again in barracks, but ignored it. If Harry wanted to sulk, let him.

A couple of days later, he was summoned to headquarters, and told sharply that he had no business taking a salute intended for his brother.

"The Duke of Gloucester has the same rank as you in the army, but as a royal duke he is your senior. He outranks you on all occasions — is that understood? You know very well that a salute is always intended for, and returned by, the senior officer present — the salute given was for him, not you. Please remember that in future if you are in his company, or that of any other officer senior to yourself, when a salute is given."

He stared at the man on the other side of the desk, his face burning, sick with humiliation and anger. The eyes staring back held unmistakable triumph; the joy of someone given a chance to cut him down to size.

Bastard, he thought. Bastard. They were all bastards. He couldn't even answer, he was too choked.

He needed the comfort Wallis could give him. Who else could he talk to? He couldn't confide this insult to anyone but her.

When he got back to the house on Boulevard Suchet, however, he had to wait to talk to her because she had visitors, an American and his wife, a plump blonde woman in a black straw hat and white dress. Her even fatter husband wore the most appalling suit he had ever seen. The material, the cut, the design of it, made him shudder.

"Where are you from, Mr Mason?"

"Harry and his wife are from Maryland!" Wallis told him, eyes bright with nostalgia. "They knew my father's family. You remember I told you about the house on Preston Street, and my grandmother Warfield? The Warfields are the *crème de la crème* in Maryland, and my grandmother was a queen in that society. I loved her more than anyone in the world, except my Aunt Bessie."

He had many times heard about the Warfields and their social status. Wallis appeared to believe they were an American equivalent of the royal family.

Mr Mason told him eagerly, "I'm in the munitions business. I'm over here to sign a big contract with the French government. We wouldn't have taken the liberty of calling on you and your wife, but we brought a message from a mutual friend — Charles Bedaux, who,

232

as you know, is also involved in the same business. We saw him last week in New York and he gave us a letter for you.''

''That was very kind.'' He accepted a glass of wine from Wallis, hoping his hand wouldn't tremble. It was difficult to be polite to strangers while he was in such a state of anguish.

They seemed to stay for ever, and Wallis was so happy to see people from her own country and to hear American voices, that she kept the conversation going although none knew better than her how to cut an occasion short and get rid of people who bored her.

At last, though, they departed. Wallis walked to the front door with them and stood there, chattering and laughing, for what seemed to him an eternity, with the cold winter wind blowing through the whole ground floor, making him shiver, although his face was hot.

Her high heels tapped and clicked back towards him, and he turned to start speaking only to find her face set in a mask of ice.

''Did you have to be so chilly with them? I was going to ask them to dinner, but you made it crystal clear that you wanted them to go, and they aren't dumb, they realised you didn't want them around.''

He was frightened of her when she was in this sort of mood, but he pretended amazement. ''I hope I did not give any indication ...''

''You made it all too clear how you felt! You were rude, damned rude. I liked them and I was having such fun talking about Maryland and my family, hearing all the gossip about old friends. And then you come in and give them fishy looks and ruin the whole atmosphere.''

His voice shook, his hands were icy. ''I wasn't expecting to find strangers here, I wanted to be alone with you.''

Her tone took on a brittle sneer. ''You're supposed to have been trained to talk to strangers, to be polite and charming to everyone, whatever their station, but I suppose that doesn't apply to Americans.''

Anguished, he cried, ''You know that isn't true! I love talking to Americans normally, but...'' He broke off, swallowed the lump in his throat, tears finally pricking in his eyes. ''Oh, Wallis ... I've been waiting for hours to get to you, tell you what they've done to me now.''

He kneeled down beside her and put his head on her perfectly polished shoe to show his total and utter contrition. When she was in this mood the only way to get forgiveness was to demonstrate that he was her slave.

''Please, please, forgive me if I've offended you. You know I would never willingly do that.'' A sob came, and then another. He kissed the slender, aristocratic foot inside the shoe.

She put her hand under his chin and lifted his head, stared into his tear-filled eyes.

''I forgive you. Now, get up and tell me what has happened.''

''H ... he's ... sent for m ... me...'' He couldn't stop stammering, as Bertie always had. Once he had heard Elizabeth say that Bertie's stammering was due to his fear of their mother and father, They had made Bertie feel inadequate, a failure. He had been afraid to speak in case he made a mistake, and so he stammered. David sometimes found it hard to speak, too, when he was really frightened, and Wallis could scare him rigid.

She put a finger on his lips. "Ssh — now, slow down, take a deep breath before you speak again. There's no hurry. I'll wait until you're calmer."

He leaned against her warm body, breathing the scent of her as he had longed to do with Mama when he was small.

Mama had been so pretty, all blonde hair and blue eyes which, when they smiled, looked like a summer sky. He had daydreamed of sitting on her lap, being kissed or cuddled, but it never happened. Even when any of them were ill Mama never hugged or kissed them. She saw to it that they had the best of care and acted as Head Nurse herself, starchy and aloof, bustling from room to room, giving out medicine, but she never showed them any love.

He took a long, slow breath and calmed a little. When he had himself under control again, he told Wallis what had happened.

She was incredulous. "And all because you answered a salute? I don't understand, why shouldn't you salute back if you get saluted?"

"I thought the salute was for me! It was automatic. But that bastard took pleasure in humiliating me, putting me in what he wanted to make me admit was my place now. Bad enough when I have Bertie being offhand with me, refusing to take my calls. Now Harry is telling tales, sneaking on me, demanding that he takes precedence just because my title isn't a royal one! I'll be having to kowtow to my own batman next!''

She was outraged on his behalf. ''How dare they? You're right, they love having the chance to spit in your eye! But you're still a king to me, you always will be.''

She soothed and comforted, stroked his hair, kissed him softly. Getting up, she made him sit in her chair, and curled up on his lap, let him hold her tight, the warmth of her body seeping into the chilled reaches of his own.

It was another hour before he read the letter from Charles Bedaux that the Masons had brought.

''Charles is coming back to Paris next week! He invites us to dinner at the Ritz; just the three of us. He wants to talk about something important, and says not to ring the Ritz because he's certain the line is bugged by French intelligence, who listen to every call he gets. They have a girl planted on the switchboard, he says.''

''I wonder if they're listening in to our calls too?''

''If I find out they are, I'll raise hell.'' But his voice lacked conviction. Whatever he said, who would listen? He was powerless. The bitterness of the realisation stung like poison in his blood.

''I sometimes wonder if our own servants are spying on us,'' Wallis said, grimacing.

He was beginning to believe that everyone around him was spying on him, checking on his every move, repeating every word he said. Even Fruity Metcalf was no longer the friend he had been.

''Even Fruity,'' he muttered, and Wallis looked intently at him.

''How many times have I told you I suspect he has

been planted on us by the secret service?''

He sighed. ''I'd hate to think you're right. I've known him so long, he's been a good friend to me for so many years.''

''When you were Prince of Wales, yes. And then King. But now you can't do anything for him any more. You have no influence, no power.''

He swallowed bile. No influence. No power. No real friends any more. They had all been fair weather friends who had deserted him when he gave up the crown. She was right.

A week later, they had dinner with Charles Bedaux, who had arrived back from America that morning and looked a little the worse for wear.

''Bad crossing,'' he said. ''We were all terrified of U-boats. Life on an ocean liner is no longer so glamorous. You can't get away from the war, even on a ship.'' He looked around the Ritz and sighed. ''At least nothing much seems to have changed here.''

The waiter arrived with champagne cocktails and Charles took one eagerly. ''I need this!''

A pianist played Cole Porter, in the little bar which led out to the walled garden. The dancing notes floated into the restaurant, which also led out to the garden, beyond whose brick wall Paris traffic echoed.

Everything seemed the same as it had been just a year ago. You might forget there was a war on, apart from the blackout curtains shutting the lights of the restaurant from the night sky above.

The waiters moved around in their discreet fashion.

The diners talked and smiled. Who would have supposed France was at war?

They talked lightly about society gossip in Paris, about the latest French fashion, about mutual friends.

"I suppose the army is keeping you busy?" Charles asked him as they ate *foie gras frais,* the liver perfectly cooked, served on cabbage sautéed in butter.

Neither Wallis nor David ate more than a few mouthfuls, although they were delighted by the *foie gras.* As Wallis always said, you cannot be too rich — or too thin. They always ate very little, but what they did eat had to be the best.

"Don't talk to me about the army," he said fretfully.

"Something wrong?" Charles asked, watching him thoughtfully.

"The French are insane, sitting in trenches, waiting for the Germans to come. All their guns point one way. If the Germans invade elsewhere, France is finished."

"This food is as superb as ever. The war has not changed that," Charles said smoothly, as the waiters swept back to them with duck from La Bresse, perfectly cooked, a delicate, tender pink, served with a tarragon cream sauce and a scattering of watercress on the edges of the plate.

He insisted on paying the Ritz bill, so they invited him to dinner at their own home two days later. He was the only guest. After dinner they sat in the drawing room and drank liqueurs with their coffee, put on a recording of French dance music. Their chairs were drawn close together. Charles talked in a low voice, pausing to listen whenever he thought a servant was coming, or even just walking past the room. The blackout curtains shut out the night, but in the garden the winter wind made leafless branches rustle and scrape against each other. When Charles arrived they had seen big flakes of snow blowing past.

"How I wish I were down at the Riviera," Wallis said, shivering in spite of the big fire burning in the grate. "I hate cold weather. Oh, David, do you remember how hot it was in Hungary, on our honeymoon, when we stayed at Charles's hunting lodge? It was so kind of you to lend it to us, Charles."

"It was my pleasure. I hope I can be of some service to you again very soon. This war will not last for ever."

"Thank God," Wallis said. "When do you think the invasion will come?"

"Not until the spring. Winter is a bad time to make war. After Easter, if I were you, I would return to the south of France. Paris will not be a safe place by then."

She looked at David. "And His Royal Highness? What should he do? They will expect him to stay with his regiment. If he tries to come with me they might arrest him."

"Oh, yes, they would," David gritted through his teeth. They would enjoy that, taking him back to Britain under guard, like a criminal. He had begun to wonder if they planned to do that before the real war began.

"Then he must stay with his regiment, for the moment, and wait to join you. Whatever he does, he must not return to Britain. If they invite him back, for any excuse, even if the request comes from his brother, or his mother, he must not go. It would be dangerous for him. He might find himself going through Traitor's Gate to end up in the Tower."

"They wouldn't dare! The people wouldn't allow it!"

"They wouldn't know. Nobody would be told. You would just vanish. There are precedents for it, in your history, aren't there? Ex-kings have ended up in the Tower, and been executed."

Wallis's breath caught. "Executed?"

Charles Bedaux shrugged sardonically. "In times of war, anything can happen. After all, they must be afraid you will come back and take your throne again. The only way they could be sure you never do that is a firing squad inside the Tower. When France falls, England will be next to go. Your Highness, it is vital that you are here, in France, ready when the call comes to take your place on the throne of England again."

FRANCE

1999

CHAPTER
ELEVEN

The police arrived next morning to take measurements and photographs, questioned Claudia for half an hour, then talked to Hugh and Louise. They became angry when told that Ben had probably already left France.

"He had an urgent message from his mother — his father is dying, he had to go home," Claudia explained.

"He should have stayed until we had seen him!"

"He can always come back, if you need to take a statement," Hugh assured them. "He is my nephew, there's no problem with making contact with him."

That soothed them down a little, especially as they had found no fingerprints, and, since nothing had been stolen, this was not a priority enquiry.

"They often come back if they fail the first time, so keep a watchful eye out, and never forget to close your shutters before it gets dark."

"I won't, don't worry," Hugh nodded. "Once burnt, twice shy."

"Good. Wasn't your name and address in the notebook of the man who was shot on the beach a few days ago?"

Hugh looked startled. "Shot? I thought he had drowned."

"No, he was shot in the head. We think he may have been a crook. If that was a list of possible houses to burgle maybe it was his partner who broke in here last night? We'll have to talk to him again. See where he was last night."

After they had gone, Hugh went up to his office and Claudia sat down with a coffee. The phone rang. As she ran to answer it she hoped it was Ben, but it was Siegfried sounding upset.

"We're in trouble. Patti has lost the month's account books. She was working on them and had them in her big black satchel. Somebody stole it."

Claudia groaned. "Oh, no, what a nuisance! Is she sure she hasn't just mislaid it in her room?"

"A guy on a bike snatched it from her as she was walking through Montmartre! It's gone, I'm afraid. What do we do about the accounts? And the worksheets were all in the satchel, too — the diary, everything. We don't know what we're doing now. Luckily, we do know there was nothing booked for today, but there is a booking for Saturday night."

"I'll come back," decided Claudia. "I'll try to get a flight this afternoon. See you."

She rang Nice airport and booked herself on to a flight at four o'clock, then ran upstairs to pack a bag.

She met Hugh as she was carrying it downstairs. He looked at the bag quizzically.

"Have you decided to take me up on the offer of a holiday?"

"No, I've got to go to Paris urgently." She told him about the robbery. "Siegfried rang because Patti was too scared I would be angry with her. I have duplicate books in my flat, but I shall need to talk to them, see the banking statements, check on the various bookings. I don't want my whole operation going down the pan just because Patti's bag was snatched.''

''Maybe it would be a good idea for you to stay in Paris. It might be safer for you there.''

She shook her head. ''I'll stay as long as I have to — but I'm coming back. This will only take a couple of days.''

''I'd feel easier if you weren't here, frankly.''

She kissed his cheek. ''And I'd feel easier if I were sure you weren't in any danger, so I'll be coming back.''

In fact she was in Paris for longer than she had expected. It took her three days to put the business back on an even keel. Patti had coped very well with the day-to-day running of the job, and she had scrupulously banked all cheques, but by losing her satchel she had got the other side of the business into a muddle, since it was difficult to be sure which of their suppliers had been paid in the last week and which had not.

It was four days before Claudia got a plane back to Nice. She took a taxi to Cap d'Antibes, and arrived on a glorious morning. Louise made her tea and sat chattering to her in the garden.

''Nothing has happened since you left. Except that Hugh had a phone call from Ben.''

''His father?'' Claudia asked anxiously, and Louise nodded.

''I'm afraid he did die, but Ben got back in time to see him alive. That must have been some comfort.'' Louise gave her a coy look. "He asked to speak to you, first, and I told him you had had to go to Paris on business, but were coming back very soon. He seemed very disappointed."

Hugh came out of the house. "So, there you are! I told you to stay in Paris!"

"And I told you I was coming back to keep an eye on you!"

He grimaced. "Did you settle your affairs satisfactorily?"

"I hope so. Patti was very apologetic, but it wasn't her fault, poor girl. The police found the satchel in a bin — along with torn scraps of papers. Why couldn't they leave them in the bag? Why tear them up?"

"Spite, pure spite. Petty thieves hate people who have things they don't have — like a job, money, credit cards. So they steal what they can and vandalise anything else." Hugh looked at his watch. "What time is lunch, Louise?"

"I'm going to serve it in ten minutes, don't worry! Do you want to eat out here, or indoors?"

"Here, I think; it's such a lovely day. Is the white wine chilled? I'll have a glass while we're waiting."

"I'll get it," Claudia said, following Louise into the house and laying a tray with glasses and the bottle of Chablis which had been chilling in the fridge.

She and Hugh talked idly as they sipped their wine and ate the simple lunch Louise had prepared — tomato and mozzarella sliced and laid out in a fan, sprinked with fresh, torn basil leaves; followed by grilled salmon with lemon and lime slices and a bowl of mixed salad leaves and steamed new potatoes.

"Has Ben's father been buried yet?" she asked tentatively.

"The funeral was yesterday." Hugh's voice was flat, cold.

She was afraid to say anything else; she felt him slamming the door of his mind and leaving her outside.

Two days later Louise had the day off, so Hugh suggested that they have lunch in Cannes. It was a glorious day; very hot yet with a crisp wind blowing off the sea.

Hugh parked in the expensive harbour car-park, then they wandered together along the harbour towards the Croisette, the sickle-moon curve of hotels, apartment blocks, luxury designer shops carrying magic names — Dior, Chanel, Armani.

This was not yet high season, so the town was not completely choked with cars and people, but traffic was always busy here, whatever the time of year, women strolled from boutique to boutique, and they had to wait some time to cross the road when they halted opposite their favourite restaurant.

Behind them somebody called. "Hugh? Hugh Hepburn?"

Claudia started to look round and felt Hugh stiffen. She quickly looked at him, but his face was blank as he turned towards the boats bobbing in the harbour.

The voice came from a very large white yacht tied up nearby. On the deck stood a tall man with silvery hair which had once been fair.

"So you've finally shown up in person, Roger," Hugh said icily.

The other man laughed as if Hugh had made a joke. "Well, you know I usually sail around the Med at this time of year. Come aboard and have a drink, a bite to eat. I'm on my own, I'd be glad of the company."

"Thanks, but we're on our way to eat in the restaurant opposite."

"May I join you, then?"

Hugh looked at Claudia. "Would you mind if he did?"

She shook her head, not knowing what Hugh wanted her to say.

"This is my goddaughter, Claudia Guyon," Hugh told the man.

"Delighted to meet you, Claudia." He looked round at another man standing on the yacht's deck. Tall, powerfully built, he wore immaculate white shorts and shirt. He was pretending to polish the already gleaming brass, but Claudia had realised that all the time he was watching them, or flicking his stare up and down the harbour, like a watchdog on the alert for danger.

"Tim, I'm going ashore. I'll be in the restaurant opposite."

"Yes, sir." Expressionless face, sharp eyes. Was he a deckhand? He didn't look like one.

As they walked across the road, Hugh asked, "I presume he's your bodyguard?" and Roger nodded.

Why did Roger Morrell go around with a bodyguard? Was he very rich? If he could afford a yacht that size he must be wealthy.

"How's your father?" Hugh asked, and Roger sighed.

"Very frail, but it's astonishing that he's still alive. He had a stroke twenty years ago. Would have killed most people, but not him. He's hardly moved out of his bed since, just lay there at first, had to be fed and moved, like a baby. Couldn't talk or move for years, but gradually, he began to recover his speech."

"How wonderful," Claudia said, touched.

He smiled at her. "We're delighted. Mind you, he doesn't always make sense. His mind's too confused. That's the trouble. We have a nurse taking care of him. He needs constant attention. My boy, Guy, sits for hours with him, he's amazingly patient."

The waiter wandered over to give them a menu each and take their order for drinks.

Hugh asked, "How many children have you got, Roger?"

"Three. Guy, my eldest — he's a historian, he's writing a book about our family. Then there are my girls — two, both married now. Clarissa had a son last year, called him Stephen, after my father."

Hugh looked at Claudia. "Roger's father is a general, served over here, in France, during the Second World War. General Morrell. One of our great war heroes."

Roger stared across the busy road at the harbour, the yachts, the blue sky behind them. Tim was still on deck, still watching them.

"Does he remember the war?" Hugh asked. She heard soft sarcasm in his voice.

On the surface it sounded so polite; the small talk of old friends. What were they really talking about?

"For years he couldn't remember anything," Roger said flatly. "We thought he had serious brain damage, but lately he has begun to remember. In fact, that's all he talks about — the past. In flashes, but still ... some days he seems better, other days he seems to be sinking fast."

"I'm surprised you aren't at Leylands, then. I'd have thought you would want to be with him as much as you could when he might die any time."

Claudia was taken aback by this cold criticism of a man whose father was dying, and she saw from the expression on Roger's face that he was angry, although his voice when he spoke gave no hint of that.

Calm and smooth, his tones were those of a politician, taught to hide his feelings.

How could anyone trust such a man? She suddenly thought. How could you tell what was really going on behind his smiling face?

"I have been with him whenever I could, for weeks, but I have my job, you know, I have to be in London when Parliament is in session. I'm a very busy man. I go up to Leylands whenever I can, but I had flu a couple of weeks ago. Run down by the strain, the doctor said. I was tired, I needed a break, a change of air. I left my son looking after my father. I ring every day to make sure there hasn't been any change."

He paused, the calm surface cracking, anger in his eyes. "I love my father very much!"

Hugh grimaced, made an apologetic gesture, a hand flung up towards Roger. "I know you do. You've always been a very close family."

"And I won't see him hurt, or distressed, Hugh."

Their eyes clashed. Hugh turned towards Claudia and told her, "Roger is a member of the British government."

She would have liked to ask what office he held, whether he was important — but at that minute the waiter arrived with a fruit sorbet in a small glass for each of them. Prettily done, she thought, looking at the pieces of crystallised orange and leaves made of angelica which decorated the top of the citrus sorbet; a mixture of lemon, orange, grapefruit, she realised when she tasted it.

"And very ambitious," Hugh said softly as the waiter left. "Aren't you, Roger? You have your eyes on the top job, one day. You were always determined to succeed, even at school. It's a family trait, though, isn't it? You inherited it from your father. And knowing you, I'm sure you'll get there, just as he did. Whatever it takes, whatever you have to do."

Her face puzzled and uncertain, Claudia sensed the hidden messages behind the words, but still had no idea what these two men were really saying to each other. Was Hugh merely making fun of Roger, or was he threatening him? And with what?

"Your father is still alive, too, of course. I saw him recently, just before I left England," Roger said. "He's pretty frail, though, and Rafe's death must have hit him hard."

Claudia tensed, looking at Hugh, trying to read how the mention of his brother affected him. His face was unrevealing, but pale.

"You didn't go home for the funeral?" Roger asked him.

Hugh shook his head.

"No, your father seemed to think you would not be there. When I told him I was coming here, and might be seeing you, he asked me to give you a message. He wants you to remember that the only real loyalty is to the family."

"Even when the family itself is treacherous?"

"Surely the family comes before anything else?"

"Even before King and country, Roger?" The sarcasm was back, but the other man replied quickly, angrily.

"You obviously think so — after all, you changed your country, moved to France all those years ago. Still here. Or are you thinking of going home some day?"

"No. France is my home now."

"You can walk out on your family, Hugh, but you can't change them. You remain what you were born. An Englishman. Their blood runs in your veins."

Hugh smiled drily. "You mean, treachery is in the genes, in the blood? Yes, I'd agree with that."

"Didn't somebody say that patriotism is the last refuge of a scoundrel?"

"Dr Johnson, but I'm sure he'd have agreed that true patriotism begins with loyalty to your friends and family. They're the foundation of your country. If you betray that, you won't think twice about betraying your country."

A red flush ran up Roger Morrell's face. "I wouldn't betray it. I wouldn't betray anyone. I loved my wife. Since she died, I haven't married again. And before you ask, I don't have a mistress, either. And I certainly wouldn't betray my country.''

There was a pause, then Hugh seemed to soften slightly. ''No, I can't imagine you betraying anyone. I'm sure you're a good son and a good father.''

''I hope I am. My family are my life.''

''Then how would you feel if someone broke into your home, trashed the place, and beat up and sexually abused your daughter?''

Claudia drew breath, beginning to shake. Don't! she wanted to tell Hugh. Don't talk about that to him. I can't bear to hear it talked about.

Roger didn't look at her. His voice flat, he said, ''I'd be violently angry. Bloody furious. You can't think I would approve of anything like that?''

The waiter arrived with their main courses. Silence fell. Claudia stared at her plate of *lapin à la moutarde*; it looked good. She took a forkful, tasted it professionally. The rabbit was perfectly cooked, and the Dijon mustard gave a mild heat and flavour to the sauce, which had been made with *crème fraîche*, she imagined, from the taste and consistency. Not bad, she conceded, although she felt she could do better.

When they had all finished eating, Roger asked, ''Will you be wanting desssert?''

Claudia and Hugh shook their heads. The menu offered only rather over-familiar puddings; chocolate mousse, *crème caramel*, apple tart. Mostly bought in, probably, and to be found everywhere along this coast.

''Come and have coffee on my boat, then. We can't talk here, Hugh. Too many people within earshot.''

Turning, Roger summoned the waiter and asked for the bill. "This is on me," he told Hugh.

"No, I'm paying the bill," Hugh immediately protested.

Claudia decided to leave them. Roger obviously wanted to talk to Hugh without eavesdroppers, which she sensed would include her. "Will you excuse me? I won't bother with coffee. I want to buy some magazines. I'll walk down to the newsagent on the Croisette, then I'll sit on a bench and watch the men playing boules. Pick me up there, Hugh."

"OK. Get me some English papers, would you? Whatever they've got." He handed her a two-hundred franc note which she stuffed into the pocket of her jeans.

Roger stood up, held out his hand. "It was a great pleasure to meet you, Claudia. I hope we'll meet again soon." He paused, said without looking at her, "And I'm very sorry to hear of your unhappy experience in Paris. I hope nothing of the sort ever happens to you again."

"It had better not," Hugh bit out.

Claudia was glad to get away. She walked along the harbour, watching the rows of beautiful, elegant, expensive yachts bobbing in the water, mast wires jangling, gulls lighting on the roofs of cabins, squawking. They were wealth and power made visible; some of them worth a million dollars, carrying a staff of four or five. Rich men's toys. She couldn't even imagine the sort of money you would need to buy yourself one of them.

Hugh had had a small boat for many years which he

kept at Antibes. They had sailed every summer. It wasn't in the same class as those anchored here at Cannes, of course. Hugh's boat barely carried three of them, the cabin was tiny and Hugh sailed it himself. His boat was no emblem of riches or power — it wasn't even a toy. He fished from it — they ate what he caught and he gave the rest to friends. He had many friends among the fishermen. There were fewer now, though. The local waters were almost fished out. Fishing boats had to go further to find their catch, and many had given up. Fish was often imported from Corsica or Algeria, across the Mediterranean.

As always, men were playing boules on the sandy ground beneath the pines and plane trees on the other side of the Croisette road. She walked across to the newsagents beyond them and bought Hugh's English papers and some French magazines for herself, then wandered back and stood under the trees to watch the boules for a few minutes.

After a while she sat down on a bench near the bus stop and opened one of the magazines, became engrossed in pages of innovative recipes with brightly coloured photographs. Now and then in these magazines one discovered an exciting new way of cooking familiar ingredients. Today she spotted an Algerian recipe using lamb, mint, apricots and couscous in an unusual combination. It sounded great. Her Paris customers might like that, couscous was very popular with some of them. She would cut it out and paste it into her scrapbook when she got back to the villa. In Paris she had half a dozen scrapbooks of recipes she had found in magazines.

As she turned the page a man sat down beside her. Rather too close, Claudia felt, moving away without looking at him. His smell was powerful; the reek of garlic mingling with musky aftershave. It was vaguely familiar. She turned her head to take a quick look at him, and at that instant the man moved too, towards her. Something jabbed into her arm. She gave a cry of pain and shock, put a hand up to touch the place; it was tender, but there was only a small red mark on her skin.

"What did you do to me?"

"What's the matter with you?" he returned coolly, and she had the same worrying sense of familiarity. She had heard that voice before, she was sure of it.

She rubbed her arm angrily. "Was that a knife you cut me with?" She had never seen him before, she was certain of it. She must get away from him, he might be a lunatic. She began to get up, and he grabbed her arm and yanked her back down on to the seat.

"Keep your hands off me!" she said and got up again.

But her knees gave and she staggered.

He got up, too, putting his arm round her. "Are you ill?"

She tried to push him away, but could only make a gesture like a weary swimmer, her arm floundering. What was wrong with her? She felt weak, dazed.

Alarm and fear beat inside her head.

What had he done to her?

She tried to walk away, but he manipulated her sagging body, towards a car parked at the kerb, behind a bus.

He leaned down and opened the rear passenger door. She tried to escape but couldn't think straight, let alone scream or struggle.

Her mind moved in slow motion, working out that he hadn't stabbed her. He had stuck a needle in her arm. She had been drugged.

Her body slumped sideways into the back of the car, and then she lost consciousness.

Tim and Roger went below. Hugh wandered around the deck, preparing himself. He knew what Roger was going to say and he knew how he was going to answer. The next half hour was going to be unpleasant.

But he still enjoyed the feel of the rocking motion, watched sunlight glinting off the brass fittings. He hadn't been out on his own boat for a while. He had been too busy with his new book. He and Claudia must go fishing while she was here. He never enjoyed anything as much as a day out on the sea in early summer, with a good, stiff wind in the sails, and sunlight glittering on the water.

None of this was Roger's fault. Hugh was angry with him for what had happened over the last couple of weeks, yet at the same time he was sorry for him. Tough luck for Roger to have to deal with it. He must be terrified.

Roger came up with a tray of coffee and a bottle of French brandy. He set it down on the table, gave Hugh that practised, politician's smile. "How do you like it?"

"Black, please, no sugar."

Roger half filled two small cups. "Brandy?"

"No, thanks, I'm driving, remember."

"Doesn't she drive?" He paused, obviously making an effort to recall the name, found it. Another politician's trick — what did he use to trigger his memory? Mnemonics? The alphabet? "Claudia?"

Hugh caught the fleeting self-satisfaction. Pleased with himself for remembering. He must meet so many strangers; hard to recall names and faces.

"Short-term memory problems, Roger?" he deliberately asked and then regretted the tease as he saw the fear and pain in the other man's eyes.

"I've always had trouble remembering names. It isn't hereditary. My father's memory went after the stroke."

"Yes, of course. I'm sure your memory is fine. And, yes, Claudia can drive. OK, then, a finger, no more."

They sat for a moment in silence, sipping. The sun was hot on Hugh's back.

"Give it back, Hugh," Roger suddenly said. "It was all a long time ago. Almost everyone involved is dead, or soon will be. All you'll do is destroy their reputations and hurt the living."

"I'm sorry, but the truth is the truth, Roger. People have a right to know exactly what really happened."

"Don't be so sanctimonious! You aren't doing this in the name of justice. You're doing it to get your own back on Helena. You've been waiting years for a chance to hurt her the way she hurt you."

Hugh's face tightened, grew white with rage and pain. "This has nothing to do with her, or my own family!"

"Of course it is. You want revenge on all of us. The Morrell family hurt you, and you're determined to get your own back. You and I were good friends once, Hugh — how can you betray that now?''

''I wouldn't use a word like betrayal, if I were you.'' Hugh was so angry now that his voice rose, and people walking past along the harbour wall turned their heads to stare.

A dark red flush grew in the other man's face. ''Keep your voice down, damn you!''

''Watch your own tongue, Roger, if you don't want me to lose my temper.'' Hugh put down his coffee and stood up. ''I'd better go.''

Roger got up, too, took hold of his arm and coldly said, ''This is my last warning, Hugh. If you don't give it back you'll regret it!''

''Don't threaten me, Roger. You're already in enough trouble. That man who was found dead on the beach — he was working for you, wasn't he? Claudia recognised him. He was one of the two who broke into her apartment.''

''I don't know what you're talking about!'' But Roger's face was pale, rigid with control. He knew something about the murder. Had it been committed on his orders, or had the man been killed by someone else?

''I wouldn't have thought you were the type for cloak and dagger stuff, Roger. Is someone else involved? We both know how many different interests could have reason to want me silenced. Am I up against the secret service? I suppose it could even be the French secret service. They'd have reasons for wanting the past buried.''

''You damned fool, Hugh! You ask too many

questions. It's dangerous to pry into dark corners. Have sense. Either destroy it, or hand it over to me.''

Hugh shook his head. ''Go back to England, Roger. If anything else happens I swear I'll tell the police everything, and after that no force on earth will get the genie back into the bottle.''

He strode down the gangplank without looking back. Roger stood on the deck, watching him go, sunlight glinting on his hair and tanned skin. Hugh felt sorry for him; he was an innocent, a decent man trapped by the past sins of his own family.

He got his car from the car-park at the end of the harbour, drove back towards the Croisette without glancing at the yacht he had just left.

As he passed the men playing boules he slowed down, but Claudia wasn't in sight. He drove further on, turned the car round and drove back, keeping one eye on the shops he passed, half expecting to see her dawdling along, window-shopping. Still no sign of her.

A car pulled out of a parking place ahead, so he shot into the space, and began searching the nearby streets without success. Had she walked into the rue d'Antibes which ran parallel with the Croisette and was full of expensive international shops? He paused to look at his watch. Nearly four o'clock! It was an hour since they had left the restaurant.

Where on earth had she got to?

Had something happened to her?

His mind filled with fears which made his blood run cold. He got back into his car and drove along the harbour. Roger was not on deck now. The vessel was moving, backing away from its mooring.

Hugh's pulse raced. He parked illegally, half up on the pavement, broke into a run but was too late. The gap between the boat and the harbour wall was too far for him to risk jumping. He would simply land in the dirty harbour water if he tried it now.

The bodyguard, Tim, was on deck, working with complete absorption, coiling rope, not even looking landward.

Hugh shouted. "Where are you heading?"

Tim looked round, spotted him, cupped his ear to indicate he had not heard what Hugh had said.

"Where is the boat off to now?" Hugh yelled, louder, but by then the yacht was turning seaward and Tim did not reply, just shrugged and waved a hand towards Nice.

Hugh didn't believe it. They wouldn't leave such a good mooring in Cannes to go to Nice. It wasn't easy to get good moorings in such a central position, for a start, and the distance, on land, between the two ports was very short. You could drive from one to the other in around an hour.

Hugh stared after the boat, not sure what to do. Roger could have given up, could be going home to England.

But where was Claudia?

Maybe she had met an old friend, was having coffee with someone in the town. She might have lost sight of the time.

Roger was a very clever man. He wouldn't make such an obvious move. He wouldn't have had Claudia snatched. He wouldn't be taking her away on board. Or would he? Was he getting desperate?

For Roger there was a lot at stake; his career, his family, his whole life.

When the villa had been sold to Hugh the old man had been out of his mind, unable to tell his son why the villa must be kept in the family. Roger had had power of attorney. He was a clear-headed, efficient man; he had tidied up the family estate, modernised the share portfolio, sold off properties his father had bought but no longer used.

Only when his father began to recover from the effects of his stroke did Roger finally hear the truth. Hugh could imagine the shock his old friend had felt. Roger was a conservative, old-fashioned patriot. He must have been appalled when his father confessed how he had acted before and during the Second World War.

How long did it take him to realise the hostage he had unwittingly given to fortune?

When they were young, he and Roger had often played chess. They had been evenly matched, had explored each other's weaknesses and strengths many times. They had been good friends then. He still liked Roger, but he knew how Roger thought, the ruthlessness he was capable of, the cool-headed logic of his game. He knew Roger was capable of abducting Claudia. But had he done so?

If he had had her snatched, and she was on board that yacht, that placed Hugh in a dilemma.

If he called the police, and they pursued the yacht at sea, there was a strong possibility Roger would get rid of the evidence before the police caught up with him.

He was capable of such brutality to save himself. She would be killed, before they threw her overboard, to make sure she could never give evidence.

CHAPTER
TWELVE

Claudia woke up with a headache, feeling sick. For a second she didn't remember what had happened. She tried to open her eyes, but her lids wouldn't move. She tried again. As she turned her head she heard crackling. Then she realised. Her eyes were bandaged with something cold and tight which ran right round her head and would not shift.

She must have had some sort of operation on her eyes, that was her first thought.

Then it dawned on her that her mouth was sealed, too, with the same thick, crackling plastic tape.

By then she was wide awake and thinking hard. Where was she?

She remembered sitting on a bench in Cannes watching men play boules. Waiting for Hugh to pick her up in his car. The sun hot on her face. She had been feeling lazy, languid, after the good meal she had just eaten.

A man had sat down next to her. She had moved along the bench away from him, but he had followed. There had been a sudden jab of pain. She had thought he had stabbed her. But he hadn't. He had stuck a needle into her.

Her mind worked feverishly. She must have lost consciousness. She didn't remember anything else. She must have fainted.

Where was she now? She tried to move and discovered that her hands and feet were bound. She was in the dark, unable to see, move, or even scream.

Like a mummy in a tomb, she thought hysterically. Except that she was lying on her side, with a pillow rammed into her back to stop her rolling off the bed on to the floor.

At least she could hear. She wasn't totally cut off from the world. Somewhere nearby a clock ticked loudly. Wind rattled a window, blew through branches outside. No sound of traffic, though. She deliberately lay still, focusing all her attention on what she could hear. No sound of the sea, which she could hear day and night in Hugh's villa, on Cap d'Antibes. She must be somewhere in the country. It was too quiet to be anywhere near a road or any other house.

She could hear a low voice talking nearby. Slowly she shuffled herself over the bed towards the direction of the voice.

Suddenly her head hit a wall. She knee-jerked in pain.

God, that had hurt. The pain throbbed. She didn't dare move again, but the voice was louder. A man's voice, deep and gravelly. She must be lying right up against the wall of another room.

There was only his voice, so he was either talking to himself, or on the phone. His voice was familiar, she was certain she had heard it before.

She couldn't remember where.

"Has Hepburn been in touch?" he growled, and her mouth went dry.

Hugh. They were talking about Hugh.

A pause, then the man said, "How much longer do I have to stay here? I want to get out of the South, go back to Paris."

It was the man who had sat down next to her on that bench in Cannes and pushed a hypodermic into her arm. But before that . . .

She had heard his voice elsewhere.

"When I've killed her, what do I do with the body?" the voice asked and panic flooded her like dank waters in a deep, deep mine, drowning everything else, making her head swirl and echo with the words . . . killed, killed.

She was going to be murdered.

Sickness rose into the back of her throat. She retched, shuddering.

How would he kill her? Would it hurt much? Would it be sudden, over in seconds? If he injected her again, with something that simply put her out of life, that wouldn't be so bad as other ways of dying she could imagine. Painful ways. Being raped, tortured. What if he cut her throat? That must be agonising. If he shot her dead it would be over in seconds, but what if she didn't die immediately, was left to die slowly, in anguish?

His voice cut through her feverish imaginings.

"No! She has to die. No two ways about it. She saw my face, I tell you. I'm not leaving her alive to tell any tales."

If only she could move. Struggle, fight him, even simply scream for help, but she was helpless. All she could do was lie there and wait for him. Wait for death.

The image of Ben came into her mind. She didn't want to die.

She thought of that strong, tanned body in the blue waters of the swimming pool, of their lovemaking in her bedroom, and ached with desire. She loved him, she had wanted him from the minute she first saw him, on the Seine quayside. She was a cool-headed, modern woman who had always believed she knew precisely what she wanted from life and how to get it.

Meeting Ben had shown her how primitive her instincts were. She felt her flesh burning, hungering. She wanted him with an overwhelming need, a desire that ate her up.

Where was he now, at this minute? She would die to see him, to touch him.

Hugh turned into the Chemin de Croe and slowed, staring at the car parked outside his villa. There was nobody in it or near it. It was the latest model dark blue Fiat. He had never seen it before.

The gates swung open as Hugh approached them — Louise must have spotted his car coming.

He parked, got out and took the steps two at a time. Louise opened the door before he got there. She looked excited.

''He's back.''

''Who?'' He threw a look past her, across the kitchen, up the stairs into the salon. His heart was beating twice as fast as it should; he felt sick with worry and fear.

Had Roger come in person to hand him an ultimatum?

"Who!" she teased, laughing, blithely unaware of what had happened to Claudia or why Hugh was so tense and angry-looking. "Her young man, of course."

He must have been listening because he appeared at that instant, at the top of the kitchen stairs. All in black. Black shirt, open at the neck, no tie, black trousers, black shoes.

Had he lost weight? Or was it just the effect of all that black? He looked thinner, anyway. His face was drawn, shadows under the eyes as if he hadn't slept, mouth tense.

"Make some coffee, Louise, would you, please?" Hugh asked.

"Where's Claudia?" she asked, looking through the window into the garden.

He didn't answer. He and Ben confronted each other on the stairs like dogs squaring up for a fight.

"What are you doing back here? I thought we'd seen you for the last time."

"You didn't answer Louise. Where's Claudia?"

"Get out of my house. I have nothing to say to you. Hugh pushed past him, walked across the salon and stood by the window staring at the sea he could glimpse through the pines. This view was different every time. It had been a hot day, but now the sea had a wild look, darker blue than usual, and the sky above it was becoming cloudy. Maybe a storm was on its way?

Through clenched teeth Ben said, "I'm not going until you tell me where Claudia is."

"I don't know."

"What do you mean, you don't know?"

He heard the alarm in Ben's voice. He cares about her, registered Hugh, he's worried, she really matters to him.

Louise brought up the coffee a second later and set it down, but didn't go back to her kitchen. He could feel her behind him. She had heard what he had said.

"Something's wrong, isn't it? Has something happened to Claudia? Please, tell me. You're scaring me."

"I didn't mean to." He turned and gave her a brief, apologetic smile. "I'm sorry. She left me in Cannes, I haven't seen her since. We may get a phone call any minute asking me to pick her up."

"You mean she met a friend? Was it Jeanne? She's in pod, almost on the point of having it, if you ask me, big as a house. We saw her in Antibes last week and Claudia promised to call on her soon and see her home."

"I don't know who she met, or where she went. She said she was going shopping, that's all, but when I went to pick her up she wasn't there. We'll pour the coffee for ourselves, Louise. I expect you have a lot to get on with."

She hesitated, reluctant to go, but in the end gave a shrug and went back down the stairs.

Ben began pouring the coffee, black for both of them. Hugh sat down, took a cup and sipped it. Scalding hot, it burned the tip of his tongue. He was almost glad of the pain. At least that was real, and he had been feeling unreal since Cannes.

"You might as well tell me," Ben said flatly. "You look like death warmed up, do you know that?"

Hugh lifted his head, shot him a grim look. "So do you. Look in a mirror. You're as white as a corpse." Then he frowned, remembering. "Sorry. That was a joke in poor taste. I'd forgotten he was dead."

His brother was dead. The fact really hit him. Death was final. No possibility of change, of forgiving, forgetting, of ever being brothers again as they had been when they were children, boys running wild over the hills, riding ponies, fishing, lying in the heather watching red grouse nesting among the clumps of grass, or the merlins darting close to the ground, hunting small birds. Rafe had always been tenderhearted, hated to see the merlin fly off with a finch in his claws.

Ben met his stare. "We buried him two days ago."

Hugh didn't answer. That small, thin, gentle boy who had been his brother was dead. It was hard to believe; brought death nearer to him, himself. He shivered, staring through the window, longing to escape out into the dark blue weather.

Ben relentlessly went on, as if determined to make him face the fact, "It rained all day. That heavy, soaking, English rain. Real funeral weather. We all got soaked walking through the churchyard. Soaked and covered in mud."

"Then what are you doing back here? Shouldn't you be in England? Who's going to talk to the lawyer, sort out the estate, any financial problems? There will be letters of condolence to be answered. Have you left ... her ... to do it on her own? She'll need you now."

"The lawyers are sorting everything out. I've paid any bills that need paying. What she needs at the moment is to get away, into the sunshine. She's exhausted. I brought her here."

Hugh took in breath fiercely, turning dead white.

"She's here? Where?"

"Staying in the Hôtel du Jardin. I left her lying down. The trip tired her, she needed a few hours' rest."

Hugh turned away again, stood with his back to Ben. "I won't see her." His voice was harsh, not quite steady. "Don't bring her to this house. I won't see her, do you understand?"

"Is that all you can think of? Yourself and how you feel? What about my mother? I brought her here because I could see she had to get away or she would go mad. If you saw her, you would realise she is on the verge of a breakdown. He died so slowly, and she had to watch. She needs a change of scene, and I need to see Claudia. It killed two birds with one stone to bring her to France with me. I was worrying about Claudia all the time, I had to know what was happening to her."

"You hardly know her!"

"What's time got to do with it? I love her. And it's time you told me what was going on. Look, Hugh, I can keep a confidence, and I think you need to talk to someone. You're looking hag-ridden, you know."

Hugh sighed. "Am I? Well, it's true, it might help to get another angle on it." He thought, phased it carefully, with deliberation. "The thing is, I have something somebody wants, and I'm afraid he may have had Claudia kidnapped."

"Kidnapped?" Ben broke out, the colour draining from his face. "My God, you must call the police." He walked towards the telephone. ''We must ring them at once!''

Hugh caught his arm and held him back, saying urgently, ''Wait. If I call in the police, they may kill her.''

''Kill her?'' Ben stared in shock, then he almost shouted, ''Give the bastards what they want, for God's sake! Don't risk her life!''

''Do you think I would? I'm just waiting for them to phone and tell me where and when I can swap the documents for Claudia.''

''What documents? Is that all they want, some documents? I thought you must be talking about money or jewellery, or a work of art, something valuable.''

''These papers are more valuable than you can imagine,'' Hugh said, and told him about the storm the night Claudia's mother died, the collapse of the chimney and what he had found buried in the rubble.

Ben frowned. ''But surely anything in the chimney must have belonged to General Morrell, if you bought the villa from him?''

''Until I opened the box, and looked through it, how could I be sure who it belonged to? This is an old farmhouse. General Morrell bought it back in 1930. The documents could have been in the chimney before that. I had to read them to be sure who had owned them. And once I had read them I knew I couldn't just hand them over to your mother's family. Most of the documents are in German. And even if I can't read German, I can recognise the signature on some of them. Adolf Hitler.''

Ben sucked in breath sharply. ''Hitler? How did

General Morrell get hold of documents signed by Hitler? When were they written?''

''The earliest letters were from the mid-thirties. The last ones were written in 1939.''

''The start of the war?'' Ben whistled. ''This sounds like dynamite. I'd love to get a look at them — what are they about?''

''Treason.''

''Christ,'' Ben said hoarsely. ''You aren't serious? The General? A traitor? I don't believe it. Are you sure these documents aren't forgeries?''

''If they aren't genuine, why would Roger Morrell be here, trying to get them back?''

''Roger?'' Ben's voice was shaken. ''He's here?''

''Claudia and I had lunch with him in Cannes, today. Afterwards, he invited me on to his yacht, where he asked me to hand back the documents. He said I was being a fool, it was dangerous to pry into dark corners, I could only damage reputations and hurt the living. I told him I intended to publish, and I went off to pick up Claudia.''

''You said she was with you and Roger at lunch!''

''At lunch, yes, but when Roger said he needed to talk to me in private, Claudia walked round the harbour to buy some newspapers at the newsagent on the corner.'' Hugh frowned. ''I realise now that he prompted her to go off by herself by saying he wanted to talk to me alone. He wanted to split us up. He left me on deck while he went below. He could have made a phone call telling someone where Claudia could be found.''

''But ... he's a member of the government!''

"And if I published these letters he'd be ruined, would have to resign! Look, I drove up and down for a while, looking for her, then I parked and searched for an hour. But there was no sign of her. When I got back to the harbour, Roger's yacht was sailing away."

"You think she was on it?"

"What do you think? Which is why I'm waiting for a phone call from Roger."

"Why wait? Why not get in touch with his yacht?"

"You mean call the yacht's radio?"

"Never mind," Ben said, walking towards the phone. "I'll ring Guy at Leylands, he must know how to get in touch with Roger."

Hugh groaned. "Why didn't I think of that? My brain is in meltdown, I'm afraid. All I can think about is getting Claudia back safely."

"That's all I can think of, too," Ben said huskily. "You will give back these damned letters, won't you? What does an old treason matter compared to her life?"

Hugh nodded. "Tell Guy I'll do whatever they want, but only if I get Claudia back safely."

Ben reached for the phone.

NORTHUMBRIA, ENGLAND

Early summer, 1999

CHAPTER
THIRTEEN

The old man lay in the great four-poster bed in the very middle of the high-ceilinged room, his gnarled hands resting on the yellow silk brocade coverlet which he had brought back forty years ago from his time of residence in Hong Kong. Embroidered red dragons coiled across the silk and up the side curtains to the canopy. When the tall casements of the windows were opened in warm weather the wind blew through the silk and made the dragons dance as he had seen them at the celebration of the Chinese New Year so many times.

"Dragon dance. Fire and wind," he mumbled. "Good luck."

There was a movement beside him. He turned his head, startled, and saw himself sitting by the bed.

"What?" he said in agitation, shrinking back into the banked pillows. "Who...?"

The man by the bed leaned over and gently touched the back of one of those frail, thin-skinned hands, so fragile now that light shone through them as if through glass.

"It's me, Grandpapa."

"Me?" the thready voice whispered.

It was like looking into a mirror. Was he seeing

himself as he had been in his early twenties? His head swam, disorientated, the planes of the room swinging from side to side. That was his face. It came towards him through the shadows and he watched it in terror. His face on another man. How could it be?

Jack. Of course, it must be Jack. He should have realised.

"Jack?"

But it couldn't be. Jack had died in the war. Blown to pieces by a landmine. They never found enough to bury, but he had never told his parents that. His mother couldn't have borne it. Some truths were too bitter to be told.

How long ago had Jack died? More than fifty years. Half a century. So this couldn't be him. Unless he was dreaming and he knew he was awake. The hand touching his was too real — young, warm, supple.

He looked at that fair, smooth-skinned face, the wide eyes, as blue as if a bit of summer sky had fallen into the boy's head.

Not Jack, but the same face; same hair, same eyes, he thought. It had to be one of the family. All the Morrells had that colouring, those fine-featured faces. Easy to recognise them. Was this his own son, Roger? Faces and names came and went in his mind all the time. Vanishing and then lurching forward out of the mist of memory.

"Is it you, Roger?"

"No, sir. That's my father. I'm Guy, you remember? Your grandson."

Sorrow overwhelmed the old man. "Jack's dead."

"Yes." There was a flicker of surprise in the blue eyes which were so like his own — before his had paled, faded, the skin around them wrinkling into a thousand lines. "That's right, Grandpapa, your brother died during the war."

"Stepped on a landmine. They said he was laughing. That was Jack. Always laughing."

Tears leaked from his eyes making snail tracks down his face. "Laughing Jack, they called him in the regiment. He was buried there, what there was left of him. My mother always used to quote some poem about a corner of a foreign field being always English, God knows why, because she came from a German family. It wasn't foreign to us. We belonged there, just as much as we belonged here."

"Yes, sir."

"Bad thing, fighting your own people. Upset my mother to know we might be over there killing one of her family. Two of them did die during the war. She's dead too, now, my mother. Died in 1950. She never got over Jack's death. I couldn't make it up to her, although God knows I tried, but she missed him too much. If I had given her grandsons ... after she died I married your grandmother. Should have done it sooner, given my mother a grandson to love, a reason to go on living. We all need a reason to live."

"Yes, sir." The flow of talk was surprising Guy Morrell. He listened intently, knowing he might never hear his grandfather talk like this again.

The old man lay still, eyes closed, and Guy thought he had gone back to sleep, but he suddenly started talking again. "Roger, that's what we called your father. I wanted to call him David, but his mother insisted on Roger."

The faded blue eyes watched a gleam of sunlight pierce the room, lighting a painting on the wall opposite. He had bought it over fifty years ago from a Paris exhibition. Who was the painter? Some French fellow, couldn't remember the name. Good artist, though.

The likeness was amazing; he looked as if he might speak any minute. He remembered that expression so well; the uncertain shyness that lay beneath his outward arrogance, the charm. He had been painted wearing a pale blue linen suit, open-necked, casual yet elegant, his favourite summer wear.

"My father hates to see me without a tie," David had said the summer the portrait was painted. Had it been 1934? Or maybe 1935? "He's obsessed with what he thinks is the proper way to dress. He says I look common in my slacks and shirts without a tie, like a workman, and when I told him that's how I want to look, I thought he'd have apoplexy!"

They had laughed together, but it hadn't been a joke. There had been a tragic gap of understanding between father and son. They couldn't talk to each other, didn't know each other. The old man had been set in his ways, refusing to move into the new century, measuring his eldest son by Victorian standards which no longer applied.

"Doesn't he understand the people love you?"

The blond head had been shaken, the blue eyes wistful.

"He only understands that I'm not a carbon copy of

him! That's what he wanted. I've never been good enough.''

That was the look the painter had caught; a sadness, a loneliness. The portrait had hung there ever since he had inherited Leylands. He had had it hung in this room the day he had moved in here as master, succeeding his own father. That was something else he had had in common with David. He hadn't got on with his own father. The blue eyes seemed to smile at him across the room. They had had so much in common.

Guy Morrell looked at the portrait his grandfather was staring at. ''He was a typical Stuart, wasn't he? Not only had the Stuart face and build but the character too; all the charm and all the weaknesses. They say he was a petulant, spoilt little man.''

His grandfather rose up in the bed, on his elbow, his quivering voice wild. ''You didn't know him! How dare you? Never let me hear you talk about your king like that. You aren't fit to mention his name, damn you.''

Face anxious, startled, the boy moved closer. ''I'm sorry. Sorry.'' He took both of the old man's hands. ''Don't get upset, Grandpapa. It's bad for you.''

He subsided, his breathing fast and irregular. He closed his eyes. His heart was beating so hard he pulled a hand free and put it on his thin chest, which was rising and falling rapidly. He tried to press down on it, to calm its rushing beat.

''I'll call the nurse.'' Guy Morrell got up, but the old man caught his sleeve.

''No. Don't want her fussing around. Sit still, boy.''

He lay unmoving for a minute or two, his mind

clouding with the past again. Sometimes he couldn't even remember what year it was. Time whirled about the room like smoke.

"What year is this?"

"It's 1999. Next year is the millennium, the end of the twentieth century."

The old man's face was blank. He stared through the tall windows at the unrolling landscape of green hills, the frilled leaves of an oak bending over hedges between fields full of grazing animals, black-and-white Friesians, small woolly sheep, a couple of fine-bred bay horses. Arab blood, bred from his father's stallion, Egypt, who had been dead nearly a century now, but whose bloodline went on and on.

Papa had dreamed of winning the Derby with him once, but Egypt had had a bad fall jumping, and been lamed, so Papa had put him to stud and had made a fortune from him over the years. Egypt's descendants were probably still running on some racecourse somewhere. The blood had not been bred out. Good breeding always showed.

Look at this boy. You could see at a glance that he was a Morrell; the family face was unmistakable; such sharp, finely defined bones under that fair skin, the blue eyes, the fine, silky hair.

They had settled here not long after the Conquest, having come from Normandy in the army of William, their Duke, helped him take England and been given this land as a reward for their services.

There had been two brothers; Guy and Charles de Maure in the beginning. They had built this house on a

282

low hill overlooking a river valley, determined to hold the estate against allcomers. For years they had been under attack from the local English. Charles had died of the ague a few years later after a campaign, sleeping on wet English ground with his men, with only his cloak to keep out the cold. He had a wife but no child. Guy had been left alone to continue the line.

"He did, too," the old man murmured. "Fourteen children, eight of them sons. Six girls. By the time Guy died he only had two sons and a daughter left. People died young in those days."

His grandson had a confused, bemused expression. What was he talking about now?

"You know it was Guy's grandson who dropped de Maure and changed his surname to Morrell when he married a local girl whose family insisted he make his name English? They're a stiff-necked lot in these parts, always were. Wonderful country, though."

"Beautiful country." The boy walked over to the window to stare out at it, and the old man watched him with pride. Fine-looking boy, with that long, straight Morrell back. A horseman's body.

"Good seat on a horse, Guy?"

The boy came back, smiling. "You put me on my first pony, don't you remember? I still ride every day. Never happier than when I'm on a horse."

Wistfully, the old man said, "I haven't been on a horse for years. Can't remember last time I rode."

So many things he couldn't remember. So many things he couldn't forget. Funny how he remembered the family history from a thousand years ago, but forgot last week.

Why did the boy keep staring at him in that strange way?

"I was born here, in this room," he said thickly. His tongue filled his mouth these days, the words came out mangled, he wasn't sure why. Had his tongue swollen, or his mouth shrunk?

"Going to die here." He held out a hand, and Guy came quickly to take it. "Listen, make sure they don't try to take me off to some damn hospital. Want to die here in this room. They all did, my father, my grandfather, and his father, all of us, back to the sixteenth century, old Simeon, but he was only carried in here to die after he had a bad fall out hunting. Most of us get born in here too. Good room for big events, this one. Being born and dying."

His gaze wandered over the enormous, draughty expanse of it: dark red walls, the ceiling so high it was barely possible to see the ornate plastering in the corners and centre.

Anxiously, Guy said, "Don't think about dying. A long time before you need to think about that."

He looked at the boy with a petulant frown. "You a doctor?"

"No, sir. You remember, I'm Guy, your grandson."

"Of course I remember that, goddammit, boy." Then the old face softened. "You're the image of my mama."

Blonde, beautiful, with blue eyes and skin like apple blossom, she had been the beauty of the county, ravishing. His father had been envied by every man who set eyes on her. Yet she hadn't been enough for him. He had had a lot of other women, all his life; the wives of his friends, servant girls, whores up in London. Had he ever loved her? Or had he married her for her fortune, which had been large, or her connections, which had been powerful? She came from an aristocratic German family with a vast estate, but their money had come from mining coal and a big steelworks.

It had been a very useful marriage to the Morrells. Love had not been part of the bargain. She was a possession they had decided to acquire, not a human being to love and cherish.

Yet on her side, there had been love. She had loved the man she married. A big, powerful, very masculine man with a reckless grin and a dangerous temper, he had always attracted women. It was not surprising that the innocent, seventeen-year-old girl he married should fall head over heels in love with him on sight, and spend the rest of her life yearning for the love he never gave her.

How many nights had they heard her weeping in her room? He and Jack, sharing the night nursery, night after night while they lay awake and heard her sobs, smothered in her pillow, while Papa stayed in London and never came home.

''My mama died out there, down in the valley. Hunting. Neck broken.'' She had taken a fence at a dangerous gallop. Suicide, people had whispered, she had wanted to die. His father was in the middle of his last, longest love affair, and she couldn't take any more. The inquest called it an accident, of course.

In those days coroners and magistrates knew their duty. The Morrells were the most powerful family for a hundred miles, their land ran from one side of this end of England to the other. Scandals surrounding them were hushed up, whispered about, never published.

His father had shot the horse, crying noisily as he did it, then knelt down and stroked the damp, silken neck saying, "I'm sorry, I'm sorry, my beauty."

He had cried for the horse for days, red-eyed, yet at the funeral of his wife, with the whole county there in black, he had been calm and dignified, accepting their condolences with a grave nod, dry-eyed.

The old man knew now what they had been thinking, all those neighbours and friends of his father. That they wouldn't miss her. She had, after all, been a German, a foreigner; they were a conservative breed these people up here, they did not like foreigners, especially Germans. The English had even hated Queen Victoria's husband, Prince Albert, because he was a stiff-necked German. Only when he was dead had they relented and, out of guilt, and knowing him better than they ever had when he was alive, mourned him publicly.

They had not mourned Mama. She had been forgotten as soon as she was buried, by everyone except her children, and her servants, who had all loved her because they knew her warm, caring heart.

"She was a very beautiful woman, wasn't she?" the old man said, looking round at another of the portraits hanging on the walls. This was a Sargent. He had seen her, painted her, as she was to those who loved her — dressed for a ball, with lustrous oyster satin setting off her warm, honey-blonde hair, those big blue eyes, her mouth pink and glowing with warmth and love. None of

286

the other portraits of her showed her true nature — only Sargent had done that.

How could Papa not have loved her?

"My father has a strong look of her," Guy murmured.

"Who?"

"Your son, Roger, sir."

"Roger? Yes, so he does. Is he here?"

"No, sir. He's in France, on holiday."

The old man looked confused for a moment. "France ... the villa? On the Cap?"

"No, you remember — we sold that years ago, Grandpapa. We have a place in Cannes now, more modern, much easier to look after. There's a resident maid and gardener, a married couple who live in a flat over the garage. We let the place out when we're not using it."

The old man clutched his grandson's hand. "Sold my villa? He had no right!"

"You gave Papa power of attorney, don't you remember?" the boy soothed.

The frail hand gripped like the claws of a dying bird. "Good God. He did what? Sold my villa? Who does he think he is? That place was mine. He had no right to sell anything of mine. Where is he? Get him here. Have to talk to him."

"Papa did what he thought was best. There's no need for you to worry. Everything will be fine."

"He had no right to sell my possessions off!"

"You gave him power of attorney, Grandpapa!"

"I don't remember doing anything of the kind!"

"Somebody had to take care of the estate. We couldn't

just let it moulder, somebody had to look after things. You trust Papa, don't you?''

"If he sold my villa ... no!''

"He was doing what he thought right. You weren't using the villa, none of us were, it was locked-up capital, and needed a fortune in repairs and modernisation. Papa decided ...''

"Oh, he decided!''

"Don't upset yourself like this! There's no need to worry, Papa is doing his best for you.''

His flurry of distress had exhausted the old man. The flicker of lucidity in the pale, wet eyes died out again. The eyes closed. He slipped away into a half-sleep, mouth open, snoring.

The door opened and two other people came into the room. The younger man stood up. "Thank you for coming, Dr Rankin. Nurse Skelton explained?''

"He's been back with us again this morning? Was he making real sense?''

"Yes, absolutely. Talking quite clearly, he even remembered his brother Jack dying fifty years ago.''

"Oh, the distant past comes back regularly, very common. It is yesterday they can't remember.''

"But he seems to be much better than he has been for the past five years. What does it mean?''

"Obviously, something has changed, but for the moment we can't be sure what's happening. I'd like to make some tests.''

"What sort of tests? Can you do them here?''

"Well, I really ought to have him in the hospital, we couldn't bring all the equipment here, it's far too heavy.''

"No. Absolutely not. He hates hospitals. He's over ninety! At that age, what's the point of upsetting him just to do tests?''

"Well, up to you. I take your point.''

They both stood looking down on the old man, whose blueish lids had the look of borage petals in ice, transparent, crepey.

"Sorry, but I promised him — no hospital. I'll leave you and Nurse Skelton to do your work, then. Excuse me. If you want me I'll be in the library. Please let me know if there's any reason for immediate concern. And please try not to distress him, won't you?''

Guy touched the few fine strands of silvery hair brushed across the pink, shiny scalp — more like a baby's than that of an old man.

"Take care of him. He's very precious to us.''

"To everyone in the county, sir. I am always being asked for news of him. People love him.''

Leaving the bedroom, Guy walked along the high-ceilinged corridor out on to the wide gallery above the main staircase. A dark red Persian carpet runner lay along the centre of the highly polished woodblock floor, smothering the sound of his footsteps. He glanced down over the mahogany banister to the enormous, echoing, vaulted hall below.

Pink marble pillars framed the closed front door; the floor was tiled in black-and-white. Two Irish wolfhounds lay in front of the great hearth in which a log fire burned although it was early summer. In this house, summer came late and winter early; the rooms were never really warm. Icy draughts whistled from the northern hills all year round.

The dogs stirred at his footsteps and lifted their elegant grey heads, their tails thumping.

When he reached the bottom of the stairs he clicked the fingers of one hand and the wolfhounds at once got up and padded after him along the corridor to the library.

Sunlight flickered on the golden oak panelling. In the carved oak fireplace the log fire was mostly ash now. Guy took two logs from the wicker basket standing by the hearth and carefully settled them on the glowing ash, picked up ancient leather bellows and blew the sparks into a flame, watched it lick round the logs and catch. The smell of burning pine wood filled the room. Drops of amber sap dripped through the iron grate into the mound of ash.

''That's better, isn't it?'' Guy said to the dogs. He walked over to sit behind his desk. The dogs, sighing gustily, lay down at his feet as close to the warmth of the fire as was comfortable.

Piles of books were lined up along the back of the desk. Guy took one with a russet leather binding, the Morrell arms in faded gilt on the front cover, flapped it open, put a ruler in to keep his place and began to read, leaning his blond head on his hand, his elbow on the desk.

He was researching for his second book, a history of his own family entwined with the history of this whole region, the borders, Hadrian's Wall, Northumbria. Very little had ever happened in this part of the world that his family had not been deeply involved in, and some of them had appeared on the world stage too, in national government, like his great-grandfather, and now his own father, or in the army, like his grandfather, who had ended his career as a general.

The room slowly warmed up, the only sounds a rustle as he turned a page, the regular breathing of the sleeping dogs, the rhythmic tick-tock of a longcase nineteenth-century clock.

He was fascinated by what he was reading, but he had spent the past few days sitting up beside his grandfather's bed, watching and waiting, under a strain that showed in his face and eyes. His lids drooped and he drifted into a light doze.

The sharp jangle of the telephone woke him. His neck ached, the hand propping his head was cramped. Yawning, he reached for the telephone and almost dropped it.

''Yes?''

''Guy?''

He sat up straight. ''Father — where are you?''

The voice at the other end had a note of irritation. ''On the yacht, on the way to Nice. God, was I glad to get away from Provence. I'd forgotten what a hellhole it can be when the mosquitoes are biting. They got me half a dozen times when I was in Nîmes, and I'd smothered myself with anti-*moustiques* stuff. Anything happening your end?''

''He was talking again today. Not much and it was hard to follow what he was saying. As you know only too well, he's pretty confused most of the time, but he has flashes of memory.'' Guy leaned back in his chair,

291

pleasurably aware of the warm, silky coats of the dogs close to his feet. He leaned down to stroke their ears. "You know what all this reminds me of? The start of that book. What's it called? Dickens." He chased the memory for half a minute. "*Tale of Two Cities.*"

"Recalled to life?"

"That's it. Recalled to life. But Rankin seems to think it could be a last flurry before ..."

His father abruptly interrupted, as though the word Guy had been about to use was a blasphemy.

"Damn Rankin, dreary old pessimist. The old man could live another ten years, in my opinion. Has he said anything new or important? Are you writing it all down, as I told you?"

"There was nothing to write down. Nothing made much sense except family stuff about the way his parents died, and I've often heard about that. He kept looking at the Sargent portrait of his mother. He really loved her, didn't he? You can see it in his eyes every time he looks at the painting."

"Oh, yes. The sun shone out of her as far as he was concerned. All her servants adored her, too. She was one of those women, not just a beauty, but really special. Yet her own husband seemed almost bored by her. She wasn't his type. Damned odd, that. People outside the family didn't take to her much, either. Funny business, life."

"How strange that both she and her husband died after hunting accidents."

"Never thought of that, but you're right. Damned odd."

292

"One of God's little jokes."

"You think God has a sense of humour?"

Guy always enjoyed one of these philosophical discussions with his father. They had only begun talking to each other like this after Guy turned eighteen, which wasn't that long ago. He settled himself even more comfortably, smiling.

"Well, logically, as he created the whole world, he must have created jokes, so he must have a sense of humour, surely?"

His father grunted. "Maybe. I must say some of his jokes don't seem very funny to me. Bit cruel, some of them. Can't see why Rafe had to suffer the way he did, for instance. He didn't deserve cancer. He was a decent fellow, I always liked him."

"Have you seen his brother yet?"

"Yes, had lunch with him."

"I just read one of his books. He's good, don't you think? I mean, really good, not just a best-seller. There's something different there."

"He's a difficult sod, I know that. I didn't get anywhere, trying to persuade him to see it from our point of view. I'm afraid we have to get tough with him."

Guy sat up, face apprehensive. "What does that mean? Father, don't do anything stupid!"

"I'll do what I have to do, Guy. Got to go, haven't got time for a long chat. Ring you same time tomorrow night. And Guy — no visitors! Understand? No visitors. Nobody at all. No matter how important they may be. Not even the Prime Minister. Not even any of the family, or his oldest friends. Keep everybody away from him, except the doctors and Nurse Skelton."

"Rankin wanted to move him to hospital."

"Good God, no! We can't have strangers looking after him. I hope you told Rankin it was out of the question."

"I did, don't worry."

"I think it would kill him to be moved, to leave Leylands."

"I'm sure it would. He wants to die in that room, you know. Said so today, said all the Morrells were born or died in that bed, and so would he."

"I hope you told him to stop talking bloody nonsense! You mustn't let him talk that way, it will depress him. Keep his spirits up, Guy. He mustn't die before I get back."

"Rankin said he might live for months." Guy paused. "Or die tonight, of course. With someone his age you can never be sure. Are your friends enjoying the trip?"

"I dropped them off at Aigues-Mortes to do a tour of Provence."

"I remember Aigues-Mortes — walled town built by some French king on his way to the Crusades?"

"That's the place. Full of atmosphere but far too touristy for my taste now."

"I remember you took me there ten years ago, for dinner one evening and we saw flocks of bats fly up out of the roofs and flap off across the marsh. Creepy. Almost as creepy as that place just outside Arles — full of broken old stone tombs. What was it called?"

"Les Alyscamps." His father's voice was flat and hard.

294

A shiver ran down Guy's back. He knew that tone —
what was wrong? If only his father would confide in
him, let him share the problem or even help, but there
was no point in asking questions, he knew he wouldn't
get any answers.

"Talk to you again tomorrow," Roger Morrell said,
and hung up.

Guy sat for a while staring into the fire. What was his
father up to? What had he meant by saying he was going
to get tough with Hugh Hepburn? Guy wished he was
there, could monitor what his father was doing. For a
very clever man, Father could do very stupid things at
times. He became reckless when he was anxious or
afraid.

The phone rang again and he reached for it.

"Hallo?"

The voice was familiar. "Hallo, Guy, it's Ben."

"Ben!" Guy sat up, his nerves jumping. He had heard
already that Ben and his mother had flown to France
that day. "Good heavens. How are you?"

"Do you want the good news first, or the bad?"

"Always prefer to hear good news."

"I'm in love. And I mean, really in love. It's serious.
I've met a girl I want to marry."

Bewildered, Guy said, "That's wonderful, Ben.
What's her name?"

"Claudia Guyon. She's beautiful and I'm crazy about
her. Now for the bad news ... your father has had her
kidnapped."

Guy drew a sharp breath. He swallowed. "Is that a
joke? Not in very good taste, Ben."

"Don't take me for a fool, Guy. I know all about what your father is up to. He had her kidnapped today. Guy, get in touch with him on this yacht of his . . ."

"I can't, I'm afraid. He rings me."

"A minister of the crown, unreachable? I don't believe you. That would be more than his job's worth. Don't waste my time, or your own, by lying. Tell him from me that if Claudia isn't safely released today I shall personally give your grandfather's story to the press."

Guy stiffened, very pale. "I don't know what you mean . . ."

"Shut up, will you? And listen. It will be on every front page tomorrow morning, along with extracts from the letters. And tell him, the letters are not here — they're in a bank where only Hugh, in person, can get them. And if Claudia isn't back with us tonight, you and your father will pay for it. I'm giving your father until ten o'clock tonight to deliver her safely to Hugh's villa."

"And . . . and . . . then what?"

"Then, and only then, we'll talk terms with your father. But first, Claudia. We don't talk until she's back."

PARIS

Spring 1940

CHAPTER
FOURTEEN

Paris in the spring of 1940 seemed to its citizens to have a doomed beauty. The Germans were poised to invade Holland and Belgium. How long before they broke through into France and this unreal, phoney war became a real one with a bitter ending? Few in Paris believed the Maginot Line would hold. Gossip had seeped out to them. Those who had not fled waited for the end, not daring to think what that end would probably be.

For the moment they basked in sunlight, like lizards, drowsed in the parks, lying on the grass or under the chestnut trees, in full, glorious leaf, their great white candles splashed with blurred red or yellow, like stained-glass windows. In the Bois de Boulogne, red squirrels chased along the shady paths. Few children came to bring them nuts, as they had in other springs; few children played there now. The squirrels were not to know that the children had left Paris, gone with their mothers to the country to stay with relatives or live in rented cottages; Paris was half empty. Old women in black sat, as they always had, on chairs in the doorways of apartment buildings, or on public benches, sewing and making lace, in the sunlight, watching the world go by with expressionless eyes. The roads thundered with army lorries and Jeeps. Young people in uniform were everywhere.

At night residential streets were quiet and police patrolled Montparnasse, the Left Bank, Montmartre, the seedier parts of Paris, where in the cabarets and bars drink was cheap and girls easy. Men were drinking more than ever, especially those whose wives and children had left. Soldiers on leave thronged the streets, picking up girls, shouting, laughing, and sometimes falling out over money or women, or merely out of pent-up aggression. Fights started most nights, somewhere, in these streets. Now and again someone got killed. The military police charged in, swinging batons, dragged struggling men away and threw them into vans.

None of that violence lapped the Boulevard Suchet where the Windsors lived. They still gave dinner parties, but fewer and fewer of their friends came. Many of them, too, had left Paris for country estates, especially those from the deep south. Those in uniform appeared from time to time, of course, among them Stephen Morrell, when he could get leave from his post at Vincennes.

May was a week old when he arrived without warning on an evening when they had no dinner party planned, meaning to eat *à deux*.

Stephen drove up in a taxi, carrying a large bouquet of flowers for Wallis and a wrapped bottle of whisky for David, who came into the elegant hall to welcome him.

"Stevie! This is a nice surprise. Just in time for dinner, too. Come along in and have a drink with us while the staff make a place for you at the table." He glanced at the footman who had admitted Stephen. "Will you see to that?"

"Yes, your Royal Highness." The footman bowed and took Stephen's army cap. He wasn't wearing a greatcoat, the night was far too warm.

Observing that the Duke was in evening dress, Stephen mildly protested. "I'm not properly dressed."

"You're a soldier. Perfectly properly dressed, my dear man."

Stephen followed him into the salon; the Duke closed the door, his manner changing abruptly now they were alone.

"Stevie?" Wallis said from the chair where she was sipping a very dry martini. "What are you doing here?"

"Is this it?" the Duke asked almost in the same instant. He knew Stevie wouldn't have come if he did not have urgent news.

Nodding, Stevie put a finger to his lips, glancing at the door. Then he held up two fingers.

"Weeks?"

"Days." Stevie walked into the centre of the room, far enough away from both door and window to make it unlikely that a servant would hear what he was saying.

"Days?" The Duke turned ashen, but still remembered to keep his voice very low. "You promised to let us know in good time so that I could get Wallis away."

"I'm sorry, I was only told today. They aren't taking any chances of word getting out before they attack. She must leave tomorrow morning, first thing. Where are you planning to take her?"

"We decided on Biarritz," Wallis said, and Stevie nodded.

"Good. Close enough to the Spanish border to make a run for it if you need to. But you'll be coming back to Paris, won't you, David? If you don't, it could cause too much gossip. At this stage, you don't want that, and, anyway, somebody may need to contact you very soon."

He nodded. "I'll come back." He took Wallis's hand and kissed it, his face lined and sombre. "I shall hate to leave you alone there, my darling, I know that makes you nervous, but I must, just for a little while."

"If I leave just before the Germans invade it will look suspicious," she said. "I shall stay in Paris until we see how things go."

He hesitated, chewing his lower lip. "Very well, but start packing now."

Three days later he rushed into the house late one afternoon and told her she had two hours to get ready to leave for Biarritz. The Germans had invaded the Low Countries; Holland and Belgium were under attack.

They found themselves on roads so crowded that traffic inched along, nose to nose, many cars ancient, loaded down with people and household goods, kettles and pots flung in, bicycles on the back, mattresses strapped to their roofs. People were on the move with their lives. Some walked, some were on cycles. There was an air of desperation and misery about them all.

Wallis shivered. "This is so sad, David."

"War is sad. And stupid. And pointless. Why do

we start them?''

"Maybe we should have gone to America before the war even began."

He gave her an odd look. "I'm not running away again."

"What do you mean — again? You've never run away from anything!"

"I ran away when they wouldn't let me marry you and keep my throne. It was a mistake. I should have stayed and fought it out with them. I won't run away again."

She put her head against his arm. "You're right. I'm just so frightened, David."

"I'll take care of you, Wallis. Don't be afraid." He was touched by her trembling, her vulnerability. She was always so strong and determined, one of the most powerful women he had ever met. Suddenly she looked like a little girl. He stroked her hair.

"Wallis, I need you to be strong. Be brave, for my sake."

It made him afraid to see her in that state of shaken terror.

She sighed. "Don't worry, David. I won't let you down."

They stopped at Blois for the night, but the Hôtel de France was packed with refugees. She vividly remembered stopping there on her way to the South of France during that bitter period before the abdication.

David had been in England, locked in battle with Baldwin and the government, and she had been a refugee herself, hounded by press and public alike across a wintry France.

"I'm sorry, your Highness, but the hotel is crammed like a Christmas goose," the landlord said regretfully.

"Can't you do anything for us?" she pleaded, and he rubbed his face and sighed.

"The best I could do is put a couple of mattresses on the floor in one of the sitting rooms, and you wouldn't be very comfortable."

She made a face, but said, "We'll manage for one night. Thank you."

"I'll get the room made up for you. I would send you somewhere else, but I'm afraid everywhere is just as crowded. These are bad times, very bad times. I have half of Belgium under my roof tonight."

The kitchen staff somehow came up with some sandwiches for them, and coffee, and they lay down half an hour later, exhausted and yet unable to fall asleep for a long time.

"You're so cold," he whispered, holding one of her hands between both his and rubbing it gently.

"When I stayed here last time it was snowing. I had the most marvellous room, with an antique bed and red velvet curtains, although I wasn't happy to be told it was the room where the Duke of Guise, the leader of the Catholics in the sixteenth century, slept the night before he was murdered. I hoped it was not an omen for my own fate the next day. The baying of the mobs as I drove across France made me very nervous."

"That must have been St Bartholomew's Massacre," he shuddered. "Horrible. Every Protestant in Paris was murdered — men, women and children. When the French ambassador came to see Queen Elizabeth the

First, the whole court were dressed in black, and turned their backs on him as he walked down the throne room.

"I didn't know that story, but you can imagine how I felt that night, knowing what was going on in England. I lay awake for hours, wondering what was happening to you, dreading the future, hoping I was not going to be assassinated next morning! It was freezing, although they had lit a fire for me."

The fire in the sitting room grate was dying down, but they could still see the room by the smouldering light of its ashes. He lifted her hand to his lips.

"You have been through so much for me! I can never repay your sacrifice."

She laughed huskily. "Compared to what you have given up for me, my little problems don't mean a damn, David."

They arrived at Biarritz eventually, only to find the Hôtel du Palais just as crowded as the hotel at Blois had been, but somehow they managed to find a room.

Face lined with worry, he asked her, "Will you be OK here, alone, darling? This isn't as comfortable as I hoped — maybe we should go on down to Antibes?"

"No, I'll stay here, and wait for news," she reassured.

Next day he had to return to Paris. It was the most painful parting they had ever had. He clung to her, trembling.

"Please take care of yourself, Wallis. I would die if anything happened to you."

"I'm sure we'll be together again soon," she reassured. It was her turn to be the strong one again.

When he had gone, she settled for what she was afraid

might be a lengthy stay. People were curious and friendly at first, staring at her whenever she was in sight, whispering, smiling at her. Until German radio broadcast the news that the Duchess of Windsor was staying in Biarritz at the Hôtel du Palais. They even gave her correct room number.

The next time she ventured out of her room, she got angry, hostile glares from guests and staff alike. They were all petrified that with her under the same roof, the hotel would be a target for German bombers.

The manager came to see her, perspiration on his brow and a nervous tic under one eye, but still politely bowing. ''Your Highness, in the circumstances, it might be wiser if you moved to another hotel, for your own sake. Now the Germans know you are staying here, they may attack the hotel at any minute.''

She gave him a scornful look. ''If they had meant to bomb the hotel they would have done so, they would not have broadcast the information that I was here! They were simply demonstrating to the world that they know everything that is happening in France. The real question is — how did they know I was here? Who informed them? They even knew the number of my room. How could they do that unless a member of your staff is on their payroll?''

The man flinched, his eyes scared. ''No, that is impossible! My staff are all French and totally trustworthy.''

''It's obvious that there can be no other explanation. I'm surprised you haven't had a visit from the French secret service yet. I shall not be moving to another hotel. Good day.''

Overawed and impressed by her hauteur and air of command, the manager bowed his way out again. Many of the refugees staying there had moved on by the evening, and a new flood of people descended on the hotel. Wallis kept her distance from them all, afraid one or other of them might become abusive or even violent. They stared whenever she walked through the hotel, but she did not make eye contact.

David telephoned every day, but, after she had told him that there was almost certainly a spy on the hotel staff, he very carefully kept to personal talk, mentioning very little about the war. Those short phone calls were all that stopped her fleeing, like everybody else, across the border into Spain. She would wait here for him.

In Paris, he had nothing to do. Now that the phoney war had become a real one, the Military Mission no longer needed the work he had been doing, liaising between the British and the French. They would not permit him to fight, either.

''If you were captured by the Germans, it would be disastrous,'' said Howard-Vyse impatiently when he agreed to see the Duke after days of being ''too busy''. ''I'm sorry, sir, but I cannot use you at the moment. The Mission may be leaving Vincennes at any time. The German advance is far faster than we had anticipated. They're overrunning Belgium, within days they will be at the doors of France.''

''I did warn you. That damned Maginot Line was a farce. The Germans can just come another way and walk right in.''

The Wombat shrugged. "I've never bothered with 'I told you so'. There's no point. We have to deal with things as they are, and at the moment I have nothing for you to do, sir."

"Then what do you suggest I do?" he asked angrily, and was given a bland smile.

"May I respectfully suggest you ask the King that question?"

Going red, David turned on his heel and left.

Fruity was waiting for him in the official car that had brought him to headquarters. "Did you see the Wombat?"

Only as they drove away did the Duke burst out, "He wouldn't give me a job, he wouldn't let me fight — he said I should ring my brother and ask him for orders. Damned impertinence. Who does he think he is? I'm not ringing Bertie. What's the point? He won't let me fight. They're afraid I might be a success and show Bertie up because he hasn't joined up."

"Churchill wouldn't hear of him coming over here to fight! The King wanted to, but Churchill forbade it." Fruity grinned. "Said England had lost one king already, couldn't afford to lose another one."

The Duke was not amused. "That's all very well, but why won't they let me come home? Oh, no, that's the last thing Bertie wants — to have me in the country, getting in his way. They'll just despatch me somewhere else before my feet actually touch English soil, send me off to do another pointless job which doesn't need doing. Well, I've done enough, put up with enough."

Fruity soothed, "I'm sure they will find you a role, sir.

It is just that at present the Wombat has so much on his plate. The Germans are just miles away from the French border. They'll break through any day, and then your regiment will need you.''

The Duke gave him a sullen look and said nothing. That night Stevie came to see him briefly, after the servants were all in bed.

"This is the key to my villa, and here's a letter for my caretaker. If you want to add any more papers to those I'm keeping for you, go to the villa, tell the caretaker to leave you alone, then feel up the chimney in the main salon. There won't be a fire at this time of year. You'll find a handle, pull it hard and a box will come down on a chain.''

"What if the caretaker knows about the hiding place?''

"I've let him see me going to a safe behind a portrait of my mother on the salon wall. He'll think you have come to get something out of the safe. Actually, I emptied it, there's nothing important in there, just some gold cuff links and a snuff box that once belonged to my father. I won't miss any of them, but they will satisfy any thief that blows the safe open.''

"You're a cunning bastard,'' the Duke said affectionately.

He grinned, looked at his watch, drained the whisky the Duke had poured for him, and got up.

"I must get back before I'm missed.''

They embraced.

"Try not to get killed,'' the Duke said. "I don't have many real friends any more. Even Fruity never stops lecturing me as if I were a schoolboy."

"Never mind me. You take care of yourself, David, England needs you," Stevie said, and kissed his cheek before hurrying away.

A few days later Fruity rang early one morning for orders and was told the Duke had left Paris and was on the way to Biarritz.

"He left without saying a word to me," Fruity wrote to his wife that night. "I saw him the night before and he never said a word, but he had already packed. He's taken all the cars, loaded down with valuables, and left me not so much as a bicycle. After twenty years' faithful service, I've been left behind like a stray dog. He hasn't given a thought to how I'm to get home. I shall have to hitch a ride with the army, I suppose, but I'm finished with the pair of them. I knew they were both self-obsessed, but this is the last straw! I never want to see either of them again."

Blissfully oblivious of everything but the joy of being together again, the Duke and Wallis eagerly left overcrowded, jittery Biarritz two days later for the Riviera in the grey light of dawn. On their way south, they passed vehicles moving in the direction of the Spanish border. Few people were going the way they were. The Italian army was massing along their southern border with France, with only a small French contingent facing them. At any moment the Riviera might itself become a battleground.

"The Wombat suggested I come down here and contact the French forces, let him know how things stand," David said as they made their slow progress

310

through Provence. "He was glad to see the back of me."

"Well, it's their loss. They only have themselves to blame," Wallis said, snuggling close to him. The weather improved with every mile; the sun was hot on their faces, they had the windows open wide to let a breeze blow against their skin.

It was easy enough on this journey to find accommodation and food. The tourists had fled, only the natives remained, although most of the young men had joined the army or navy, and it was the very young or very old who were left behind.

Each new familiar landmark in that sun-bleached vista made their hearts lift, even the strange, gorse-rough, dusty, ant-infested hills of the Estérel, were a welcome sight because it meant they would soon be home.

The vegetation down on the coast was quite different to anywhere else in France. Cypress, olive and pine trees on either side, they came down the hill towards Cannes as the afternoon wore on towards twilight, sighing in delight at their first glimpse of the tranquil blue sea. White gulls flew like mobile question marks in the dusky sky.

"It seems unbelievable that there is a war on," Wallis said wistfully. "If the Italians don't invade, the Germans aren't very likely to come here, either, are they? We could just stay here until the war is over."

He didn't answer. She shot him a look and sighed again. "You don't think we should be too hopeful?"

He silently shook his head, touching her hand. "Let's just enjoy this time together while we can, and wait and see what happens next."

They settled into la Croe again within a day. Food and wine were plentiful in this fertile region, not that either of them ate more than a mouthful at any meal. But they liked to offer friends a good table. What was served to guests had to be of the highest quality; Wallis tasted every dish, and woe betide a chef who sent up food she did not pass as first class.

Other refugees began to arrive, mainly wealthy Jews from Holland and Belgium escaping from the Germans, who took up residence in local hotels. They believed the Italians, if they did invade the region, would leave them alone. For the moment life was peaceful and pleasant on Cap d'Antibes.

They lazed by the pool, built at the far end of the garden above the sea, swam, did a little gardening, sunbathed on the rocks beside the pool, read in a desultory fashion, and, like everybody else in the world, listened to the news on the radio. It was impossible to tell what was really happening back in Paris; the bulletins were carefully written to keep the French people from knowing the true situation.

There were still some British residents down on the coast, who came to lunch or dinner, and a few wealthy French friends who lived down there now, and couldn't decide where to go if they left.

Maurice Chevalier came to lunch on the 10th of June and kept them laughing with his stream of jokes, while they ate out on the terrace, shaded by umbrellas.

"We must hear the latest," David said, switching on the radio he kept beside his chair, the lead stretching back into the house across the pavement of the terrace.

At first all they heard was music, rather serious classical music, with what Wallis thought was a graveyard sound. Suddenly, the announcer interrupted with the news that the Italian army had crossed the border some forty miles from Antibes. Fighting had begun.

Chevalier jumped up, pale and agitated. "*Excusez moi*," he muttered. "You understand ... I must go ... thank you, your Highness ... you must go, too ... *bonne chance* ..."

He was gone before they realised he was abandoning his lunch and heading home to pack.

"What appalling manners!" complained David. "He might have finished his lunch first."

Wallis laughed. "Poor Chevalier, he does not have your advantages, David."

"What?"

"He's French, not a stiff upper-lipped Englishman."

"Oh, many French soldiers are the same, but they call it *sang froid*, cold bloodedness."

"Well, I'm proud of you, but I have to admit, I'm as scared as Chevalier, I have no *sang froid*, or stiff upper lip!"

He knew she was always terrified — of flying, of crowds, of the war. She looked so strong and confident, yet she was consumed with fears. He found it moving, it aroused all his tenderness towards her.

Yet in other ways she was stronger than him; at times he was frightened of her, troubled by her almost masculine power, her dominating personality.

She was a very complex human being.

They stayed in their chairs and finished their meal before going back indoors, where the phone rang endlessly all afternoon. Their British neighbours, too, were packing and hurrying away. Soon only the native French who worked here would be left, some of them without jobs or an income, if they had been employed in the tourist industry.

"The Italian army will need feeding," Wallis coolly pointed out. "An army marches on its stomach, they say, and the Italians love good food. The locals will soon have jobs again."

"Except that Italians will flock across the border after their army, and take all the jobs down here," David shrugged, and she laughed.

"You're so cynical! But you're right, of course."

Overhead in the blue sky war planes droned back and forth, heading from their base at St Raphael along the coast to the Italian border, to attack the Italian positions.

"What are we going to do, David?"

"I'd better ring the British consul in Nice, he may have an idea how the battle is going and what the outcome is likely to be."

The phone was ringing as he walked into his office. A British neighbour, calling to say he was leaving at once for Spain.

"What are you going to do, sir? I think you should leave now, don't you?"

"Probably. Maybe we'll see you in Spain before long. Good luck, anyway."

The British consul told him briskly, "I'm very busy, your Highness. I have to clear the decks in the consulate, burn all our papers, but we're on standby to leave for Spain, and I think you should do the same.''

''We'll wait and see how the battle goes, Dodds. The French may drive them back into Italy.''

Major Dodds laughed. ''I wish I was as optimistic, sir. You'll have heard the radio news — the French are collapsing like a pack of cards. France will be entirely in the hands of Germany before very long, I'm afraid. And down here, the Italians will be in charge in a matter of days, in my opinion.''

That evening as they sat alone at dinner, they heard the roar of naval guns from somewhere far out at sea. The horizon was lit up with wild, spreading flashes, red, blue, orange.

''It's like the Fourth of July,'' Wallis said. ''Without the fun.''

''It reminds me of the Aurora Borealis, darling. You see it best up in the Hebrides; the sky lights up like this some nights, although the colours aren't as sharp. I suspect it is the French and British ships out at sea, bombarding Genoa. I heard a report on the radio saying we were attacking the Italian fleet at Genoa. Strange to sit here, eating grapes and drinking the last of our vintage champagne, while over there men are fighting and dying.''

They had decided they would drink their best wine rather than leave it for the invading Italians, and had given bottles away to friends earlier.

Wallis shuddered. ''War's beastly, isn't it?''

One of his hands clenched into a fist, he struck the table, groaning. ''If only Bertie had allowed me to be useful! Harry is allowed to fight, George is flying with the Royal Air Force, but they won't give me a chance.''

''You know why. Bertie's wife hates you because you landed her and Bertie with the chores of being King and Queen. She told me once that it would kill Bertie if he had to do that job, but I don't imagine it will. He'll enjoy the power and having all the attention, the flattery. But Bertie is afraid of you, he's scared people will compare him with you, and find him wanting. And they will, too. He doesn't have your ability to get on with people, or your charm or charisma; he's too shy and awkward, socially. He's like an insurance salesman. The crown doesn't sit easily on his head.''

''Poor Bertie,'' he murmured, remembering his brother as a very small, lost, pale boy, trembling in front of their roaring father, scared to death of their remote mother, in fear of their nanny, their tutors, the servants — everyone they came into contact with!

What sort of childhood had they had? Once Bertie had told him he wished he was a poor boy, like those they saw running wild in the streets as they drove around London, or playing cricket on the village greens across England. Those children looked happy even when they were fighting each other.

Had Bertie had fantasies about being a country child growing up in a cottage with a huddle of other children and parents who loved him?

None of them had had a happy life, certainly not poor, despised Bertie, certainly not he himself.

Suddenly wanting to talk to his brother again, filled

with warm tenderness for him, he rang the palace that evening, but they would not put him through.

"His Majesty is very busy, sir, conferring with the War Cabinet," he was told in a cold voice.

He replaced the receiver, body stiff with wounded pride. When would he face the truth? None of his family wanted him in their lives. He was in exile in every sense of the word, and would be, now, until he died.

Two days later, Gray Philips appeared at their gates. They had thought him still in Paris if he hadn't returned to England, and almost did not believe it could really be him.

When the footman ushered him into the salon David jumped up to shake hands, beaming with delight.

"Gray, you look terrible!" he teased, eyeing him from head to toe. "Your uniform is dirty and crumpled, and you need a shave badly."

"I know, sir. I'd give my right arm for a hot bath! But first, I suppose you haven't any food? I haven't eaten properly since I left Paris, and I'm starving."

Wallis rang the bell, staring at him. "Gray, what on earth have you got in your pockets? Your luggage?"

He laughed and pulled out of his bulging pockets half a dozen George II silver saltcellars. "You left these behind, sir. I didn't see why the Germans should get them, so I stuffed what I could into my pockets."

The Duke picked up one of them in disbelief, caressed it with loving fingertips. "I inherited these from the Duke of Cumberland, you know. They've always been in the family, since they were made. Thank you, Gray. It was very good of you to think of them and bring them to me." His eyes glistened with unshed tears. "God knows when we'll ever see our home in Paris again, or what sort of state it will be in when we do!"

Wallis pressed his arm, leaned on him. "Don't, darling."

A footman came into the room. Wallis ordered food and drink for Gray. "Whatever you have that can be ready as fast as possible. Major Philips is famished. After that, he will have a bath — make sure there is plenty of hot water, and prepare a bedroom for him. Gray, have you any luggage? Any clean clothes?"

"I've got a clean shirt and underclothes in an army fatigue kit, I left it in the hall as I came in."

"Unpack for Major Philips and lay his clean clothes out in his room," ordered Wallis, and the footman bowed and withdrew.

While they waited for the food Gray bleakly described the situation he had found as he crossed France.

"They've caved in, like a rotten apple. I can't believe what I've seen. The railways have stopped running. Roads have bomb craters in them; many shops are running out of goods. People have panicked and bought whatever they could get, they're stockpiling them in secret."

"Can't the government stop that? They could pass a new law making it illegal to stockpile food or goods."

"Too late now, they should have done that months ago. I think the government has collapsed, too. There's absolutely no control; the police have stopped trying, many soldiers have begun walking or driving home, taking food at gunpoint when they need it. The people are terrified and gloomy, for which you can't blame them.''

"How did you get here, without a car, in God's name?''

"Hitchhiked. I got rides on lorries and in French ambulances. Took me four days. I hope you aren't planning to leave here for a while, because I could sleep standing up, I'm so exhausted.''

"We'll stay, while it's safe.''

When he had eaten he went to bed and slept until well into the next morning. The weather was still hot and cloudless, typical Riviera weather at that time of year. The war seemed a million miles away, but they knew it was coming closer all the time, the radio droned out bad news throughout the days. It was obvious that they could not stay on there for much longer.

The Duke's piper and manservant, Fletcher, who had been living at la Croe since they had bought it, giving the Duke lessons whenever he had free time, spoke to him during the day to say he had been offered a place on a ship sailing for Britain.

"I'm packed and ready to leave, sir, with your permission.''

"You can come to Spain with us, Fletcher, you know.''

"I would rather get home, sir. I'll rejoin the regiment. That's my place.''

"I've enjoyed your lessons on the pipes, Fletcher. Thank you for everything you've done.''

"Aye, sir.'' Fletcher withdrew with dignity.

The Duke sighed. ''He disapproves of us going to

Spain. Thinks I should do what he's doing — go home to England and join my regiment. He has no idea how much I would love to do just that, if only they would let me."

"How many times must I tell you — they don't deserve loyalty from you when they don't give you any loyalty."

The phone rang all day. British people saying goodbye, French people asking if they needed help. Finally Major Dodds rang them from Nice to say that he and his party would be leaving for Spain, in convoy, with the Vice Consul from Menton, on the following day.

"I have had a message from London, urging that I take you with me, sir. It will not be safe here for you and your wife once we have left."

"Look, Dodds, la Croe contains most of our most valuable possessions. I don't want to lose them all by leaving the house unprotected."

"I've considered that, sir. The American consul here isn't moving out. They're still neutral, and he doesn't believe they are in any danger. He has offered to come along and put his official seal on the gates and the door of your house, with a notice affirming that la Croe is under the protection of the United States."

"That's very good of him. I'll ring him myself and confirm that I would be happy to accept the protection of the United States. I know my wife will be delighted to hear that news."

After ringing the American consul, he spent the afternoon destroying papers, locking some more

320

important ones in a big metal box, or stacking them all in the strongroom.

"Although, if the Germans really want to get at them, the room won't withstand a direct hit from one of their big guns."

Wallis laughed merrily. "Darling, that would blow the contents to kingdom come! No, the Germans are too practical to do that. They'll just bring in an expert safe-cracker."

"Well, at least the strongroom will withstand the average thief! The German army are another matter."

He took some papers over to Stevie's villa. The caretaker was obviously curious, but obeyed his curt request to be left alone. David felt up the chimney and at first couldn't find the handle Stevie had described. He stretched up higher, grimacing as his fingers reached through soot. At last he touched cold metal, his hand curled round the handle, and pulled hard.

A rattling sound, and a square metal safe descended inch by inch. He unlocked it and put the documents inside, locked it again, then began to wind the chain upwards out of sight.

It took him another five minutes to clean his hand with his handkerchief. He did not want the caretaker to notice soot on his finger, so he put on his leather gloves before leaving.

Ladbrook, the Duke's chauffeur, supervised the packing so that they were ready at noon next day to join the convoy of vehicles led by the Vice Consul.

Fletcher, and many other British residents, were already on board a couple of battered, rusty old cargo ships sent by the British government to Cannes to bring them home.

"Couldn't they do better than that?" Wallis asked contemptuously, as the convoy drove through Cannes and glimpsed the cargo ships which hadn't yet departed. "I wouldn't want my dogs to sail on those old hulks."

The dogs were curled up around her feet, so used by now to long journeys in the car that they were fast asleep within minutes of leaving.

"They need every ship available, for war duty, your Royal Highness," Gray Philips told her in a voice loaded with disapproval of her complaint.

She ignored his retort, closing her eyes and sinking down under the travel rug wrapped around her in spite of the heat. Always a bad traveller, her nerves played up under the added stress of the war. She found it easiest to try to sleep as much as possible.

The convoy drove along the southern coast into Provence. They spent the first night at Arles. Wallis ate a tiny meal and went to bed. The Duke talked to the others for a while, then said goodnight and left them. As he was about to go upstairs a porter sidled up to him and slipped an envelope into his hand in a surreptitious manner.

Startled, he asked, "Where did you get this?"

"Delivered by hand, sir. An hour ago. I was told to make sure I gave it to you and nobody else, and not to let anyone see me do it."

The man's hand came up again, suggestively open.

The Duke fished into his pocket for a few coins and dropped them into the palm, although no doubt the porter had already been handsomely paid to deliver the letter.

He opened it in his room, where nobody could see him. Wallis was fast asleep. The Duke put on a coat, turned the collar up to half hide his face, put on a hat and pulled it down to make it hard to see the rest of his face, then wrapped a scarf around his neck so that he could pull that up if he met anyone. As an afterthought he put on dark glasses too. Then he quietly went out again.

He met nobody on his way out of the hotel. The rest of their party had obviously gone to bed; the bar was empty and shut up for the night. The porter was back on duty, but he was half asleep, a newspaper spread over the desk he sat behind, his head nodding. He didn't even look up when the Duke slipped out.

The night was clear and cool, he could see the stars in amazing clarity as he walked through the backstreets and out of the centre of Arles. There were no streetlights here and no traffic.

He had been here before, with Stevie once, years ago. Stevie used the place as a rendezvous; here he met people he did not wish to be seen with, people whose friendship might be dangerous for him. Stevie had a wild, reckless streak; that was what made him a brilliant soldier, that touch of bravado, the devil-may-care dash that took him through the bloodiest battle. Yet he had a tender heart, too. He was an odd mixture of male and female.

In silence David pushed open the iron gate of the Alyscamps. There was a faint, protesting whine. Within, nothing stirred. Ahead of him lay a long, narrow alley fringed with shrubs and trees; laurels, pines, lime trees, birch.

He had a torch in his pocket, but when he got it out found he did not need it. There was enough light to see by as he walked slowly, his feet sinking into the soft, pale sand covering the path.

On either side marched lines of ancient stone sarcophagi, a few Roman, most medieval, some with carved heads at the corners, sphinx-like faces glittering in the moonlight, staring with blank, blind, carved eyes.

By day he knew there were ants everywhere, the relentless crooning of wood pigeons among the trees, sage-green lizards basking in the open spaces between trees. By night, rats thronged the place, slithering across his path once or twice, making him jump. An owl gave a long, melancholy cry from a lime, its great eyes glowing. Owl moths, who came out only in the dark, floated silently past; their great wings brown and yellow, but when they heard the owl cry, they broke into more rapid flight before dropping to the ground behind the bushes to hide from predators, folding their wings over in the hope of becoming invisible.

He wished he could imitate them. In the dark the alley was a haunted place, full of disturbing shadows and sounds.

The Duke stopped half-way and flashed his yellow torch beam once, twice, three times, then turned it off and put it back into his pocket.

After a moment he heard a faint sound, saw a dark shape ahead of him, then a brief, answering flash.

He walked into the cover of the trees and sat down on one of the broken sarcophagi, took off his dark glasses, got out a cigarette and tapped it on his gold cigarette case.

He was joined a second later. "Don't light that, sir. It was dangerous enough shining a torch. We don't want to attract attention if we can help it."

The Duke smiled at the face he saw dimly by moonlight. "Hallo, Charles. What on earth are you doing in Arles? I couldn't believe it when I got your letter. You're like a will-o'-the-wisp, flitting about everywhere."

Charles Bedaux sat down beside him, shuffling up the sandy dust with his toecaps while his eyes flickered all around, up the alley to the gate, back again to the big, black shape of the church further along.

"I had to talk to you, you left Paris before I got the chance."

"But how do you come to be in Arles? Where are you going?"

"I'm on my way to the Italian border."

Startled, the Duke said, "Haven't you heard? They've crossed it, there's fighting going on there now. It would be dangerous for you to go anywhere near the border."

"I know, sir, but I have letters for the Italian commander there. Then I heard you were staying at Arles for the night."

"How did you hear?"

Bedaux smiled a little smugly. "Oh, I have friends who hear these things. I wanted to hear your plans — is it true you're going to Spain?"

"Yes, in a convoy led by the British consul from Nice."

"You must not go to Spain, sir, stay on at la Croe."

"And be captured by the Italians?"

"Certainly not! That would never do. It's a pity you left Paris. It would make life easier if you were on hand, ready for when you were wanted."

"I wasn't risking my wife's life! She had to leave Paris, and she wanted me to go with her. I could not let her travel alone. You've crossed France. You know what madness has taken hold of the people, all over this part of Europe. You advised me not to return to England, so we came down here, and we've hung on at la Croe as long as we dared, but if we hadn't agreed to go to Spain now it would have aroused suspicions. We were under pressure to get out of France at once. The consul insisted. And Spain has a friendly government, after all."

"Yes," Bedaux slowly agreed, without enthusiasm. "But what if they decide you are too valuable to be allowed to leave again? They might put you under house arrest and make us pay heavily to obtain your release to us."

He drew himself up, eyes blazing with indignation. "They would not dare take me hostage like that!"

Bedaux gave another of his smug smiles. "I'm afraid you underestimate how much other people will dare when they see a great prize dangling under their noses. And you are a glittering prize, David. If England falls as easily as France — and all the signs are that it probably will, the English people don't want war, and we have many friends there — the Spanish government might seize you and hold you hostage.'' His voice grew harsh. ''I must insist, David. Berlin thinks you should stay in France. Do not go to Spain.''

''Are you threatening me?'' The Duke was taken aback by the man's tone. Bedaux had never spoken to him like that before.

Quickly, Bedaux said, ''Advising you, sir. For your own good. Don't leave France. Any day now, your time may come. You may be back in England, back on the throne. Don't risk that by going to Spain.''

The Duke gazed ahead of him at the soft breathing night, the stone sphinx faces staring back at him, the owl moths hunting through the warm air.

''If I pulled out now the British consul would cable London, might even arrest me and force me to go with him. And Wallis would become frantic if I didn't go on, she's very worried and frightened. I must go to Spain. I'll wait there for news.''

Threat showed itself again in the other man's face and voice. ''The Führer will not be pleased. He may change his mind about putting you back on the throne of England.''

''When he has conquered England, let me know,'' the Duke said with a sting in his own voice.

''You've seen how corrupt and weak France is — do you really think England can hold out against us? We will be the masters of Europe by the end of this year.''

The Duke had flushed at the other man's tone. This was a new Bedaux, one he did not like.

He got up abruptly. He was afraid of losing his temper

and saying something he could never take back. So without saying another word he walked back along the alley of the sarcophagi, through the sand which smothered his footsteps, moonlight filtering down through the leaves of laurel and lime, whose fragrance brought back memories of his visit to Germany, when he was nineteen, and up at Oxford. They had stayed at one time in Wurtemburg, where he had had to go on long, tedious drives with the King. There had been an avenue of limes nearby, and when he had a headache and felt sick after one of those interminable state meals, a German nurse had fussed around him, put him to bed with a silver-wrapped glass full of pale, golden tea made with dried lime flowers, promising that it would cure his headache and help him sleep.

That was what he needed tonight. Some lime tea, to help him forget the tangle and complexity of his life.

He had never intended any of this to happen. One step at a time, he had come this far along a road he had set out on in anger and bitterness. He could not guess where his path would end, but he felt cold and sick as he made his way back to the hotel.

The warm Mediterranean night to which he was so accustomed was suddenly alien, hostile.

He would have given anything to be back in England.

FRANCE

1999

CHAPTER
FIFTEEN

Claudia had never before realised how much she depended on her senses — on seeing, touching, hearing. Lying in the dark unable to move very far or see or make a sound, all her fears and anxiety were concentrated in her ears. She listened intently to every tiny sound, interpreting it, trying to understand what it might mean. The smallest sound could make her nerves jump erratically, and the intensity of her emotions was making her heart race.

Her captor was still in the next room; he was listening to the radio or watching television. Voices, music, boomed and faded as he turned it up or down. He walked around, opening cupboards, moving chairs, which scraped on the floor. One fell over. He swore viciously. There was a clattering of cutlery and plates; he was eating.

How long had she been here? It seemed days since she had eaten that meal with Hugh and the Englishman. Not that she wanted to eat; the very idea of food made her feel sick, but her professional interest in food remained. She wondered what he was eating and if he had cooked or simply made a sandwich. He could have a freezer full of microwave junk food, of course.

He poured himself a drink; she heard a bottle clink on a glass, then the gurgle of his throat as he swallowed. Beer? Wine? Beer, probably. He was the type. What type, though? How did she know what type he was?

He opened another bottle, filled his glass again. The sound of the running liquid reminded her that she wanted to go to the lavatory.

She wouldn't think about it. If she did, the discomfort would get worse.

She wished she had taken more notice of what he looked like in those few moments on the Croisette before she had passed out. Whatever he had injected her with seemed to have wiped out her memory of the time just before she had the needle thrust into her arm. Or was this blankness due to shock? Whatever the reason, she simply could not remember what he looked like; his face, his clothes, his shape — anything.

Maybe if she concentrated she might bring that face up from the deepest level of her unconscious, but when she tried, it would not come.

So for now she just listened to him. It kept her sane, trying to work out what he was doing. If she let herself think about what she had heard him say earlier, it would make her feel even worse. Death had always been a far distant future event she did not truly believe would ever happen to her. She had agonised over her mother's death, but she still had not imagined herself ceasing to be; her mind no longer working, her memory unrolling to the last second of time and then that cold, dark silence.

She groaned, eyes desperate to penetrate the darkness

all around her. If only she could see!

But she could think. And she had to think about something other than dying.

Hugh, for instance — what was he doing at this moment? He would be looking for her. She could be sure of that. Would he call the police? Probably not. He would be too afraid of the consequences. These were ruthless people who would stop at nothing.

Even murder.

Hugh knew that and he wouldn't want to push them into killing her.

How would she die? God, please, something quick; being shot in the head would be over in a second. She would hardly know what was happening. She hoped he wouldn't unbind her eyes first. She didn't want to know it was coming.

She wasn't brave enough to bear pain, die slowly, knowing she was dying. She knew she would go to pieces, scream, beg ...

She was such a coward.

No, stop thinking about dying. Think about ... Ben ...

Tears suddenly welled up in her eyes and seeped down her face, under the plastic bandage, warm, salt tears that made her skin feel sticky.

Ben, Ben, Ben, she thought, conjuring up an image of him in the villa garden the day he heard his father only had a few hours to live. Ben, almost naked, his body wet and golden under the southern sun, touching her, kissing her, their bodies clinging, skin on skin.

She would never see him again.

Never. Pain throbbed inside her.

Since she had met him she had never felt so alive. And now she was going to die.

"This waiting is a killer," Ben said, pacing backwards and forwards like an animal in a cage.

Hugh stood by the window again, staring out at the night sky. "I hope to God you haven't pushed Roger into doing something stupid, that could end in Claudia being killed. If you had told me what you were going to say I'd have stopped you."

"Doing nothing at all would have been even crazier," Ben snapped.

The electronic buzzer went and they both jumped.

"I'll get it." Ben walked quickly out on to the landing above the kitchen to press the button that made the gates swing open, and stood there watching Roger enter. He was alone. The gates swung shut behind him, nobody else came through.

Louise was having a bath, the kitchen was empty. Ben went down to open the door to Roger.

"How dare you leave a message like that with my son?" Roger icily accused, coming into the house. "You scared the life out of him. He was afraid I was in terrible trouble."

"You are." Ben let the door slam and saw Roger jump. His nerves were in a bad way. Good, thought Ben. I hope they are. We're obviously going to have to lean on him to get Claudia back.

"Come up, Roger," Hugh said from the top of the stairs, running a narrowed stare over his face. "You look as if you need a drink."

In the salon Roger confronted him, bristling. "Look, I asked this firm to locate you and try to get hold of the safe containing my father's documents. I told them to be very discreet. How was I to guess they would turn out to be blundering thugs?"

Ben snapped, "We want Claudia handed back, safe and sound first. Tonight. Now."

Roger said to Hugh, "Do we have a deal?"

"Claudia for the papers?" Hugh took a deep breath. "And you accused me of blackmail? God almighty, Roger, I wish I could think of a way out of this — your family deserves to be exposed. But while Claudia is in danger I'm powerless, so OK. You hand her back, I hand you the papers."

"When can I have them? Can you go to Paris tonight and get them?"

Ben leaped like a wolf, took Roger by the throat and shook him. Flailing around, Roger tried to break out of his grip, making choking noises.

Hugh said quietly, "Let go of him, Ben." He took hold of Ben's shoulders and dragged him backwards. "You'll kill him! That won't help get her back."

Released, Roger reeled away, coughing, leaned on a chair, fighting for breath.

After a minute, Hugh said flatly, "OK. The deal is, we get Claudia back, you get your papers tomorrow as soon as the bank in Paris opens."

Roger had a hand at his throat, massaging the redness Ben had left. "There's a problem. Before I came here tonight, I talked to the man who's holding her. He's demanding that I pay him in full at once."

"Then pay him."

"I will, but..." He broke off, sweat showing on his face.

"But what?" Ben demanded, eyes narrowing in suspicion.

"He's threatening to..." He broke off again, swallowing visibly.

"Stop pussyfooting around. What is he threatening to do?"

"He says she saw his face, and he can't risk her telling the police."

"He'll kill her?" Hugh guessed, ash grey.

Ben was shaking with rage and fear. "My God, if he hurts her, I'll kill you, I swear I will."

Again Hugh talked over him. "Roger, you say he wants his money — have you got to take it to him in cash, or is it a bank exchange?"

"Cash. He doesn't trust banks."

"Tonight?"

Roger nodded.

"Where have you got to take it?"

"He has rented a house on a back road to a village called Gourdon — you know it? I had to look it up on a map.

"I know it very well, it's a perched village above a valley, the Gorge du Loup, they call it — the valley of the wolf. It's still pretty wild territory, although in summer they get a lot of tourists."

"Well, this guy says there's a narrow, winding road from Opie to Gourdon. The house is set back from the road about a third of a mile, in some rough scrubland.

The name is painted on a sign down by the road. Les Oliviers. It was an olive grove once, and there are still quite a few olive trees around the house, he said.''

Claudia was so exhausted by fear that she kept dozing off, but when a door banged she woke up with a start.

Her captor was in the room. He walked over to the bed. She couldn't see him, but she hated the smell of him. Sour alcohol, sweat, garlic, the smell of unwashed flesh.

He leaned down close to her. ''Fucking bitch, I owe you for trying to put my eyes out.''

So it had been him in the villa. It hadn't been an opportunistic burglar. She should have picked up his smell then, but she recognised it now, her gorge rising.

He grabbed her hair and yanked her off the bed by it, her trussed body helplessly swaying.

She felt cold metal touch her forehead, above her taped eyes.

A gun, she realised, shaking. He was going to kill her now.

''I thought of fucking you first, but I don't want to leave any DNA on you, anything that can tie me to your body when they find it. Goodbye, you bitch.''

The round cold hole in the muzzle pressed into her, she heard the slow squeeze of the trigger and her knees sagged in terror.

At night the Gorge du Loup had a wild, primeval feel to it. There were few houses and no street lighting, just the tangle of trees, bushes, rustling grass through which a narrow road ran. There was no other traffic on it at this time of night. It took them a long time to find the turning, but at last Hugh's headlights illuminated the sign. Les Oliviers. They turned on to a rough dirt track half buried among trees.

After five minutes they caught sight of a faint light shining through closed shutters. Hugh slowed down even more.

"Out you get."

Ben kept his head down, opened the passenger door and rolled out into the long grass. Hugh leaned over to close the door again, very quietly, without stopping the car.

He halted in front of the house and switched off the engine. As he got out, the front door jerked open. Hugh and the man, framed in a light from the house, stared at each other.

"M'sieur Morrell?" the Frenchman asked. He openly held a gun, black and shiny in his hand.

Hugh nodded. "Yes."

"I'll use this," the other said. "Don't think I won't. No tricks. Come forward slowly, hands up where I can see them."

Hugh raised his hands and walked carefully towards the man, who stepped back to let him pass. As soon as he was inside the house, the front door slammed behind him.

The gun was jammed into his back. "Walk."

Hugh obeyed without replying. The man had talked to Roger, might remember his voice. It would be wiser to say very little, give him fewer chances to suspect that it

338

wasn't Roger he was dealing with.

The house seemed to be completely dark except for this one room they were entering. He was aware of passing two other doors. From outside he had realised the house was small, one storey, built like a box, with two windows at the front and, no doubt, two at the back. There would probably be two small bedrooms, a bathroom, a kitchen and a sitting room. The construction was common enough in France.

Where was Claudia? Was she in one of the other rooms? She might not be in this house at all. What if she weren't? How were they going to find her unless this man agreed to take them to her.

"Put the money on the table," he was ordered in that rough accent, the tone of the backstreets, slum Paris, where the gangs operated, where great swathes of the population were criminals. Or was that a trace of *Niçoise* he heard? He thought it might be.

The Mafia still dominated some of this area. There had always been a strong Italian influence down here, particularly in Nice, the richest, most crowded city on this coast. Had this man originated in Nice and moved to Paris later?

Hugh steadied his voice, spoke with the English public-school accent Roger habitually used.

"Where's the girl?"

The Frenchman growled. "I told you, she saw my face, and I'm not risking her talking to the police."

"I didn't hire you to kill anyone! If you got caught I'd end up in court charged with murder too! Where is she?" Hugh was sweating — was she still alive?

"Hepburn knows me, he'll tell the police if I don't bring her back."

"*Dommage,*" the Frenchman said cynically. "That's just too bad, but I am not leaving any witnesses behind to identify me. So, put the money on the table, M'sieur, and be on your way."

"Not until you bring her in here."

The man stared at him, mouth tightening. "I think maybe I'm going to have to kill you too."

"Don't be a fool, man. Somebody will know you rented this place. The police know you're down here on the Riviera, they know the name Hepburn was in your partner's notebook. They told Hepburn they had interviewed you about his death. He's an old school friend of mine, he knows I am seeing you tonight. If I turn up dead, your name will head their list of suspects."

"They won't find your body. Or hers. I've got a good hiding place worked out. Stop wasting my time. Where's the money?" He raised the gun to Hugh's jawline, cold metal on warm flesh.

Ben had got into the house from the back and was coming up behind them, taking one soft, silent step at a time, closer, closer.

Ben took another step. A floorboard squeaked. The Frenchman whirled, swore, fired in reflex action. Blood welled up in Ben's shoulder, a spreading red stain on his jacket. He looked incredulous, as if he couldn't believe he had been shot.

Hugh grabbed the arm holding the gun, knocking it upwards.

In that small room the sound of another shot was deafening.

The Frenchman stood very still, then went down like a felled tree.

Shocked, Hugh stared at the body. There was no face. It had been blown away, leaving just a bleeding red mass.

Ben swore hoarsely. "Jesus!"

"I didn't mean to . . . it was an accident"

"Will the police believe that?"

Hugh rubbed his jaw where the gun had rested. Odd, he still felt the pressure of it. Maybe he always would.

"We won't hang around here to explain. Don't touch him, or the gun. We'll leave him where he is — he's still holding the gun, only his prints will be on the trigger. We must find Claudia and get out of here, but first I'd better look at your shoulder."

"No, let's just leave it, we can deal with it when we get to your villa. First, let's find Claudia."

Claudia was lying very still on the bed, where she fallen. When she heard footsteps, then felt hands touching her, she writhed on the bed, trying desperately to scream. Was this it? Was he going to shoot her now?

"It's me, Claudia, you're safe," an English voice said, then the tape over her mouth was wrenched away.

"Ben?" She couldn't believe it. Wished she could see him, staring into the darkness behind the tape over her eyes.

A warm mouth brushed hers; the soft touch hurt because the skin around her mouth was so sore, but she didn't care.

"That man may hear us . . ."

"Never mind him. He's dead."

Relief made her muscles relax completely.

Ben had a Swiss Army knife in his back pocket. He carefully cut the tape which covered her eyes, cutting through some of her hair in the process.

She winced as she felt the strands part, as the tape tore away from her skin. It hurt badly, but what did it matter? She was alive. Her hair would grow again. Her skin would heal, although it was very sore around her eyes, but she could open them at last. She looked up at him, inches away from her, smiling.

Her heart moved painfully. He was so beautiful. "Ben, oh, Ben."

He bent to kiss her again. Under his passionate mouth she felt life flowing through her.

While he finished cutting the tapes, she stared at the torn shirt, the blood slowly seeping out, wondering how badly it hurt.

She fought not to cry out as each piece of tape fixed to her flesh was stripped away. It was amazingly painful.

Ben shot a look at her mouth; she had bitten the lower lip, it was bleeding.

"I'm sorry, I know I'm hurting you, I'm trying hard not to." He tore away the final tape; she gasped in pain, then stretched her aching body.

"Oh, it feels so good to be able to move again!" Lifting her arms, she put them round Ben's neck, taking care not to touch his shoulder. "We must get you to a hospital."

"No, safer not to," Hugh said from the door. "I know

a retired doctor who'll look at it, no questions asked. He used to work for the Mafia in his spare time. Are you OK, *chérie*? He didn't hurt you?"

"I'm sore from head to foot, but I'll survive." She sat up unsteadily, put her feet on the floor.

Hugh came to bend down and kiss her hair. "Ben and I have been frantic about you." But he was abstracted, in a hurry to get away. "Can you walk, Claudia?"

"Just watch me!"

They made a slow progress through the house, into the car. Hugh drove off slowly, his headlights not switched on.

"I don't want to attract attention. We'll use the headlights once we're back on the road to Opie."

There were no other cars on the road down through the gorge, back to the coast Claudia sat in the back with Ben lying across her lap, his shoulder pillowed against her, so that nobody they passed should see that he was wounded.

As they reached the winding road down through the gorge, Claudia asked, "What do we say if the police come to the villa?"

"Why should they?"

"Well, they came to the villa the other day."

"Because my name was in his partner's notebook. But so were a lot of other names. You, me and Ben have been together all evening. That's our alibi. Louise will back us up. But I'm pretty sure we won't hear from the police."

Half an hour later they drove through the villa gates and parked. Hugh helped Ben out. Louise was asleep in bed by now. The house was dark, empty and silent downstairs. Claudia made coffee and sandwiches, while Hugh rang his retired doctor friend.

The old man only lived in the next road. He arrived ten minutes later and tut-tutted over Ben's shoulder. "Messy but just a surface wound, it will heal quickly. I'll have to put some stitches in it."

It took him half an hour to clean the wound, give Ben a local anaesthetic and make a curved sickle moon of neat stitches. Hugh poured the doctor a brandy and some coffee before he went home.

"He didn't ask me a damn thing," Ben said, when the three of them were alone again. "But he must have realised I'd been shot."

"I told him it had been an accident while you were cleaning your gun."

"And he believed you?"

"Probably not, but he's an old friend. He was in the Resistance as a boy, and cheerfully did jobs for the Mafia in Nice. He's not the type to ask questions."

They had a brandy themselves. Claudia gasped at the heat in her throat, felt it sink down into her body.

"Ben told me you were handing back the documents to Roger Morrell. I'm sorry you had to do that, Hugh. You won't be able to write that book without them, will you?"

He sat staring at the moon above the sea. "I no longer want to. I've wasted years hankering for revenge. Now I've realised what a fool I've been. I told myself my wife had ruined my life, but the truth is I ruined it myself, by refusing to forgive and forget I've spent nearly thirty years in a prison of my own making. Well, I've come to my senses. I shall turn my back on the past and walk away. It's not too late to start again. I have years of life ahead of me. I'm going to make sure I enjoy them.''

Ben quietly said, ''I hope that means you'll forgive my mother. If you just saw her, for a few minutes, it would help both of you to go on without all this bitter past business dragging behind you.''

Hugh sighed. ''Can we talk about that tomorrow?'' He got up, putting down his glass. ''I'm off to bed. You two should get some sleep too. Claudia, put Ben in the spare bedroom. Goodnight.''

They sat in silence listening to his footsteps on the stairs.

''Will you come with me tomorrow to the hotel to meet my mother?'' Ben asked. ''I need you to like her, I want her to like you.''

''I'm longing to meet her.''

He reached for her hand and carried it to his lips. ''If only Hugh will agree to see her!''

''Oh, I think he will. What else did he mean by saying it wasn't too late to start again, and he had come to his senses! He's going to forget what happened, forgive her, and your father. Tomorrow is the start of his new life.''

''And ours,'' Ben said. ''I want to get to know you much better, at a slower pace.''

''It has been pretty hectic, hasn't it, since we first met in Paris?''

They had got to know each other faster than they would have done if fate had not thrown so much at them. She felt very close to him already, and she wanted to get even closer.

"You look feverish — loss of blood can be dangerous, Ben, you should go to bed and get some sleep."

"You, too," he agreed, and they went to bed leaning on each other. She showed him into the small, spare bedroom — the mattress only had a sheet and a pillow on it. She found a duvet for him, then went to her own room.

Claudia slept very late next morning. Her dreams were chaotic and frightening. They made her glad to wake up at last.

The hot sun streaming through the shutters made yellow bars on the walls. She lay, weak and drowsy, but very aware of being safe, listening to the sound of voices downstairs. She could not hear what they were saying, but she felt too languid to move. First she must shower, wash off the smell of fear on her skin.

Out on the terrace, Ben and Hugh were talking after breakfast. Louise had left to do her morning shopping run. They had told her only that Claudia was back, and that Ben had had an accident in his car. "A broken shoulder bone, not serious, it will heal soon," Hugh said.

"Was Claudia with him?" she asked anxiously, and they shook their heads. Louise sighed with relief. "Well, I must get on with the shopping. I'll try to get a nice plump duck — *magret de canard* today, and tomorrow I'll make a *suprême de canard,* in a white wine sauce."

"Sounds good," Hugh approved, and she bustled away, beaming.

As she drove off, Ben said, "My parents never told me anything about you. I had no idea my mother had been your wife." He paused, tentatively said, "I suppose you aren't Claudia's father? The two of you are so close, you're obviously very fond of her."

"Her father was a very good friend. He was a journalist, too. We worked together, we were about the same age, we had a lot in common, except that his wife was a wonderful woman."

Ben flushed angrily. "Don't start insulting my mother!"

"I wasn't going to. But I admired Claudia's mother. She never married again, wasn't interested in anyone else, right up to the end of her life. I'd become very cynical about women, but she was the shining exception."

"Is Claudia much like her?"

"Oh, yes. Family resemblances are odd. Claudia said that the moment she saw you, you seemed familiar, although she couldn't think where she had seen you before. She picked up on some sort of likeness to me, obviously. In fact, you're more like me than your father, I think. He and I were never that alike."

"If he was my father."

The words dropped into a long silence, like coins falling down a well, making a resounding splash.

"What is that supposed to mean?" Hugh asked, sounding shocked.

"The dates don't fit. I was sorting through my father's

desk to keep myself busy, and found my birth certificate. I was born just two days after they were married. All these years they lied to me. I never saw their wedding certificate until then; I thought they got married a year earlier.''

''Have you asked your mother?''

''How can I, when she's so upset? But, don't you see, when I was conceived, she was still your wife. So I started to wonder if...''

''We managed to get a quick divorce because she was pregnant by your father. We hadn't slept together for months.''

Ben gave a sigh of relief. ''So my father was my father, after all? You can't imagine the shock it gave me. I've been reeling ever since.''

''I've heard that close family members could have confusingly similar features. And it isn't unheard of for people to get married just before a child is born. These days they often don't bother even if they have children.''

''But why did they lie to me? They told me I was born a year after they were married. Why did they do that?''

''No doubt they were embarrassed. My parents were old fashioned, they wouldn't want any gossip about their one and only grandson being born just two days after his parents got married!''

''I suppose that could be it.''

They both turned, hearing footsteps in the salon, and saw Claudia coming towards them wearing a short, silky blue tunic and white sandals. She had one hand lifted to shield her eyes from the bright morning sunlight. Ben's heart lifted. She was so lovely.

Hugh got up. "How do you feel, *chérie*?"

She smiled at them both. "I've never been so hungry in all my life!" She looked greedily at the croissants in the wicker basket on the terrace table. "Is the coffee still hot?"

She would never tell them how close she had come to death. The moment when that man had had his gun to her head, and was about to pull the trigger when he had heard a car outside, had been the worst experience of her life. She had believed she was about to die. She didn't want to talk about it, she just wanted to forget.

"I'll get a fresh pot." Hugh took the cold coffee pot into the house.

She sat down next to Ben and took a croissant.

Ben put a finger under her chin and turned her face towards him, kissed her lingeringly on the lips.

"You smell like spring."

She smiled at him. "How's your shoulder?"

"Painful, but I'll live. I'm full of painkillers. Are you coming to see my mother this morning?"

She nodded. "I'm looking forward to meeting her. I only hope she won't hate me on sight, for stealing her only son!"

His eyes glowed. "She already knows about you, I talked about nothing else as we flew here. I wanted to stop her brooding over my father's death, and give her something hopeful to think about. She was eager to meet you as soon as possible. I rang her half an hour ago to say we would be coming to the hotel sometime this morning."

Hugh came out with the fresh coffee. "I just heard the morning news on local radio. There was a brief announcement about a body of a man found in a house off the Opie road. The police apparently are not treating it as a murder. Suicide is suspected. They said he was believed to be the partner of the man found dead on the beach. The way the bulletin was put together hinted that the two cases were connected, so let's hope the police think he shot his partner, then shot himself."

He poured out the coffee, and Claudia picked up her cup, cradled it in both hands and took a sip, her eyes half closed.

"Oh, that is so good! Don't you love the smell of the first coffee of the day?"

"Love it," Ben said, watching her with a heart-wrenching intensity. Without taking his gaze off her, he told Hugh, "I'm taking Claudia to meet my mother. Will you come?"

Hugh stared across the garden like a sailor gazing at the wide, open sea. "I don't know if I'm ready to see her again — or if she would want to see me."

"She will. Why else do you think she came back here with me? It may sound weird, but I think she could talk to you about my father, about how it was when you were all young. Nobody else really remembers those years."

Hugh nodded. "I've been thinking about him a lot lately, remembering when we were young. Stupid, the waste of all those years."

Ben watched Claudia eating a crumbly, buttery croissant. Her mouth would taste of that now. He couldn't wait to find out.

Hugh said flatly, "I have to go to Paris with Roger today to get the documents from my bank."

"Go tomorrow. Make the bastard wait."

"No, I'd like to finish with Roger and the Windsors, and I have some sympathy for Roger. He's scared for himself, true, afraid of being exposed. That's all politicians really do fear — being found out, having the media on their tail. The truth is always an enemy, to a politician. They live on lies and call it spin-doctoring. But Roger is trying to protect his father, too. He really cares about that old man, I had no idea how much."

"Guy's the same — almost obsessed with that barn of a house and their centuries of history. They're a weird family."

"They're your family, your mother's family." Hugh smiled. "And I think it would be better for Claudia to meet your mother without me there to confuse the issue. I need more time."

Claudia put her hand out to him. "Why don't I invite her to dinner here, maybe tomorrow? Louise and I can cook a great meal for her. You'll feel easier on your own ground."

He smiled at her with love, but his face still held troubled uncertainty. "Is it important to you?"

She put her other hand out to Ben, who took it firmly, holding the small, capable fingers between both his hands.

"Very important, Hugh. To all of us."

He looked from her to Ben and then shrugged. "OK, *chérie*. Invite her to dinner tomorrow and I'll be here."

He turned his eyes to the distant, glimmering sea. "I wonder if I'll recognise her, after all these years?"

And how will I feel? he thought. His heart was already beating far too fast, his mouth was drying. At his age it was ridiculous to feel this way. Anyone would think he was a boy of twenty again.

The publishers hope that this large print book has brought you pleasurable reading. Each title is designed to make the text as easy to read as possible.

For further information on backlist or forthcoming titles please write or telephone:

In the British Isles and its territories, customers should contact:

ISIS Publishing Ltd
7 Centremead
Osney Mead
Oxford OX2 0ES
England
Telephone: (01865) 250 333 Fax: (01865) 790 358

In Australia and New Zealand, customers should contact:

Bolinda Publishing Pty Ltd
17 Mohr Street
Tullamarine Victoria 3043
Australia
Telephone: (03) 9338 0666 Fax: (03) 9335 1903
Toll Free Telephone: 1800 335 364
Toll Free Fax: 1800 671 4111

In New Zealand:
Toll Free Telephone: 0800 44 5788
Toll Free Fax: 0800 44 5789